6-07

THE ENGLISH HORSES

THE ENGLISH HORSES

A WESTERN STORY

WILLIAM A. LUCKEY

FIVE STAR

An imprint of Thomson Gale, a part of The Thomson Corporation

THOMSON

GALE

LIBRARY OF CONGRESS CATALOGING-IN-PUBLICATION DATA

Luckey, William A.
    The English horses : a western story / William A. Luckey. — 1st ed.
    p. cm.
    ISBN-13: 978-1-59414-509-4 (alk. paper)
    ISBN-10: 1-59414-509-1 (alk. paper)
    1. Ranch life—Fiction. 2. New Mexico—Fiction. I. Title.
PS3612.U265E54 2007
813'.6—dc22   2006036245

First Edition. First Printing: April 2007.

Published in 2007 in conjunction with Golden West Literary Agency.

Printed in the United States of America on permanent paper
10 9 8 7 6 5 4 3 2 1

To Katherine Osgood, with thanks to Janice Scarpello

AUTHOR'S NOTE

Barbed wire was introduced in the mid-1870s. By trial and perseverance, the sharp wire traveled into the cattle regions of the West and Southwest, and its use forever changed the lives of the numerous men who babied, doctored, and branded the free-roaming herds.

Open range was effectively ended by the wire's introduction, and the blizzards of 1886-87 were terrible examples of the need for ranchers to monitor their stock more closely. Thousands of cattle in Montana and Wyoming drifted before the winter storms, only to be caught up against long miles of wire fence and frozen in their tracks.

During the period after the American Civil War, stories of the vast fortunes to be made from cattle on the endless Western plains induced a number of European gentlemen, most notably the English and Irish second sons of titled families, to venture into the American wilderness.

In the southwestern part of the New Mexico Territory, several English and Irish sons came to ranching. These men were articulate and well schooled, and wrote of their experiences with great excitement. Their stories have been told and retold, and the accounts are still highly entertaining.

Prologue

He wished he had kept a journal. The facts were simple and easily remembered. It was in trying to commit them to paper that he began to see how little he knew for certain about the important matters.

He'd come to this country a scarred veteran of an ugly war. As a young man he'd entered into military life vigorously. That he'd been successful surprised both his elder brother and their parent. His career had been assured until a Sudanese marksman shot off the tips of two fingers on his right hand and placed a bullet in the long muscle of his left thigh in such a manner that the leg healed without full mobility. Thus his service in Her Majesty's forces had ended.

In the summer of 1889, Gordon Arthur Charles Meiklejon sailed from England aboard the *Rockingham*. He carried with him promises of financial assistance from an anxious older brother, as long as he remained away from the British flag.

This year, 1912, the Territory of New Mexico would become a state, a public declaration of civilization despite the irascible nature of its inhabitants. Gordon Meiklejon had played a minor part in the land's taming, but he wished to keep that part clearly delineated. He was in neither form nor content a coward. He had medals and scars to prove his valor, yet he'd been shaken by the complete separation from the laws and regulations of other worlds that most clearly defined the New Mexico frontier. The men and women, whose faces appeared upon reflection, had known their own law, bowed to their own rules, and thus lived lives worthy of the greatest philosophers and scoundrels.

Meiklejon had time now. His English wife had returned to her homeland on her annual pilgrimage, since New Mexico winters were too severe for her constitution. He would sit and write, perhaps only to scratch out the raw story that still puzzled him. In writing down long-ago occurrences, he might finally reach an understanding of the events that at the time had completely eluded him.

Meiklejon sat at the desk. The kerosene lamp flickered mute encouragement. There was wood beside the library stove, more wood stacked outside within reach. He had endless time facing him, enough time to outline the bones of an intriguing, basically unsolved mystery.

★ ★ ★ ★ ★

OCTOBER 1889

★ ★ ★ ★ ★

CHAPTER ONE

Normally time meant little to Gayle Souter. His cattle herds told him what was needed, so he worked from their bovine calendar. But he knew this day's date, October 16th, and even the day of the week, Tuesday. It said so in the barber's window right next to where it said the doc would pull teeth after three.

Souter was waiting out his misery at Billy McPhee's stable, trying to interest himself in watching the street fill with too damned many folks. The inbound train was whistling its business. Souter paid attention; he wasn't used to empty time.

"Next stop Socorro!"

Gordon Meiklejon woke up disoriented but only for a moment. "Socorro . . . next stop!" The conductor's loud words were what he'd traveled a long way to hear. Meiklejon stared out the window and found he did not care for what greeted his burning eyes. It was a land thinly soiled, mostly sand, with a covering of dark green brush. Yet he'd been told Socorro was good ranching country.

He was the last person off the train, and a small boy grabbed for his bag. "Mister, I can take you to the good hotel. It ain't far . . . I can carry them bags. Good food and not many fleas. Best place in town I promise you, mister."

It was simple enough to accept the urgent recommendation. "Fine, child, you take the bags. But go slowly, please, I wish to study your town."

Such a request should not be confusing, but the boy stared openly at Gordon and cocked his head when Gordon continued to speak.

"I gather this town exists for the ranches which surround it. I cannot help but notice the pens, constructed for what I would assume would be large numbers of cows."

The boy grinned. "Sure we got cattle comin' through. They ain't cows though. Them's kept up to the houses . . . women say they needs the cows"—he breathed in—"for givin' milk to babies. Cattle use them pens, mister." The boy hefted one of Gordon's bags that weighed half as much as the child himself. "This way, mister . . . said I'd do you right."

Meiklejon's room at the Southern was perhaps excellent considering its surroundings. An ugly little man had brought him to the room, a man who would not cease talking. "Good to see new faces in town, sir. Yes, sir, Socorro's growing, and growing fast." Gordon had taken the front room, which was wide and spacious and offered a fine view of the town's main thoroughfare. He unpacked his stale clothing, and, with the scent of frying meats and freshly boiled coffee in the air, he began to feel an enormous hunger. It was early, not quite eight o'clock, on what was promising to be a hot day.

In the dining room, an older woman, dowdy and well-padded but of good cheer, greeted him. "Yes, sir, yes, Mister Meiklejon. My husband said we had a distinguished new lodger and I saved you our finest table." The woman, too, promised to talk forever until Gordon raised a hand.

"Thank you kindly, madam. I am quite tired, and rather hungry."

She spoke no more while leading him to the table of honor. A full breakfast quickly manifested itself.

Quite unexpectedly an enormous loneliness overwhelmed him; he wished to feel a human hand, the safety of a gentle arm, the touch of loving fingers along his jaw. Fear gripped him, intertwined with the gaping loneliness, but any stir of emotion among strangers would be most shameful.

"Mister, you want more coffee? Or a piece of pie? Mama bakes the best pie in town. Lots of travelers have a piece to finish off their breakfast." A new barbarity couched in words from a pretty mouth intended to gorge him. But these same words gave him distance from his feelings and allowed him the grace of patting his emotion back into place.

"Thank you, miss, but . . . no. I have taken in all the sustenance my long-abused body may absorb."

He rose from the table to wander out of doors. He had come here on impulse; he had chosen to place faith in this one town. He would purchase land and settle. Now he needed to learn about his proposed home. In furtherance of this challenge, he approached a supposedly unoccupied gentleman.

"Sir, could you tell me the hour?" It was said politely and Gordon received an ill-tempered look.

" 'Bout nine."

That was all he garnered before the man moved to a circle of other men beginning to form. Careful to avoid the widening group, Gordon set an even pace along a boarded street, curious to look in each window and know the business within. He was careful, easy on his stiffened leg, and after some time found himself returned to the same spot where he had previously learned the time.

A deep, full voice spoke harsh words: "Damn him for ridin' in like we ain't nothin' to him. Damn him for all the trouble he's gonna cause."

Gordon looked where men were pointing. A horseman had appeared at the edge of town, and the group, surrounding Gordon, drifted apart, faces turned to the approaching rider.

It was the first riding animal Gordon had seen in several

weeks that he thought worthy of notice. Most of what was available had been scrub stock, such as usually found in hot climates. Heads too large, ewe necks, narrow-chested, and goose-rumped. Indeed, the most redeeming features of these animals were the ease with which they covered unyielding ground.

This horseman rode a tall, long-legged sorrel marked with too much white for Gordon's taste, but the animal was well formed and sturdy. The rider's gear was of the local variety, but its construction and decoration were exceptional. The rider himself possessed a grace not seen in many men, perched as they were on their scrawny mounts. The usual wide-brimmed hat shadowed much of the face, withholding the eyes from Gordon's study. The head bent down, the eyes appeared too briefly, a light shade of blue startling in the darkened face.

" 'Mornin', mister. Nice day . . . for buzzards and weasels."

Gordon wisely said nothing. Although the rider's clothes were mended and patched, the bridle held medallions of silver and the saddle was carved with ornate flowers. Even the handgun was nestled in its scrolled holster. Gordon noted that the rider's free hand rested near the pistol at all times. As horse and rider proceeded, Gordon recognized a marked change in the group of men—their sound had muted, their hands had stilled. It became difficult to draw in a breath. Gordon's heart raced, his pulse thumped as he watched the sorrel horse strut. He waited. Still nothing happened, no one moved.

Then a voice crackled and stopped the prancing horse.

"Well, there, Mister Holden. You come to be miserable with me or to make the misery worse? Sure can use the company while I wait."

An older man, heavy-set and in some obvious discomfort, had emerged from a building marked Livery Stable. One hand was set tentatively against the swollen side of his reddened face. This sudden presence knocked air into Gordon's lungs and stirred the group of silent men.

"Hey there, Souter. Ain't seen you since I got this bronc'. You had some strong opinions on my choice, I remember."

The two men laughed, even Gordon smiled, and the endless traffic around them resumed. Words were exchanged between the two men that Gordon could not hear. Then the sorrel horse became agitated, shifting its weight, stamping a front hoof to paw the dirt. Sweat showed thick and white between the animal's hind legs as its tail slapped wet hide.

The man addressed as Holden nodded to his older companion, then touched long legs to the horse's sides. Nothing else seemed to move as the big horse skittered down a convenient alley. Even Souter remained watchful until Holden disappeared, and then he went inside.

Gordon's leg trembled, his eyes fluttered, and he could feel that thump inside his chest. He would try a café across the street for a glass of something cold. Then he would resume his quest. But a commotion behind him forced him to look back as a thin horse ran past him. A scrub barely thirteen hands, ears flat, tail high, the pony responded frantically to the lashings of its fat rider. Horse and rider skidded into the same alley that minutes before had received the sorrel gelding and its commander. Gordon hurried in a painful run, determined not to miss the inevitable confrontation with Holden. Short of breath, he stopped, wiped his wet eyes with the back of his sleeve.

Mouth gaping, reins flying, the thin, yellow pony now raced toward him. Freed of the rider's bulk, the saddle rose and fell with each stride, its heavy stirrups unnecessarily goading the pony's flight.

When the pony was close, Gordon jumped to catch the bridle. His fingers felt the wet muzzle, the pony's breath close on his face. The pony slowed, then reared against Gordon's grip.

Yanked off balance, Gordon caught the saddle horn and righted himself. His heart and breath roared, but he heard the words.

"Now that's not the smartest thing I've seen a man do. Jumpin' out to catch that scrub could get a man killed." It was the rider on the sorrel.

Gordon shrugged as he drew the reins over the pony's head. He used his damaged right hand to withdraw his last linen handkerchief to wipe his face.

The man continued: "That bronc' belongs to Melicio Quitano. Obliged if you'd take it to Billy's stable. Melicio don't need it right now, but when he wakes up, he'll be wanting to ride on." Derision laced the words.

This Quitano was alive or he would have no further need of the yellow pony, Gordon surmised. Choosing carefully to exhibit himself as a thoughtful man despite such risky behavior, he said: "I shall see to the pony, sir."

Laughter made the retort barely comprehensible. " 'Shall' is it? You're that Englishman." The laughter stopped. The sorrel's horseman leaned back in his ornate saddle, rubbing a place high on his arm. "I commend you, Englishman, for catchin' that pony."

Gordon passed the stunted fingers across his jaw. It was his ruse for stalling.

The rider hesitated, then spoke: "It's not likely *Señor* Quitano would enjoy seeing my face right now. He spoke hard words and paid for them. Some kind citizen will be glad to tell him where his pony's gone . . . since we're gatherin' an audience . . . and you can be sure these boys'll be eager to talk. Once I'm gone." A bitter note tinged the last words.

Gordon's instinct as he looked directly into the handsome face was one of pity. That a man so young and well apportioned should know the world in an ugly manner.

"I won't tell you my story 'cause folks'll tell you. All about

Jack Holden and his outlaw ways."

Gordon held his breath at the man's honesty.

"Don't fret now. They're likely to drive me to my death with words, Mister Englishman. You take note and tell me sometime who speaks up and what story they tell."

Gordon Meiklejon could not doubt that the townspeople were wise to fear the young man, and wiser still to let him ride on. Holden tipped his hat and reined the sorrel around Gordon and the yellow pony. Horse and rider reached the main street, turned left, and walked down the exact center of that broad path while the town held its breath.

It was the man with the swollen face who took the pony's reins and led it inside the stable. Gordon followed, curious as to what questions would be asked.

The older man was decisive. "There here's Melicio's bronc'. How'd you come by it?"

"Sir, there was an unplanned meeting between this beast's owner and the gentleman, Jack Holden." He waited. "Holden has now ridden from town and the pony's owner lies in the dust. As Mister Holden and I exchanged words, I could see Mister Quitano, down the alley, recovering his senses, and it was apparent he was not interested in continuing the quarrel. I believe the pony will be picked up when its owner is so inclined."

Unexpectedly his voice wavered and he was familiar enough with battle and its aftermath to recognize he was suffering an attack of delayed fear. The trembling was a reasonable result of the circumstances. He only hoped the man he now faced did not question his courage or honor.

"I come in from the ranch 'cause I got a bad tooth." The voice was muffled. "Been waitin' for the doc or the barber. Fella owns this place's a friend. He'll be wantin' cash for holdin' Quitano's bronc'."

He smiled and Gordon found the smile allowed him to relax.

He extended his hand. "Sir, my name is Gordon Meiklejon."

The proffered hand was mostly thick fingers attached to a callused palm. Gordon bowed slightly, careful not to give offense. His hand was pumped twice and let go. The man spat into straw piled high in a corner.

Gordon spoke cautiously. "What can you tell me about Mister Holden? He's quite interesting."

"Holden's a known cattle thief, no worse than most, better'n some. He don't take too many. He ain't likely to hurt a man for defendin' his herd. And he's been known to take on work for a ranch needs the help. Keeps his stealin' over to Arizona or Texas." The man's voice slowed. " 'Ceptin' for Son Liddel. Them two feud over horses, and the rest of us watch."

Gordon kept his judgment private.

"Quitano lives a hard ride from here. He runs a livery . . . a hole full of sorry bronc's." The broad hand swept widely and Gordon saw the marks of work and years on the raw knuckles. "Melicio says he's a businessman, but I don't trust the son far as I can throw him . . . one-handed." He waved his left hand. "There's times a horse goes through his place with one brand, comes out marked for 'nother. Lame bronc's come back sound."

"I shall keep your observations in mind, sir. Your name . . . ?" Direct and simple, Gordon ticked his fingers on his jaw and saw the older man's eyes follow the maimed hand. Certainly now the inevitable question would follow.

"Name's Gayle Souter. How do?"

Gordon snorted. It seemed almost necessary to shake hands again and both men raised their arms slightly.

Souter grinned. "Meiklejon, you've had your introduction and I hope you 'preciate it. There's good land here, and good people. This place'll make any man more'n he thought of himself."

Was the man a seer, able to speak so directly to Gordon's

desires? A younger son cast from the family with little result from his short life other than to follow orders, first from parent and brother, then the military? Now life was of Gordon's own choosing, such as the foolish gesture of grabbing a runaway's bridle. A reckless deed, yet, once done, it earned some small approval.

He matched Souter's grin. Once begun, the grin became genuine and for a moment Gordon's heart lightened. "Mister Souter, it is indeed a pleasure to make your acquaintance."

Pompous as usual, yet Souter's grin grew even as the man grasped the intended sentiment.

"We shall speak later, Mister Souter. I believe I have a few obligations that must be met, sir."

When they opened the livery door, sun hit them directly and hard wind scurried dust about their boots as the sound and motion of Socorro returned. Meiklejon left with renewed purpose, knowing he would seek out and listen to Mr. Souter when the time was right.

CHAPTER TWO

A chair against an inside wall in the hotel lobby offered succor. The girl from the morning meal reintroduced herself, and Gordon learned that nothing in this country could be counted upon to behave as it should.

"Mister, you look pale. Let me get you some of Papa's whiskey." She was young and pretty, he mused. She handed him a chipped glass half full of amber liquid. "My name is Rose Victoria Blaisdel, Mister Meiklejon. Please call me Rose. Welcome to the Southern Hotel."

When he glanced at her pleasing features, he was startled by the knowing eyes.

"Mister, you weren't smart to go catching up Quitano's pony. That puts you between him and Jack Holden, and it's no place for a greenhorn. You could have been hurt, and you still might get shot."

Her observations told Gordon that word of his escapade had spread through town. And here was a female, albeit a very attractive one, expressing doubts on his ability to care for himself. She was questioning his experience, assuming that only those rough men clad in leather and outsize spurs could take care of themselves. The remainder of the masculine population must be at terrible risk.

He had fought the enemy and survived, 9,000 miles or more from here; he had been wounded and crawled to safety; he had killed while bleeding into baked ground; he had fought hand to hand and was still alive. She had no cause to judge him on such flimsy evidence as today's one act. He must correct her impression.

"Miss, I would not allow you to think so little of me. Neither of those men could outshoot me, if it were to come to that." A rebuke of slender proportions. His voice carried weight and dignity to ease her concern.

"Mister, you ain't carrying a handgun."

Gordon laughed. "Miss Blaisdel, you are correct." He handed her the empty glass. "Thank you for your concerns, and for the liquor. I shall be fine with a few minutes of peace." He made a great fuss of folding and returning the disgraced linen to his breast pocket, and, when he again raised his eyes, the girl was gone. Whiskey roared in his nether parts, and he felt a sudden need to use the outhouse.

He returned within the half hour, limping slightly. When no one lurked in the hotel lobby, Gordon struggled up the stairs, seeking his room and its isolation. The journey had been difficult, and, by the time he reached his single room, he was desperate to lie down and stretch his leg, loosen his clothing, and accept the luxury of rest.

For those moments between being awake and asleep, Gordon's restless mind presented repetitious musings. He was the frail, stranded younger son, caught now in a wilderness from which there was little chance of escape. He could not return to England.

He slept. Sweat soaked into his loosened collar and spread dark circles at his folded arms, banded the unbuttoned waist of his woolen trousers. He rolled his head and fought the demons each man brings to his dreams.

Rose Victoria Blaisdel studied the mound of spoiled potatoes. She and her sisters prepared all the meals, laid out the tables, served the customers, and were told to cleanse their thoughts of any man they served. Rose Victoria hated putting a plate in front of the pink-skinned, sweating men who leered and pinched, if only with their eyes.

"Yes, Mama, I'll hurry. But the potatoes are spoiled and I can't peel them fast."

When she married, it would be to a man with servants for all these disgusting jobs. Mama taught her girls that they should be gracious and inviting without making any promises—until they attracted a suitable husband. Suitable, of course, to Mama's taste. Mama was strict in those choices—no cowboys or mustangers, specifically no drifters. A ranch owner, a salesman if the company was reliable, not a schoolteacher even though Mama said learning gave a finer sensibility. But schoolteachers were too often soft men, unformed and without ambition. Unlike the women who taught, who often grew whiskers. Mama had set opinions and she instilled them in each daughter, until the girls trailed unquestioningly behind their mama. Except for Rose Victoria, who read too many books, thought too many thoughts, and puzzled over ideas far beyond her mother's reach. These ideas were from her few school days, taught by the spinster

Miss Katherine Donald.

The Englishman was presentable. He could not be faulted on manner or money as he had come to buy an established brand. He was not unattractive, with fine light hair that fell across his slender forehead. He was tall and well fashioned in his foreign suits. And physically whole despite a few minor flaws, unlike some of the locals who were crippled and unable to care for a healthy wife.

As the eldest, Rose Victoria had first choice. She sighed as the last of the potatoes were peeled and she swept the remains into the slop bucket. She hated pigs, hated their smell, their noise, and the fact that she must tend to them as she tended to customers. She would marry and there would be no pigs to slop on her wedding night.

Gayle Souter had been a long time in this country, and he liked what played for him this very morning—lines drawn, views exchanged, two men of mettle gauging the other's strength. He hoped the Englishman stayed. Times changed and a few civilized men could make a difference. Souter rubbed his graying jaw, edging carefully around the broken tooth. He'd been fighting the tooth for a month, had gotten so he couldn't eat or sleep. He was wishing for soup, and passing by good steak, even pushing off from dried apple pie.

Hell of a thing when a man didn't want to eat his fill or do his work, not for a man like Gayle Souter. He was in his mid-fifties, bowlegged from carrying weight all the long years. Stiff when he walked, slow to talk his mind, but solid and knowing the worth of responsibility.

He rubbed his hands and the smell of horse liniment rose from the friction. Hands pained him in the chilled mornings. He hurt most places a man could name, from breaks and cuts, bones jammed out of place. And he faced another birthday in two weeks. He was plumb getting old.

His boss, Ransom Littlefield, owned 150 sections of the roughest, most unforgiving land Gayle Souter had ever ridden. And Littlefield's cattle were like their owner, continually on the prod. Had to be to keep their babies from being coyote dinner. Ten years Souter had worked for Littlefield. Littlefield didn't like talk, so Souter ordered and the men followed. It was a bargain in both directions.

Two days past, Littlefield had said he was selling out, did Souter want to buy? Souter had glared at the old man, then grimaced as slow comprehension dissolved the anger. Littlefield was ancient, and Souter had never seen it. Face seamed, teeth long gone, shaky hands, neck turkey-wattled. Only the eyes showed a memory of youth. The man was maybe dying, and Souter hadn't known. But Souter said no, he couldn't buy.

He had ridden into Socorro, using the broken tooth as the need. Rubbing his bent hands over bits of hair, Littlefield had said it was best Souter got the tooth pulled. " 'Bout time, son, you been mean all summer."

Littlefield needed to sell; the Englishman wanted land. 150 sections. Made sense for Souter to sit down at a table and study those pale eyes, see if there was enough backbone.

He watched a young girl cross the street and rubbed his jaw, felt pain branded on inflamed bone. It was one of the younger Blaisdel girls. Growing up nice and sunny, not like the older girl, Rose Victoria. Couple a times he'd found himself eyeing that oldest girl with indecent thoughts. She moved slow, looked up through long lashes, and stared sweetly. The younger girls weren't that way at all.

Old man rickety and bowlegged, hands sprung wide and bent from work. Old man was a fool for thinking like a young buck. The oldest Blaisdel girl did that; man had his nature, couldn't change now.

He could fancy the Donald woman. She paid her bills while her old pappy left behind gambling debts and whiskey bottles and more promises than any man could collect. The Donald woman could do as a wife. A man with sense, he could see her refusal to be judged by her pa. She was a woman warm at night, clever all day. But even she was too young for Gayle Souter, and he'd had his share of wives. Still the oldest Blaisdel girl got a man to thinking.

He watched the Blaisdel youngster cross the street, carrying a package that leaked thin blood. Souter chomped down on a chaw that reminded him why he was standing in the livery door watching the doc's window. Then the doc's buggy made its appearance. Souter spat out the chaw, wiped his mouth, and felt the tooth rise in protest.

The following morning Gordon Meiklejon drank deeply of bitter coffee and winced at the scalding taste. Souter entered the dining room, stared at each occupant before heading straight to Gordon's table. Souter's face was lop-sided but no longer swollen, and his recent affliction did not prevent him from speaking clearly.

" 'Mornin'." The head tilted briefly but there was no "sir" following.

"Good morning, Mister Souter. Please join me."

The old man put on quite a show. One large hand was placed on the table's edge, and the rest of his considerable weight leaned on that hand while the body was lowered into the chair. "Had a horse turn on me 'bout a month past."

Gordon empathized with the terse explanation. The Blaisdel girl served more of the bitter coffee, which Souter drank in great gulps.

The Englishman was a good listener, his narrow face white, his pale eyes steady on Souter's face. Souter put the end to his selling and sat back, laid both hands on the table. He saw their knots and scars, and shook his head, blaming any failure of his yarn on coarse words. But Meiklejon was interested; Souter read that much in the slender face. Souter sat quietly, knowing a whole lot rested on a few words.

"I will want to talk with your Mister Littlefield. When do you think we might leave?"

Souter grinned to slow it down. "Mister Meiklejon . . . ah . . . sir." He swallowed some on the last word but it was right this one time. "There's a horse Billy'll let you use. We can ride when it suits you."

Within a half hour Gordon emerged from his room and began his descent, eager to step into the lobby where he found Souter waiting. He anticipated the ride, fresh air, and exercise. It would be a treat after his confinement in the train car.

The eldest Blaisdel girl held out her hand to Gordon. "Mister Meiklejon, please be careful. I will worry until you return."

A pretty speech for a pretty girl. He was touched by what he read as genuine distress. "Please, miss, don't fret on my account. I will be with Mister Souter."

At the hitch rail, Souter held the reins to a solid bay gelding of some quality. The animal wore the usual contraption of leather and wood, all of which sat on two folded blankets. Souter took possession of a squat horse with the head of an elephant on a mottled body. A canvas bag of food hung from the saddle's horn. The man pointed to a similar bag tied to Gordon's saddle. Behind the cantle were tied a blanket and what looked to be an oilcloth. "For sleeping out," Souter remarked. Gordon looked into the endlessly clear sky.

Another ten minutes was wasted in the local emporium purchasing one of the ubiquitous broad hats. That being accomplished, the two men rode out single file. Immediately the land climbed and evidence of mining corrupted its beauty, but

Gordon could not prompt Souter into speaking on anything but cattle.

Magdalena was reached well after noon. It appeared to be a highly industrious town, surrounded by miles of pens clustered near new railroad tracks. Gordon wished to stop, but Souter showed no inclination to do so and Gordon remained wisely silent about his needs.

The bay gelding had a quick trot, which Gordon would have enjoyed had the saddle been more comfortable. He rode more like a child aboard its first pony than an officer from Her Majesty's forces. At times he envied Souter on the mottled pony. The old man sat the animal's singular pace with no apparent effort. Gordon Meiklejon felt abraded pain in his knees and backside after several hours and began to wish for another method of travel.

By mid-afternoon, Gordon was aching to set foot on firm ground, needing greatly to relieve himself. Souter showed no such signs of distress and Gordon would not be outridden by an older man. At dusk they came to the downslope of a long hill; beyond them was a great expanse of flat, treeless plain. White patches were visible among sparse grass. There was nothing else for any appreciable distance.

Souter wiped his face with his shirt sleeve. "Them's the plains o' San Agustin. We'll ride out 'fore sunrise."

Camp was reached none too soon. After tending to the bay, Meiklejon saw to his pressing needs in the dubious privacy of brush oak. He had misgivings about his mount; salty foam had been under the saddle pad when he removed it. Perhaps Souter would be more tolerant tomorrow. As Gordon passed close to Souter's pony, he noticed that the horse showed few signs of fatigue. It tore into the thin grass eagerly.

"You know ranching, Meiklejon?" Now that something

28

bubbled and smelled intriguing over the camp's fire, Souter would talk.

Gordon edited his response. "My family has run cattle for several hundred years, Mister Souter. I am familiar with keeping records and using the best bloodlines. Does that answer your question, sir?" All his English displeasure was in that last word.

Souter picked over the words. "I don't think you got the idea of what we're ridin'. It ain't polite to ask a man how big his spread is, but Littlefield's got title to some hundred 'n' fifty sections. Here a section is six hundred 'n' forty acres."

Gordon would not accuse the man of lying. "How do you keep track of the cattle, Mister Souter? And the bloodlines . . . so you know which bulls are producing the best stock?"

Souter opened a can of thick milk. "We let 'em breed, brand the calves, push the mamas onto new range, and let the bulls do their job. Then we gather the crop come fall and sell 'em. Keep back a few promisin' bulls and start again."

Gordon was aghast at the laxity of methods. "Do you not use fencing to maintain certain lines?"

Souter snorted. "Think o' fencin' this much land, findin' the trees big enough to hold back a longhorn bull. Hah!"

"Surely there must be some way. . . . I intend to bring in Red Durhams. Our family has used them for several generations." Gordon hoped to introduce sanity into the absurd conversation. Mr. Souter confounded him.

"The only way I know is barbed wire. A beef hits that, stays on its side of the fence." Souter paused. " 'Course you lose stock, and good men."

"Mister Souter, could it be effective here?"

Souter looked up from rotating the pan. "Meiklejon, I'm an old man been ranchin' one way all his life. You're askin' me 'bout a fence that tears man and beast apart, causes wars, some of them deadly. Ain't no one tried the wire down here. The land's too rugged." He allowed a long pause. "Me, I hate the wire for what it does." The anger was real. Meiklejon had his answer, until Souter surprised him, saying: "If it were me, I'd wire a few sections, buy a damned good bull. If it were my spread. . . ."

Gordon admired Souter. He was above all practical. But there was a second note to the speech—Souter wanted to own the place and said as much by his comments. Later that wish could color his judgment, but, for now, when Souter spoke, Meiklejon intended to pay attention.

"Meal's ready. You hungry, you better eat."

Over a second cup of coffee, Gordon asked his question: "Why do the ranchers tolerate Jack Holden? If you banded together, you could stop him and put him in jail, and your Mister Liddell wouldn't lose any more stock. No one would."

Souter looked over the rim of his fire-blackened cup. "Well, now, Meiklejon, it's early yet, but I figured you'd be tellin' us what to do."

That stung. Gordon half raised his right hand, let it drop. Souter was absolutely correct.

CHAPTER THREE

Gordon woke before dawn and all his effort went into getting up. Leaning down to his gear, he was convinced he couldn't raise any item high enough to slide it on the horse's back. He knew better than to ask for Souter's help.

The plains were visible as Gordon's bay lethargically followed Souter's mustang. Souter's pony paced smoothly; Gordon's bay lumbered into a choppy trot. After miles of sand and sun, the grass and soft trees were a blessing. But it was the hint of water that raised Gordon from a half sleep in the saddle.

Souter reined in his eager pony. "Well done, Meiklejon." *For a foreigner* wasn't said. "Sleeping in the saddle's the mark of a man's ridden some."

Gordon licked his dry lips. "There's water?"

Souter grinned.

As they rode, the smell became intense. A shallow well greeted them around a clump of lush juniper. Beautiful water surged from the ground.

After wetting his lips, spitting out the first mouthful of water, Souter elaborated: "This here's Datil Wells."

The two horses were watered, and, with a full measure in the canteens, the men rode out energized. The land erupted in tall grass and high pines where the ground rose and fell in hills bounded by steeps cliffs and rock outcroppings. Several times Souter dismounted and ran knowing fingers through scuffed dirt. Gordon watched, and, when Souter looked out to the land they'd crossed, Gordon listened.

"Ground's dryin' too fast."

They rode from before sunrise into the early night. High up in a chilled meadow, Souter made camp. The fire got built while Gordon cared for his bay. Beans, bacon, coffee. Gordon was content.

"Hey the fire!"

Gordon remained on his log. Souter's hands moved toward the rifle too far out of reach, then stopped.

Souter spoke: "Come in careful."

Gordon readied himself. Souter shook his head in warning.

The horse appeared first. Its eyes were red, its forelock tangled. The animal blew slobbers of thick foam as it walked toward them. A man was barely visible on the horse's offside. As Gordon stood abruptly, the horse shied and a hand reached for its muzzle. A voice spoke softly and the horse quieted.

"Coffee?"

It was then that the man appeared. The fire's shadows drew

out each spare line. Gordon thought of the tribesmen he'd fought on other continents and figured he was about to see the American counterpart. He had believed the manifestation would be a red Indian, yet this was a white man. A small man, nowhere near Gordon's six feet and not wide and blocky like Souter. Narrow, face burned by raw winds.

Souter spoke. "You'll be wantin' this." Deliberate movements to pick up a tin cup and pour it full, lace the coffee with canned milk, and extend the cup across the fire.

The man stepped closer, the horse stepping with him. A soft word stopped the horse, a hand took the cup, brought it to a thinned mouth. White teeth glowed briefly, then were covered by the raised cup. The noise of drinking was all Gordon could hear.

The eyes circled the fire and found Gordon. All color was lost in the flames, then a turn of the face, a differing light, and the eyes became a harsh green. The man set the cup down, returning his gaze to Gordon in unsettling inspection. Gordon drew a sharp breath.

Under the shapeless hat, the hair was black. The slight frame was weighed down with an animal-skin coat that dispensed an unpleasant odor. The exposed shirt was stained and badly mended. The pants were hard wool, layered along the inside with leather.

While the horse snorted, the man spoke: "Obliged." Then he backed the horse, making a *clucking* sound until the pair disappeared. Souter and Gordon could hear a few hoof steps and then nothing.

"Who was that?" Then Gordon rephrased his question: "What was that?"

"Mustanger. Don't see many of 'em." Gordon cocked his head. "Locals call 'em *mesteñeros*. I heard 'bout this one. He's been after a small herd." Souter hesitated. "Not many of the wild ones left. That wire we talked 'bout . . . it's takin' their range."

Gordon wasn't certain if "wild ones" related to horses or the singular man.

"You see him . . . stay upwind of the smoke? Sure smelled ripe. Yep, he's after a herd. A *mesteñero* picks a bunch o' bronc's and follows close. Don't wash, don't cook. Smells like a bronc' . . . gets the herd use to him. Guess this one got cold and took the risk. Coffee'll do that to a man if he's ridden long on cold camps."

"You mean he follows the animals until he quite literally wears them down? But how could he catch an entire herd by himself? It isn't possible."

"He'll take the young 'uns hangin' 'round. Young 'uns ain't got their own bunch yet. It can be good pickin's. It's a rough life, but he's his own boss." Souter paused, a peculiar light in his eyes. "That 'un looks as old as a *mesteñero* ever gets."

Souter retrieved the cups and filled them. Gordon accepted the dollop of canned milk. Then Souter carved out burned beans and bacon. "That horse he was leadin' . . . mustang. Same's the pony I ride. Hell, Meiklejon, you know." Gordon would never dismiss the small local ponies after this arduous trek. "The man's got a good hand. That roan listened to him, wasn't feared of us, neither. Says a lot about a man, the horse he rides." Souter actually grinned. "Best turn in now. More miles tomorrow."

They had been seeing cattle all morning. As Souter described the qualities in each herd, Gordon marveled at their fine condition despite what he considered an appalling lack of decent grass. A good bull or two put to these hardy cows, and the improvement would be dramatic.

Ransom Littlefield proved to be bowed in the legs and

browned to a dark patina. The old man coughed and spat, looked up only when Souter made his introductions. His face was collapsed on a barren mouth. Littlefield talked only to Souter.

"Don't matter how funny the man talks, iffen the money's good, we'll cut a deal." That sounded as if an agreement were already in place. Littlefield cackled. "Sonny, the word come in yesterday, so I got Miss Katherine to cook up a meal in your honor, seein's how you been eatin' Souter's grub the last day or two."

A woman appeared at the main door. Gordon surmised she was another pretty Western woman. The country seemed well populated with attractive ladies. As she walked into sunshine, he was forced into a reappraisal. Her features were severe, the eyes unremarkable, the sorrel hair pulled back into an unflattering knot. But her figure was excellent.

Littlefield's face twisted with glee. "This here's Miss Katherine Donald. Keeps me from goin' back to the wild 'fore I die."

The woman directed her eyes toward Littlefield. She might be a hired woman, but she had her own mind, and her stare quite plainly told Littlefield to watch his manners.

Gordon climbed down from his bay and the woman produced her hand, waiting for Gordon to accept the gesture. He must revise his opinion once again. She was neither plain nor shy; there was high intelligence and sharp wit in her face. This was a woman who looked straight into a man. Her hazel eyes crinkled and softened, and her hand was strong as it gripped his. The scent of soap and fresh bread moved with her.

Littlefield purely cackled with delight. "That's enough, sonny. Don't you be courtin' our Miss Katherine. She's right persnickety. Given time she might take to you, but don't go bettin' on that. She's smart by damn, our Miss Katherine is."

She neither demurred to the old man's frankness, nor blushed at his affection. "Gentlemen, dinner will be ready as soon as you see to the horses. Mister Meiklejon, there is a room for you in the house with hot water and towels."

A ranch hand took the bay's reins, saying: " 'S all right, mister."

Souter, too, gave up his mottled pony. Walking alongside Littlefield, they entered the house, moving slowly to accommodate the old man's staggered limp.

After a meal of spiced stew, fresh biscuits, and a yellow cake covered in syrup, Gordon joined his host outside where a group of men were assembling. He recognized the horse handler from earlier. Bit Haven he was named, bandy-legged and smiling. Haven nodded eagerly when introduced.

Next was Stan Brewitt—tall, with sloping shoulders and a protruding belly, hands as slender as a woman's. Red Pierson was no more than a boy, seventeen he admitted when Gordon asked, but his eyes were clear and few doubts showed in his face.

The last man was also tall and lean, with straight blond hair thinning at his brow, a small, childishly round face set atop a long, awkward body. There was a calm certainty in the hazel eyes. Davey Hildahl he was called. A man worth keeping, Gordon decided, and recognized that he had accepted ownership.

He walked with Littlefield while Souter discussed acres and sections, concepts so immense that Gordon struggled to visualize the breadth and width of his purchase.

In the morning he and Littlefield spoke privately. An agreement was reached. Littlefield was to be paid half the purchase price now and the remainder over ten years. It was a deal that benefited both sides.

As Gordon accepted the reins of a horse chosen by Hildahl, he felt the effect of his decision. His life now depended on luck, weather, cattle, and the loyalty of his men.

The new horse was an animal of fourteen hands, a clay color with a black mane and tail, a black stripe down its back. As Gordon settled into the saddle, the pony plunged forward and kicked out. Gordon hauled up the big head and steadied the excited animal. Then he turned to Souter, who sat on his mustang.

"I'm ready now. Lead on, sir."

Katherine Donald would have a job, or she would not. Ransom Littlefield rarely let her clean the ranch house. He wanted only her company and her cooking. Now, watching the English gentleman move among the hands, she knew she had to decide whether or not she wanted the job before being asked.

She had seen Jack Holden at her father's cabin. Jack was a gossip by nature and had talked incessantly about the Englishman. Her papa, Edward Donald, had been out making rounds. It usually took him a week or more as he sold horses to the poorer ranches and sheepherders. But it was due to Katherine's hard work and persistence that she and her father had been kept from debt. Consequently she kept her friendship with Jack Holden a secret. Furthermore, if the good women knew of Katherine's involvement with Jack, they would brand her indecent.

Jack didn't often come to Quemado. He and Melicio Quitano were enemies, and Jack rarely invaded the man's home territory. Despite his reputation, Jack owned a rare delicacy and chose to leave Quitano some pride.

Katherine decided that if she began scouring the place, she might create a need for her services in the Englishman's transition from itinerant lord to local rancher. She would be surrounded by men and left alone by her unassailable virtue. And Jack Holden would not venture here. By making the decision, she would force herself into solitude while retaining a worthless dignity.

She opened her eyes, closed by her thinking, and found Davy Hildahl watching her. Katherine glared at him. "Mister Hildahl, you must get back to work. I do not care for idle men." With that she returned to the Littlefield house, and started putting into effect her plan for insured employment.

On the return journey, Gordon asked well-intentioned questions. He had bought the ranch, now he needed to gather as much information and as many facts as he could process.

Souter's blunt fingers pointed out distant landmarks, ticked off sections of the land named after physical oddities. Each section was used for a certain length of time. They passed a water hole, and, when asked, Souter replied that the water hole was on Littlefield graze, and then proceeded to name the varying ranchers whose stock were enjoying Littlefield largesse.

Introducing the wire could cause a war. Gordon, having just purchased the ranch, would begin by breaking all traditions. If he was successful, he would become a hero. If he failed, he'd be disgraced. Forcing change marked a man, isolated him from his less venturesome neighbors.

Horses harnessed to a creaking wagon interrupted his thoughts. Behind the wagon a string of horses trotted to keep up. The *crack* of a whip over this ensemble sent the grullo pony into frenzied bucking. Gordon rode out the storm with ease.

The team came to a ragged halt. After the dust settled, the foreman made his introductions, saying to Gordon: "This here's a neighbor. Lives up by Quemado." That was all, and Gordon could tell nothing from Souter's expression.

The gentleman himself explained: "Edward Donald, sir, at your service." There was an air of faded gentility about Donald's person—a stained tie, a white shirt with soiled sleeves and cuffs, clerk's hands holding the lines. The man could talk, however, and Gordon traded a grimace with Souter.

"My daughter cooked your meals . . . up to Littlefield's . . . begging your pardon, Mister Meiklejon . . . your place now. When she has a mind to, Katherine works for the old gent. She was teaching school till that fellow started his academy. His own boys burned the place, but Katherine wasn't asked back, no, sir. Too proud to admit they made a mistake."

He paused and Gordon thought they'd escaped, but it was only to get a second wind. "I'm all for education . . . got myself one back East. My Katherine works more to be doing something. Now, Mister Meiklejon, it is a pleasure, sir, to meet you. And when you get tired of riding that bronc', let me know, and we can find you a suitable mount. *Señor* Quitano and me, we got some fine animals to sell or trade, and a gentleman deserves better than that Spanish pony."

Gordon laughed, an unseemly response. It was impossible to purchase the necessary qualities in one horse. Vanity urged the acquisition of a handsome saddler and common sense led to the Spanish ponies. And here was a horse trader telling Gordon what he needed to suit his station.

"Most folks, they own a pony for distance, a stout bronc' for roping, and a Sunday horse for the neighbors. You see, Mister Meiklejon, no one horse can satisfy a man's needs, just like no one woman can."

It was an unpleasant moment. Gayle Souter reined his pony into its running pace. Gordon lifted his hat in politeness, a gesture that Donald tried to return but Gordon was already gone.

A good ten minutes down the trail, and Souter reined up. "Donald, him and Quitano, they only know one end of a horse." Gordon agreed, and Souter continued. "The daughter's hard-headed and some of the boys tried courting her, but she turned them down. If I was younger . . . hell, Meiklejon, you best watch yourself. Ain't many women out here like Katherine Donald."

They camped in the hills before Magdalena. The fire offered comfort as Gordon watched the sky. His mind unfolded around the people he'd met—smiling, frowning, waiting for orders. There was Gayle Souter, and the redoubtable Katherine Donald. The ranch hands, especially Davey Hildahl. He'd met Edward Donald, yet could not sense more than rudeness. He envisioned Rose Victoria Blaisdel—her father an unlikely sire of her beauty. Jack Holden was amusing—the stalwart virtue of an honest outlaw. But it was the eyes and hands of the *mesteñero* that stayed with him as he drifted into sleep.

★ ★ ★ ★ ★

ROSE VICTORIA BLAISDEL

★ ★ ★ ★ ★

CHAPTER FOUR

She preferred plain Rose. Rose Victoria was a little girl with china eyes. There were times she felt like that doll, but she would not be called by the silly name. The town boys called her Rosie and lingered wherever she was, pushing each other while they tried to ignore her. Rose usually tossed her head, knowing the effect of such an action.

Today Mama brought the news: the Englishman had purchased Littlefield's ranch. Rose purred. She had already scolded Mr. Meiklejon for the tired lines around his eyes, and he had listened. It had been an intimate exchange, standing so close. The lump in her throat, the beating of her heart. Rose was honest with herself if no one else. It was the thought of freedom that had her heart pounding.

Rose could read—magazines, old newspapers, ladies' journals loaned to her mother by friends. Reading gave you more places than you could otherwise see. Learning from Miss Donald had left Rose aching. It hurt to cry quietly, it soured in the mouth, burned the eyes, flooded the heart. Rose would not be hurt, not even by her dream.

Mostly Rose did chores: new sheets for the drummer in Room 4, a bucket of milk from the Swede who kept three cows at the edge of town. Rose particularly disliked going to fetch milk. It made her hate the town, her mama, even the patient cow. The Swede would pull at that great udder and grin while she waited.

It came by chance, her first brush with loving. Mr. Meiklejon needed fresh milk for his tea. She let the bucket swing beside her, felt the metal bail shift in her hand. The wind twisted and wove her dress between her legs despite heavy petticoats. She was conscious of the rubbing between her thighs.

She came around the corner into an unmoving object. Rose dropped the empty pail, a strong hand picked it up.

"Here, miss, I think this is yours."

Looking through her loosened hair, she saw him. Tall and straight, dark hair curled under his hat, eyes that laughed. Rose frowned; no one laughed at her.

"Aren't you a pretty one? I bet you're Queen Victoria."

She giggled. "I'm sure I don't know you, sir. Please let me pass." She shoved at him.

He laughed and stepped aside. "Good day, Miss Rose, or do they call you Queenie?" He bowed and removed his hat with a grand sweep and Rose could see his mass of curly hair. She reached to touch that hair, but he replaced the hat. She bit her lip with wanting.

"Miss, you're too pretty to be mad." He winked one blue eye and she knew who he was. Talk was all over town but the law never arrested him.

"You're nothing but an *outlaw*." Rose spat out the last word. She said it again: "Outlaw!"

A funny expression passed over his face. "You do speak your mind, girl. Wouldn't have thought it of a youngster like you."

She lashed back: "I'm seventeen!" She took a deep breath. "You haven't any manners." He laughed and Rose congratulated herself. Men liked fire in a girl. In their women, she silently amended.

The man wiped a hand across his mouth, then he kissed her. It tasted of whiskey and tobacco and a sweeter taste. A chaste kiss, with his mouth gentle on her closed lips. Rose wiggled against him and his mouth went to her neck. He pulled until she was standing up against him. Buttons from his shirt touched her neck, pressed against her jaw, and she could feel him breathe in and out.

"You're quite a girl, Rose. Quite a special girl." His head came down and he used his chin to guide her until he could reach her mouth again.

When they parted, Rose saw her tall outlaw through blurred eyes. She was pushed back so gently that it was not an insult. Her outlaw grinned, wiped his hands on his pants again and bent down, picked up the tin bucket, and placed it in Rose's hands.

"Now you don't want folks wondering where you are, Rose. You tend to your work, and I'll take care of mine." He walked past her and she could hear him say: "You're quite a girl, Queen Rose Victoria."

Rose dropped the miserable bucket and rubbed her hands over her arms where he had pulled her close. She shivered and felt a new ache beneath that place, and she wanted to cry and laugh.

There was laundry to be done, Mama informed her, once back home. Then Mama took Rose's face by the chin and laid a hand to Rose's forehead, bit her lip in concentration. When Rose said she'd run part way and was out of breath, Mama let her go, glad to be relieved of parental concern.

Meiklejon needed his clothes washed. It was Rose's job to wash a stranger's soiled clothing, to ruin her hands on the board, scouring with strong soap. Rose did not avert her eyes as she'd been told to do when she hung up a gentleman's undergarment. Men were no different than the ugly range bulls, snorting and pawing where females were concerned. Mama made such a fuss about propriety, so Mama should hire a less lady-like town girl. Rose stuck her hand back in the hot water, pulled out a pair of blue cotton drawers with buttons and lacings, and laughed.

Rose might be seventeen but she knew about men. Mama lectured about the ideals of pure love and motherhood, a woman's duty to her husband. She never mentioned the tingling heat, the emotions that even now stirred in Rose's belly.

Papa was yelling at his wife to hurry and get the gentleman's bill. She watched Mama scribble on the paper, with Papa leaning over her. There was no touching between them, no shared smile. No love, only commerce.

The Englishman appeared at the doorway, saw the Blaisdels, and said he would be staying an extra night, would they mind? Papa immediately smiled, his ugly face glowing. Of course, Mister Meiklejon, sir, could stay as long as he liked.

He stayed another week. The town was slow to accept his ownership of the Littlefield ranch, and Rose saw that this reluctance bothered him. The Englishman rarely spoke to her, but Rose knew he watched her, taking note of her dealings with the customers, probably deciding whether her manner was well suited to his new life.

When Mr. Meiklejon did leave—well into November—Rose purred as he leaned over her hand, raised it to brush its back lightly with his mouth, and murmured how much joy she'd given him. Rose blushed, knowing it set off her hair and features. A maidenly blush—a phrase she had read in a book from Miss Donald.

Surprisingly the gentle kiss had the same effect as Jack Holden's mouth had had on hers. Mr. Meiklejon also kissed her mama's hand and patted each of the younger girls, thanking the family for their kindnesses. Papa then ordered them all back to work as he marched off to add up the bill.

They were busy that winter. Twice Gayle Souter had driven into

Socorro to pick up wire, which was the talk of the whole area. The Englishman was fencing his land, including several springs. He was shutting off water to cattle and wild horses. Folks were downright mad.

Christmas morning came with no word from her outlaw or the Englishman. Four customers were in the dining room and Mama was fashioning a hurried meal. The Blaisdel family would share their few presents and a platter of leftovers in the evening when the travelers could want nothing more.

Rose went outside, stared down the deserted street, and shivered. But she did not return to the stuffy warmth of the hotel for her shawl. A dog trotted sideways toward a dead rabbit. Rose watched the dog circle its prey, sniff, and jump back, then dig at the corpse and jump again when the fur moved. The dog lay down, took the rabbit carefully in its mouth, and chewed slowly, making no holes or tears. Finally the dog rose with the rabbit in its mouth, and trotted toward an alley. Quite unexpectedly Rose wished she had that choice to trot down a street, turn a corner, and disappear.

"Ma'am?"

Rose jumped. She had thought herself alone, yet a man had been watching. She turned to inspect her inquisitor and was disappointed. He was small, mostly tendon and bone. She stared rudely, saw a pair of pale green eyes looking back. He had black hair and a dark beard, making his thin face even less respectable. She wondered where had he ridden from, why he was here on Christmas day? His horse was covered with dried sweat, the man's clothes caked with dirt, boots worn through, hands badly scarred. She kept staring, and he watched her until she became flustered. The eyes widened, then narrowed, and she saw his face twitch, his mouth open slightly as if catching her scent.

"Ma'am. The name of this town?"

When he spoke, there was humor in the lift of his mouth. He

noticed everything she decided, and hugged herself. He would know all about her. "This is Socorro. Where're you headed?"

"What territory, ma'am?"

Rose's arms folded directly beneath her bosom. "How could you not know where you are? Don't you know to ask someone?" Now she was angry.

He looked at her, his eyes glittering. "That's what I'm doing now, ma'am. Asking someone who knows where I am."

When she hugged herself, it wasn't for warmth. Christmas Day on an empty street and she was confronted by a wild man who didn't know the day or the country he rode. He scared her—those steady eyes, his reddened hands crossed on the saddle horn. He wouldn't let her go. She cried out: "It's Christmas Day, don't you know that at least? It's Christmas and you're alone."

"Ma'am." The man tipped his hat, stroked his nervous horse. The horse quieted, those large, scarred hands lay on the saddle horn again, and Rose licked her lips. "Maybe you best get in with your own family. Ma'am. Good day." He reined the mustang around and rode at a steady, deliberate walk down the long main street, headed toward the mountains.

Mama's voice called for potatoes. Rose licked her lips, tasted salt. "Yes, Mama." New discoveries moved within her, new emotions and feelings. The harsh eyes remained with her; the deep sadness when she spoke of Christmas. Cruel, but the words had been forced from between her lips. She needed to know his name. She could feel those ruthless hands outlining her mouth.

Her movements as she went for the potatoes were pure memory. The door pushed open, the weighty lid of the vegetable bin raised, the potatoes dug free of their sawdust bed. She watched her hand as it reached and closed the heavy wooden lid. She swallowed and thought of other things. Then she ducked through the low, root-cellar door and blinked as she reëntered sunlight.

Jack Holden was there, leaning on an old cottonwood trunk. His tall form relaxed as it graced the gnarled tree.

"Darlin' girl, you look a picture." He held out one hand.

Rose licked her lips as Mama's voice came through the high window. "Rose Victoria, the potatoes! There's another guest wanting a meal and I've got. . . ."

Mama's voice was gone, buried with Jack's mouth. The potatoes fell from her arms; his mouth parted her lips with his tongue.

"Girl!"

The voice was angry, and Jack moved aside, but his hand grazed her hip when she passed. "Good bye, little girl." He was gone as suddenly as he had appeared.

Rose got to the kitchen door and Mama took the potatoes.

CHAPTER FIVE

The fast-walking sorrel took Jack Holden from Socorro, with Jack laughing at his folly. It had been a stupid thing to do on a Christmas day but it had given him great pleasure. It pleased him to tease the caged animals. He knew that these actions would one day get him killed, but there had to be a way of dying—loving with a pretty girl would do him fine. Courting kept him from dwelling on the loss of Katherine Donald. The Blaisdel girl was more his style—flash and little substance—like his choice in horses.

The sorrel shied at a blowing weed and Jack spurred the big horse back into line. He would not ride one of the small Spanish pacers; they did not suit his wry vanity. It took a blooded horse to carry all of Jack Holden.

Several hours from town, the sorrel went to its knees. Jack stepped down as the horse buried its nose in soft sand. He grabbed the head and yanked until the horse stood. The right front tendon was thickening. *Bowed*, he thought. He undid his rigging and pulled off the bridle, then drew his pistol, wavered, and slid the weapon back. He'd leave this horse to fate.

The saddle was a burden, and walking was never good. Jack managed a mile, which ate up the bleak warmth of the afternoon. He put the saddle down, sought out a comfortable tree, and decided to wait. The territory was full of people, and some didn't know it was Christmas.

He hadn't counted on the particular horse and rider that finally approached him. Jack was in full sight of the trail, smoking a cigar. The small horse, a dark roan, was just sturdy enough to carry Jack and his saddle until he got to Son Liddell's pasture. But as Jack watched the rider, he figured he'd have to share the roan, not steal it. When the horse and rider got closer, Jack saw nothing to change his mind. The man was small but he came at Jack without hesitation.

Jack saw the watchful eyes, the nerveless hands gentle on the reins. He'd not get the roan by sweet talk or a gun. He'd have to fight, and it could come to dying. The rider stopped the roan out of reach. It was Jack's game.

"Mister, you see my trouble. Got any ideas?"

"Walk." That was all.

"Hell, mister, I done that." Damned if he'd walk when there was a horse this close. "Give a man a lift?"

The vivid eyes drifted down Jack's length, then looked at the mountains, the low sun. The eyes came around to Jack. "Tomorrow."

Didn't want company, didn't like folks much. Hell, Jack had felt it many a time when he had been threatened with a rope. The man was a mustanger—he knew by the intense smell. Best to keep upwind of his company. It would be a cold camp. Damn but he was hungry.

Before daylight, Jack slid from his blankets and approached the roan. He wiggled his fingers under the pony's nose. The roan shifted his head so Jack couldn't reach him. Jack persisted and the roan bowed his neck, touched Jack's cold fingers with a dry muzzle, and blew warmed air across Jack's palm.

"You ain't gonna steal him, mister. Get back to your sleeping." The voice came from an undetermined direction.

The son-of-a-bitch had moved his blankets. Jack lied, knowing it would make no difference. "Thought I'd make friends since he's goin' to carry double, come morning."

The knowing voice answered: "Yeah, and I just needed a softer place for my bedroll. Lie back down, mister. That roan ain't your friend."

Jack had given his name maybe three times last night, and still he got called "mister". He eased away from the roan and lay down. The blanket felt good; he was shivering from the new-dawn chill. Jack rolled up tight, cursing softly.

Cold beans, hard biscuits—at least the fellow wasn't against sharing. Cold camps didn't set well, but a mustanger couldn't risk the breath of fire on his hide. And this one was the pure quill.

The roan watered out of the rider's punched hat. This was a tough pair. It was going to be hard separating them. Jack got his saddle in one hand and came up next to the mustanger. It wasn't till then that he saw how small the man was. Not even up to Jack's chin. Yet the man didn't shrink from the threat of Jack's presence.

The mustanger pulled the cinch tight on the roan, slipped a ring bit in the horse's mouth, and buckled the headstall, held on to the split reins. Each move was spare. Then the man turned to him, eyes going up to Jack's face. Hard green eyes. Jack didn't like what burned there, knew the mustanger saw the same thing in Jack's face.

"You leave your gear, come back for it." He nodded at Jack's heavy saddle. "Ain't asking the roan to carry that thing." Jack's rig was real pretty; he'd never felt nothing but pride for the gear before. The man paused. "Bring a bridle."

Jack Holden was a lot of bad things and most he'd admit to, but he wouldn't kill a man over one horse. Not when the man looked into Jack and understood and still doled out cold beans, made the offer of a ride.

The mustanger swung up on his horse, kicked out one stirrup. Jack let his saddle drop and slid his leg over the mustang's rump. The pony squatted, ears flat back. The mustanger touched the roan's neck, spoke a few words, and the roan ears swiveled rapidly. Then Jack settled on the slippery rump and grabbed the saddle's high back. The mustanger allowed the roan to step forward. The pony half jumped, stopped, shook violently, loosening Jack. Both men laughed; the pony's ears went back again.

After a morning's ride, they climbed a small hill, and below them a band of horses grazed in a narrow cañon. Jack slid down as the mustanger spoke.

"Best think 'fore you pick out your next horse."

Jack grunted: "I got a supply some miles from here. Only needin' a lift. I'm thankin' you for the ride." He couldn't resist. "And the fine company."

Hell, Jack thought as he slid down into the cañon where the horse band grazed, *I still don't know the son-of-a-bitch's name.*

CHAPTER SIX

Jack Holden rode into Socorro once more that winter. Rose heard the horse's footsteps come around the root cellar where she was cleaning up a spilled pickle jar.

The buckskin horse Jack rode was skittish and he had his hands full as he leaned over and put his hand on her. Then he was down from the buckskin, kissing her, and Rose kissed him back. She clung to Jack, and there was nothing else in the world—until Mama's voice came from the back door.

"Rose Victoria, you get away from that man." Then it was a wail. "It's Jack Holden!" Mama's desperation was proof; Rose was no longer a child.

Jack slipped back onto his horse, looked down at Rose with those wonderful eyes. "Darlin', your ma'll bring the whole town here. I'll be ridin' on, but you keep that place warm." He smiled, and she tried reaching him but the skittish horse bolted.

Rose swept the remains of the pickle jar into a corner of the cellar and ventured out, passing by her family with a knowing smile.

Meiklejon returned to the Southern Hotel in late February. The whole town knew he had wired for more money. He spent his time at the dry goods store where Harnett would order anything for cash up front. They discussed the merits of wire while waiting for the cash to appear.

Rose didn't care about the wire or any of the talk that went with it. She only wanted Gordon Meiklejon, the suitor. He appeared lonely but that was impossible, for daily he talked with the banker and even saw the town doctor several times. Words went back and forth to England, the telegraph operator told her father. Couldn't say names for it was against company policy.

Occasionally she glimpsed him in the stuffy room Mama called a parlor, seated in a worn chair, holding a book. Those soft eyes looked out a shuttered window without blinking. She was curious to know what he thought, guessing it would be men's business.

He stopped her one evening and asked if he had offended her, for she seemed distant of late. Could he be of help? He had come to depend on her smile, he said, to brighten his days while he waded through the drudgery of finance.

Rose tucked back her hair in that practiced gesture, and smiled. It was fine, she murmured. He was busy and had little time, so much to consider, she reassured him. This pleased him, so he returned to the parlor in command of another book, with a sweater around his shoulders. An odd man, she thought. Still he was kind and owned a big ranch.

Then Jenny Miller's pa decided they best have a dance. He owned Miller's General Mercantile, where he'd started carrying newspapers and weekly magazines. Mr. Meiklejon went to the establishment daily. The dance was to be held Saturday night. Mama allowed Rose to make a new dress, and Rose chose a bright yellow, for spring. She made the dress low in front, and it was lovely.

Now all Rose needed was an invitation.

Gordon enjoyed the Southern. He even appreciated sharing a table with one or more of the hotel guests. He learned about the land, that there were places neither man nor horse could penetrate, yet cattle thrived under these deplorable conditions. Gordon listened and made his own decisions.

He should ask the Blaisdel girl to the dance. She expected such. But she was seventeen, marrying age, a child not to be trifled with unless his intentions were honorable.

It was only mid-week and word had gone out, by what means he did not understand. Outlying ranch families began to appear in town already. Gayle Souter and the hands were stringing wire and cursing their new boss. They'd been promised a bonus when they finished fencing, as Gordon wanted to insure the paternity of the next calf crop. The men did their work, but Gordon knew by their grim faces that he was not endearing himself to their winter-starved souls.

Souter came in to Socorro early Thursday to report that the wire was strung and he'd given the men off the night of the dance. It was Souter's first disobedience and a direct flaunting to Gordon's ownership of the L Slash Ranch. He glared at Souter, who glared back.

A cowboy intent on an early celebration raced a terrified horse down the long street as the townspeople ran for cover. Mrs. Blasingame, a woman of great proportions, tripped and fell in fresh manure, and the cowboy's horse bolted, depositing the eager horseman at Mrs. Blasingame's posterior. Gordon laughed. Souter was right—the men deserved their night of dancing.

Thursday afternoon word came in that the money was on its way to Silver City where it would await Gordon's arrival. It meant a ride to that town for Souter as well as Gordon. When Souter was told, he grinned at Meiklejon as if to acknowledge that he'd been outfoxed.

Mr. Meiklejon approached Rose in the hotel lobby. "My dear child, I had hoped you would understand. The bull is arriving and I must have the cash with which to finalize the purchase."

What was he talking about? No gentleman would speak of such a matter in front of a lady. She allowed a small smile to grace her features before she walked away. Her mama was calling, she said. There was work to be done.

The dance drew people for seventy miles. Rose laid out white cloths on the tables, placed candles and lanterns where Mrs. Miller pointed, and chewed over Gordon's defection while she worked.

Rose found she began to enjoy the preparations and didn't even pout when her sister Hester teased her for not having a beau. Hester was going with Jeb Miller, all spotted face and huge feet. The youngest Blaisdel, Sally, would be with the children. Rose would go unchaperoned.

The dance was, of course, very crowded. Rose did not look

for Jack Holden—he would slip in later when the men were mellowed by their liquor. The Littlefield hands were there. Red Pierson caught Rose's eye and she could not stop blushing. Finally it was Richard Blasingame who asked her to dance. He held her at arm's length and whirled her much too fast, but they danced two dances and she liked the swirl of her new dress. Heads turned to see her. Then others asked, and it was past midnight. The men's faces were flushed from their trips to the shed back of Miller's store. The younger children were asleep, lined in rows with coats thrown over them for warmth. Sally and Hester Blaisdel had been sent home.

Rose danced not caring who her partner was but quick to follow the steps. She was swept into a different world. Then the music quieted, and Rose's partner slowed. Heads came together in quiet whispers, and Rose witnessed Katherine Donald in the arms of Jack Holden.

Katherine had danced only twice. Both times the man had kept his distance and refused to make conversation. She had watched Orlie Judkins take a half step toward her, but his swollen wife had grabbed his arm and pulled him back. But at least she had danced twice, and it had felt good. Then Jack Holden stood next to her, brushing that lock of hair from his forehead, before formally asking. She glided into his arms, let him spin her away, draw her back, almost touching along his entire length. She heard the gasps—Jack Holden was dancing with Katherine Donald!

Rose smiled bravely as they whirled past, but her Jack did not return the smile. It was painful enough to make Rose push through the crowds and escape outside where she could breathe and didn't have to see them dance.

Chapter Seven

They had ridden hard. At one point on their return, when Gordon looked up from a half doze, he caught Souter in profile, ahead of him. The man cradled a rifle across his saddle, and only then had it occurred to Gordon how much danger they were in. The purpose of their trip to Silver City had been well known.

They came out of the steep hills around the lights of an un-named village. There were places where the ponies slowed to pick their path through tumbled shale. The grullo stopped abruptly, bumping into Souter's favored pony. Then Gordon heard the stuttering voice and saw the blurred shadow of Sout-er's head swivel as if trying to locate their attacker.

"I say it again, *señor*. Give me the money."

Souter's head moved slightly—Gordon could see that much— but the man said nothing, and his rifle did not shift to focus on a target. Gordon's heart pounded. A rifle trigger cocked.

"*Señor,* the money."

Gordon watched Souter. The voice was close.

"You . . . not that old man . . . you have the money, *señor.* Give it to me."

Gordon fumbled with the pouch on his saddle.

"I will kill you, *señor.*"

Gordon put effort into his tone of voice. Still it sounded as if he were terrified. "I am trying, sir. But this . . . pony will not remain still." While he spoke, he pricked the grullo with one spur. The pony kicked out and Gordon made a great show of grabbing for the reins with both hands.

"*Señor,* get off that horse."

The glint off the rifle barrel was close to the pony's skull, and Gordon stopped his ruse. The pouch slipped back onto the grullo pony's hindquarters. The pony humped its back. Gordon felt the pony's head shake through the reins.

"Ah, *señor,* it is not so difficult, after all."

Gordon raised the pouch as high as he could, for it was quite heavy, thinking to throw it into the dark and charge the enemy. The act would be futile, but he held the pouch a moment, bearing its precious weight for the last time.

Souter's pony swung its hindquarters, blocking where Gordon would throw the pouch. The mottled pony's ear were pricked and the pony let out a short nicker.

Then an almost familiar voice interrupted: "Mister, you get!" The voice was strong, clear.

Gordon could hear and feel more than see anything. A man cursing—a horse's irregular gait.

Then Gayle Souter swung his pony around to face Gordon. Souter's voice was not steady. "What happened?"

Gordon shook his head while he lowered the pouch.

Both men turned at the sound of an advancing horse. Gordon heard a shift from Souter's mount, saw the barrel of Souter's rifle raised once more. Such vigilance had just proven ineffective, but it gave a solid feel to the moment.

The rider and animal stopped. The familiar voice again: "I couldn't catch him, but he won't be back."

A hint of amusement colored the words, and Gordon finally recognized the speaker—their *mesteñero*. "Thank you, sir, for your assistance."

There was a long silence. Gordon had to trust his senses, which told him the horse and rider were still there, had not walked away.

Finally: "It weren't a Mex . . . that robber of yours."

Silence, then Gayle Souter spoke. "Glad you agree. I'd hate to accuse the wrong man."

"He rode a runt bronc', not more than thirteen hands, from the stride," advised the *mesteñero*.

Gordon nodded, although he wondered why the detail would be important.

Souter laughed. "That eliminates one suspect."

The *mesteñero* laughed, too, and it took a few moments for Gordon to get the joke—it could not have been Jack Holden.

Gordon pushed his horse until the animal greeted the roan mustang. "Sir, I am grateful to you for your rescue. Please, if there is ever anything I can do . . . ah. . . ." He expelled a hard breath, having come close to offering money, a terrible breach of ethics. "Gordon Meiklejon, sir." He knew never to ask a name, for it could be written on a poster or nailed to a wall.

The answer—"Burn English."—was spoken quietly.

"It is my pleasure to make your acquaintance, sir."

No response other than the sound of crackling branches and clipped rocks.

"I do believe he's gone, Mister Meiklejon," Souter said.

Gordon expelled a repressed sigh, and stroked his pony's neck. The animal warmth reassured him, and he was able to find enough saliva in his mouth to form the words: "Let me re-tie the saddle pouch, and then we will be going."

Meiklejon and Souter reached Socorro before dawn. They rode up the middle of the empty street, up to a crowd of tied saddle horses and harnessed teams that reminded them of the dance they had missed.

Gordon turned in the saddle, feeling every movement of the bones in his seat and legs. Music came from Miller's General Mercantile, half tones awkwardly tapping a ragged beat. Souter's face registered dismay when Gordon spoke.

"Just one dance, Mister Souter. To celebrate our successful return. I shall see you when the bank opens, which I suspect will not occur on time this morning."

He allowed Souter to lead the clay-colored pony beside his mottled cream pacer, and noted, as if from a great distance, that he had no qualms in trusting Souter with the hard coin packed in the saddle pouch. That money was as safe as if it were ensconced in the Bank of England.

He spent time at a water trough wetting back his hair, washing his eyes and hands. Finally he buried his face in the icy water and came up refreshed. Water dribbled inside his shirt and tickled his back and ribs. It felt good to be among the living.

Inside the mercantile, the musicians pulled at their instruments by reflex. Dancers spun awkwardly on the floor. Gordon paused, looking for his partner. He walked directly to her through the path of dancers, and bowed as he came within her gaze. Cautious lest his sudden appearance might upset her, he held out his hand.

She slipped into his arms, and it was a distinct pleasure, as light-headed, exhausted, dirt-stained, and sore as Gordon Meiklejon was, to be dancing with Miss Katherine Donald.

Mama was already busy when Rose walked in the kitchen. Rose took a deep breath and released it, congratulating herself when Mama barely looked up at her eldest child.

"Did you dance all night, Rose Victoria? I saw you with that Red Pierson. I don't think he's suitable. Now the Blasingame boy. . . ." Mama went on while turning the potatoes expected by the Southern's guests. Almost everyone in town had attended the dance and hopefully there would be few who would rise early to savor Mrs. Blaisdel's cooking.

Rose knew what men and women did now. Jack had played with her outside where no one was watching. She studied her mother. It wasn't possible that Mama and her father had done what she'd done tonight.

"Mama, let me help." Rose picked up a knife and went to peeling, and her mama came close to her and sniffed. Rose's heart beat hard as she prayed Mama would not smell what her precious daughter had been doing with her sweet outlaw. But it was only Mama's winter cold, which would last until the warmth of mid-April, that made her sniff.

"I knew we could trust you at the dance. Missus Miller said she would keep an eye on you, but that she had to leave early and it wouldn't be right for a girl as pretty as you to be out by herself. She was worried."

Later, when the revelers had recovered from their festivities and the town streets and businesses began to see some activity, Gordon Meiklejon entered the Southern dining room and asked Mrs. Blaisdel for a meal for himself and Gayle Souter, as they had a long ride back to the ranch.

It was two meals at double cost, because of the extra work, but it was requested by Mr. Meiklejon. Rose was sent in to serve, and she saw the change. Gordon's hands seemed steadier despite the missing fingertips, and his mouth was set in a constant smile. She found herself looking at him quite differently.

Now that she knew what men wanted, Rose couldn't help but wonder what each would be like with his pants around his ankles. Such a picture did not leave much dignity to the males; they would all be equally silly when they wanted a woman. How could her mother take it so seriously when the act was such a foolish, awkward plunging.

While she was in the dining room folding napkins, repeating the chore that took up a good part of her long days, a man entered and headed directly to Meiklejon's table. She kept folding and refolding a particular napkin while she listened.

The man was compressed into a hard woolen suit. Rolls of fat burst above his shiny collar. His hands thickened across the backs where tufts of hair decorated each knuckle. Rose was called to bring over another cup and more coffee. The man's name was Ben Stradley.

Rose fussed with the coffee, pouring while the men talked.

61

Mr. Stradley was the law from Silver City and had ridden in on a tale of an attempted robbery. Stradley tipped his head in silent questioning.

The Englishman's voice carried well, so, even as she retreated, Rose could hear the details.

"Yes, we were held up. But the would-be bandit did not get anything. I think he was more terrified by what happened than we were." Here Meiklejon looked at Mr. Souter, and the man nodded, pushed his chair back, and picked up his coffee cup.

Still Stradley did not ask questions, but Rose saw the fat along his jowls tremble.

Meiklejon continued: "A man came to our rescue, although I can't imagine what he was doing in such inhospitable terrain."

Rose watched Stradley's face. It wrinkled and frowned as Meiklejon raised his hand and continued.

"I realize you did not come here for opinions, sir. Please let me gather my thoughts. I've had little sleep and yet feel quite revived. Our savior rode up and told the so-called thief that he would be killed if he continued. The thief evidently was not so stupid that he mistook these words for a casual threat. He ran. That is all, Mister Stradley. An uninspired, though melodramatic, event."

Stradley took a gulp of coffee, then beckoned Rose to refill the cup. His voice was wet. "Mister Meiklejon, do you have any idea who would know you carried that money, and do you know who your savior actually was?"

Rose took her time pouring the refill.

"Well, sir, I do know that the erstwhile thief was not one particular man."

Stradley wrinkled his face at the odd statement and stuck out the tip of his tongue. There was a long pause. Rose held the pot above the filled cups.

Meiklejon smiled, looked at Souter, and said: "It was not

Jack Holden."

At the name Rose's hand skipped and she spilled coffee on Mama's white tablecloth. The men paid no attention.

Stradley's voice deepened. "How could you know such a fact?"

"Because the robber rode a small horse, Mister Stradley, as our savior pointed out."

The men laughed. Rose wiped at the spreading coffee stain.

"Well, then your robber could be anyone but Holden." The fat man looked directly at Rose. "Miss, do you have any fresh milk? I like fresh milk with my coffee."

When she returned with Stradley's request, Meiklejon was telling the lawman how he had first encountered the mustanger, and his voice was excited. "The first time I saw him was in the light of a campfire and I could not now swear to his individual features. He is a small man . . . that much I know . . . and at the time he smelled quite badly, which Mister Souter informed me is the mark of a true *mesteñero*."

"Why do you think he intervened?" Stradley asked.

"That he stepped in and confronted the thief is all that matters to me, but, to answer your query, I believe it is that we shared our coffee with him last fall."

Stradley nodded.

"Did he give any indication as to his direction?"

Meiklejon snorted, then took a long sip of his cold coffee. "Mister Stradley, we did not discuss itineraries. The gentleman made his intentions known to the robber, who then fled. That is all I can tell you. We were saved by his generosity and offered him our gratitude."

But Stradley was not to be silenced. "Did this man tell you his name?"

The Englishman sighed deeply and placed both of his hands on the white tablecloth, a gesture calculated to draw attention to his maimed fingers. He was using what he had to make his statement more important. Rose recognized the act. It was what she did with her deep breaths and hair-tossing.

"Mister Stradley, I did ask his name in accordance with your range etiquette. And he answered me with no rancor. I cannot imagine a man who would so simply pass on his name would then lie about it. And as the name is unusual, I do not think it a false one."

"Well, sir, tell me and we both will know."

Stradley's jowls quivered as Meiklejon answered, his voice abrupt and tired. "His name is Burn English."

★ ★ ★ ★ ★

BURN ENGLISH

★ ★ ★ ★ ★

CHAPTER EIGHT

It was good range. Where the grass changed abruptly to desert, the dark mouth of a cañon opened behind a spring. Around the resulting pool, rock walls shaped a small valley. Burn English and his roan kept watch from a high bench. The gelding's small ears swiveled endlessly; the shaggy body quivered under its rider's hand.

The mustangs grazed as Burn judged them. Finding the valley had been pure luck. He'd dogged the band for six months when he could endure the loneliness. Until he lost them south of Springerville. There were a thousand miles of tracking to the heart of these hills. He'd ridden east by instinct, following greening grass and the scent of water.

The valley where he found the herd fanned out, then abruptly narrowed between rock walls. Burn could make out a number of well-defined paths that disappeared into the cañon itself. Lush grass, water bubbling from the spring—sanctuary for the mustangs and Burn.

Burn coughed and spat. The red roan jumped and then settled. The sturdy gelding had been captured as a long yearling, and Burn had ridden him four years. Only the slightest of trembling along the deep rib cage, the wet hide on the rigid neck betrayed the roan's excitement.

Wiping his mouth, Burn felt the brush of his sparse whiskers, and the growth brought home to him the endless isolation he'd endured. In the past months he'd met up with more humans than he was used to seeing in a year, but he'd been driven by a tormenting ache. He still cursed himself for riding into town on Christmas. The girl's words had hit hard. He'd violated his own rules by needing coffee, giving a drifter a ride, and he dismissed his good citizen act in stopping a robbery.

He studied the wild horse band. There were maybe fifteen horses scattered in small groups, with the few two and three-year-olds bunched together. Most were mares heavy with foal; two early foals clung to their mamas.

It was bitter cold in late March. Caught in the plains between Datil and the Gallo Mountains, the wind blew hard ice that stiffened in the roan's thick mane. The valley might offer shelter to the mustangs, but for Burn and the roan there was no warmth or safety. Wind lifted strands of Burn's frozen hair across his face. He had to concentrate on the horses, he had to pay close attention and make a decision based on instinct and knowledge. But he was damned near too frozen to think.

The stallion was a dark bay in his prime. Burn would take only mares. The best ones would be fat and heavy, even after a long winter. He had to make his choice, but in his heart he wanted to race the roan into the center of the herd and chase them to where nothing could threaten their freedom.

As if the roan felt Burn's edginess, the little horse rose quickly on his hind legs, squealing as Burn fought to keep his seat. He needed to concentrate, to pick and choose, to figure out where to build a horse trap. *Damn.*

Burn slowly reined the mustang through a break in the rock. It was not yet time to confront the stallion and his mares. More of the miserable hail clattered on Burn's frozen face and he laughed, a sound that the roan did not hear often. The gelding bucked, almost unseating the rider. Burn slapped his hand against his frozen chaps and the sound rattled the mustang. The horse bolted and Burn let it run. Then Burn reined up; no sense in using energy, not when there was so much work ahead.

He stepped down from the roan, weary, always hungry. He'd eaten a stale biscuit, drank a few sips of water earlier. Not enough after watching the horse band through the cold blustery night. The horses had slept; he'd kept guard.

He offsaddled the mustang, rubbing down the wet back with a fistful of dead leaves. Slender icicles frozen under the roan's chin jingled with the roan's head shaking. Burn hated the sound. He hobbled the roan and hung his saddle and the wet blanket from a lightning-struck cottonwood. If he didn't, squirrels or maybe a skunk or a raccoon would come for the dried sweat and he'd own a chewed saddle, ruined reins, a handful of blanket. Without his gear, a *mesteñero* was useless.

Chewing on the last of a biscuit, washed down by teeth-jarring cold water, Burn studied the land. No fences, no ranch houses or soddies, only miles of rock and steep cuts, thin streams, and high grass mixed with cactus. Rolling sandhills broke the smooth horizon. It was good country for trapping wild horses, or grazing cattle. Not much good for anything else.

Burn got up, mindful of the aches and pains he needed to ignore. He checked on his gear, went to the stream, knelt, and splashed water on his face, scrubbed his hands clean with coarse bottom sand. He couldn't wash all over. For now he could barely tolerate his own company.

He stretched and put both hands to the small of his back. He was getting old in a young man's game, but he knew no other way to live. In the past he had ridden broncos for a rancher, and left when the boss tried to stick him with cow work. He'd been seventeen when he struck up a partnership with a *mesteñero* who knew the old ways. They partnered for three years, until a bronco broke the *mesteñero*'s neck. Burn buried Enrique, spoke a few words of rough Spanish, and rode on.

That was five years ago. Now he chased the wild ones—being

accepted into their society was easier than mingling with his own kind. The mornings were hard climbing up from sleep, pained by mended bones, recent wounds, scars that ran deep. He was coming to a bad time, when he would be lamed and crippled, too old to do what so far had given him a rough freedom. He needed to claim land and live in some bare comfort. His bones told him it was becoming a necessity.

The skies spit hail, the clouds rolled overhead like phantom waves, hiding and then revealing the almost full moon. Burn laughed. Burn English, alone since he was thirteen, thinking he could pick out land and build a house, live in the rest of the world, when in truth he couldn't buy a simple meal or afford a hot bath.

Burn sat against the old cottonwood and ran his fingers through his shaggy hair, sweeping it out of his eyes like a horse's forelock. He needed a good shearing, never mind a bath and a meal, a house of his own. He snorted and the red roan snorted back.

Burn caught and saddled the roan. It was hunger again, and a strangled anger he could not quench. He smoothed out the still-damp saddle blanket and twisted the *cincha* to flake off caked salt. He couldn't afford to gall the roan. Anger goaded him. He was being driven out of his familiar haunts by the damned wire fences. He swallowed against a dry throat, hating the weakness. Fences were inevitable. He knew that not making the same choices as other men gave him no special rights. There was no room for blame—it lay on him and no one else.

When horse and rider slowed at the valley's entrance, Burn was pleased. The mustangs slept in pairs, one on guard, head hanging, legs locked in readiness; the other tucked neatly on the ground, safe against the high wind and predators.

Burn guided the roan past the water hole, where the moon's twin floated in the icy pool. An owl spread out its wings and drifted above the reflecting surface. He listened for night sounds—the owl's cry, a coyote's call, small rodents brushing through tall grass.

He pushed the roan to follow a faint trail behind the pool into the cañon's maw. The trail looped and twisted, presenting many places where he could cut off the possibility of escape. He returned past the pool, checking the different breaks in those high rock walls. He'd have to fence those escapes, a section or two of high rails would keep the wild band in the valley. Dead junipers lay among the rock, a few straight pines that had fallen. He hated building fence.

Burn guided the roan among the sleeping mares. The stallion raised his head in exhausted challenge. Burn rode back to the crude camp, tired enough maybe to sleep. The moon disappeared behind quick clouds. Burn once again hobbled the roan, hung up the gear, rolled in the smelly, wet blanket, and went to sleep quickly, a thin smile on his tight face.

The band was gone for four days and it rained the whole time. Burn shivered in his wet slicker, barely alive inside the saddle blankets and his stinking sheepskin coat. When the horses returned, a mare was in heat and the stallion came courting. As the stallion caught and mounted the mare, Burn had to look away.

He saw the stallion slide off the mare. When she turned her head, whickered, and touched the stallion's wet muzzle, Burn felt an old ache pulse in his belly, and he wanted to frighten the band and let them run far from his plans.

The next morning they were gone—he guessed for two or three days again. He pulled out a number of dead trees, dug holes with a crude shovel. Had an axe, too—tools of a *mesteñero*'s trade. He planted posts at three breaks in the rock wall. The band had gone out past the pool, and before that they had come back on the west side. So he put up a five-foot barrier at one of the eastern breaks, and left the two western breaks open, with only the posts to mark his intentions. The horses would return from the west, balk at the posts until the stallion determined the odd objects were no threat, then they would spill into the valley and get back to grazing.

Time worked for him now, time and the harsh spring winds that dried up what winter snow remained. The spring-fed pool was a constant. The stallion knew it, returned his band to it when other water was sucked dry.

The band returned in three days. The lead mare quit at the posts, refused to let the band pass. The stallion came up snorting, pawing at the posts, and, when they did not fight or run, he swept past them into the cañon, arrogant in his victory.

The bachelor colts came in from the east. At first they came to the new fence and stopped in a tight group. A dark colt, colored much like his sire, came forward to do battle. Striking wildly, the colt rattled the fence rails but could not move them. He retreated, and, as disciplined as a flight of birds, the bachelors turned and ran to the valley's wide end. They swept down onto the ripening grass, the dark colt bucking and kicking.

As the colts raced through the grazing herd, the dark colt strayed too close to the stallion, who charged the youngster and caught him on the flank, tore a wide, bloody hole before letting go. The band stayed one day and was gone. Burn tracked sign, read that one horse limped badly.

He worked doggedly on the fence, built a second panel, five feet and solid with rails he could bully into place. Blisters covered his palms and fluid seeped into his ragged shirt cuffs. He slept through the night and into the next day. The horses returned to the water, then left two days later. The mares went to the east side and found themselves trapped. The stallion pawed at the rails but there was no escape, so the mares spilled down the sandhills, dodged the furious stallion, and went out through the west gate. The trap was closing.

Burn drove himself to finish fencing the mouth of the valley, sleeping in brief naps when he could no longer carry a railing. He had to rely on the roan's instinct to warn him. He kept the mustang hobbled in close and studied his attentiveness.

The horse herd came back but the new fence galled the stallion. The herd moved past the pool through the narrow cañon. After the horses were gone, the roan whinnied, and a single horse answered. Burn jerked the Spencer from the roan's saddle, jacked a shell in place, then backed up until he felt a boulder behind him.

"You . . . I got a Spencer and it ain't on you yet."

"Friend, the boss sent me looking for strays," came an answering voice. "This's our summer range. I lost track of a few cows . . . one a big brindle should have a week-old calf with her."

So, he was on some rancher's summer grass. It was spring by the months and winter by the cold, so Burn waited, but the rider was shy about making an appearance. Burn thought to shoot, but, with his luck, he'd hit something. He tried again.

"Mister, I ain't seen a cow, but I seen tracks."

Burn heard the horse start walking, and pointed the Spencer down—a friendly gesture, but he could raise and fire quickly. He needed a few more days, a week or two, until the band was trapped and branded.

The horse appeared. A good-headed bay that started when it saw Burn. The rider himself wasn't as much as his horse—long-legged, curled boots hanging to the bay's knees, long arms folded across a lean chest, with a round face more like a child's sitting under a too-big hat. The man looked straight at Burn. Burn drew back his shoulders and thought to raise the Spencer, but it would be a fool gesture of faint pride. The rider wasn't as young as his round face indicated and he carried deceptive muscle on his lanky frame. He could step down and break Burn in two.

"I been watching you some the last few days. You got a lot of work done all by yourself. You caught any of them bronc's yet? By the way, the name's Davey Hildahl and I ride for the L Slash."

The bay stretched down for a bite of grass and Hildahl let his boots swing out of the heavy stirrups. His eyes said he was no stranger to the work; they watched Burn carefully. Burn's mustang hobbled up to greet the visitors, but the bay paid no attention.

Hildahl tried again. "Now my horse, he's got the right idea. Past noon it is . . . going to be past the next meal if I don't keep better time. Some eating don't look like it would hurt you neither, and it sure would make me good company. Coffee's always a good place to start."

Burn raised the Spencer, let it drift before settling on the bay's chest.

The visitor shook his head. "That ain't friendly. You got to eat same as me. Even if you sleep out here with the bronc's. Try letting that Spencer look at the ground again."

Burn spoke: "No cause to come down on a man doing his job." He was as surprised by his voice as was the visitor. Hadn't spoken to a two-legged beast in three weeks, and now he was snapping. "Hildahl, ride on if I don't suit you." He allowed the Spencer to point south again, and Hildahl let out that breath.

"All I was asking was about a brindle cow and if you got a biscuit or two I could chew on. I get hungry riding up here . . . never do pack enough grub to last. Besides, you're on Meikle-jon's land. He owns title to all you can see."

Burn got angrier. "Not the horses he don't! I tracked 'em,

and I'll brand and ride 'em. They're mine!" He tried to settle his temper, but this mealy son-of-a-bitch. . . . *Ah, hell,* Burn thought.

The man seemed to understand. "Horse chaser . . . since you ain't give me a name yet . . . maybe I won't say nothing about the bronc's and your fencing. Not for a while anyways. In your traveling, you seen this big brindle cow and her calf?"

Burn steadied the Spencer against his thigh as he spat out the words. "I saw sign two days past, going north. Big cow dragging afterbirth. Couldn't tell if she was brindle."

"Thanks, horse chaser, for the report. Ain't been up north . . . never figured she'd strike out for there . . . ain't much graze. But if she's in trouble . . . hell, cows ain't too bright." Hildahl's long fingers picked up the reins and instantly the bay was ready. The horse took several steps, then Hildahl stopped it, swung around in the saddle, and stared at Burn. "Now I know you been out here too long, horse chaser, and I know you think you own that band. But I still don't have a name for you. I'll set real peaceable, so you don't have to raise that damned Spencer."

Burn told the short truth of the matter. "I come up from Texas following these mustangs. The name's Burn English. You tell your boss these bronc's're mine."

Hildahl wouldn't let it be. "Now I heard that name before. Seems a man stopped a robbery. That was the boss he saved from being robbed . . . foreman was with him . . . and the name was Burn English. Could be you . . . it ain't a name too many folks'd use." Hildahl continued: "I don't know the boss all that well. He's an Englishman. The foreman'll honor the debt, but he won't take kindly to your using summer graze. You best walk careful, Mister Burn English."

Burn rubbed his whiskered face hard with his left hand.

Hildahl didn't stop. "English, listen to me . . . it's been a dry winter and spring so far. That grass'll be needed sooner than usual. You ride careful." Then he grinned, let his long legs swing free of the stirrups. "Too bad you ain't one for eating. Other that that, it's been a right pleasure talking some with you. English, you take care."

Burn watched Hildahl turn the bay gelding north after the brindle cow. He'd meant to chew on some jerky, take a short rest before he got back to work. Hildahl's visit left him in a hurry to catch the horses before some fool laid claim to them. He forced himself to saddle and ride to the section of fence he intended as a gate. It was a too-familiar act as he laid fresh-cut juniper over the poles; he'd done this too often, trapped too many good horses.

The mustangs returned while Burn slept. He was out of biscuits, had only one strip of jerky left, so he made do with too much water and small bites of the beef. The roan looked good—grazing on the lush grasses around the lightning-struck tree was keeping him fit and eager.

Burn woke with a strip of jerky in hand, the canteen emptied across his knee, one pant leg soaked. He'd been snoring. Drool stained his chin whiskers from the half-chewed jerky in his mouth. *A god-awful picture,* he thought, mad at himself for having fallen back asleep.

The band drifted between the empty posts, careful to shy from the fencing across the valley end. They were gaunt and thirsty, yet the stallion made them wait, circling the mares and foals, nipping any mare too eager to drink. Alert despite evidence of exhaustion, the stallion was certain the fence meant harm to him and his harem. Finally he let the mares go down to drink the good spring water.

Burn waited until the mares were full. He was counting on the bloated, water-filled bellies to make his work easier. He'd planned well. The horses had come in over the railings with tired, choppy strides. Now, as they drank their fill and splashed in the pool, Burn eased along the ridge, cursing when he kicked a slide of pebbles loose that spiraled down onto the grass flooring. The stallion's head came up at the sound; the horse quickly began to drive the mares toward Burn and their last chance to escape.

Burn shouted. The mares kept coming, then the herd swirled back around the stallion and into the valley toward the wider, fenced end. The mares ran the height of the long fence where some slowed to a trot, muzzles scraping the fence's top rail. Burn dropped the first gate pole in place, threw in two more, trying to keep an eye on the stallion.

The dark bay rushed Burn, but skidded to a stop at the mixture of scents. The horse made a tight circle, came back as Burn kept stacking rails, feeling small and useless alongside the horse's rage. Burn wrapped a rawhide strip around the top gate pole as the stallion charged. Burn yelled and the horse slowed. Burn slapped his leg, and the stallion reared. Then Burn skidded his battered hat at the horse and the animal sat back on his haunches, pawing at the shapeless hat.

A few mares grazed, some whickered for their foals, some stood quietly, still carrying a foal, too tired to eat. The stallion exploded downhill toward the pool of water and the entrance into the narrow cañon. Burn waited. The mares watched but did not follow. The stallion was gone several minutes, then returned at a slow trot, head high, tail switching restlessly.

The mares lowered their heads to the grass. Nothing would disturb them now, not the angry stallion and especially not the small battered figure, who stood on braced legs near the railed gate.

Burn caught up the roan mustang and rode back to his poor camp. This time he stripped off his clothing and went into the stream, splashed the icy water all over himself and scrubbed off as much dirt as he could with fistfuls of sand. At night, after lighting a fire, he shot himself a rabbit, skinned and roasted it, pulled it apart with shaking fingers, and ate every last bite. Chewed the bones and sucked the marrow. Then he slept, knowing the horses waited.

He woke before sunrise. The roan was edgy, so Burn let him run until the horse easily responded to Burn's touch. At the edge of the valley, Burn laid down the gate rails. The stallion caught wind of Burn, and rushed forward, stopping only ten feet away. Burn led the roan through the gate, replaced the poles, and mounted cautiously, feeling the roan tremble from the stallion's presence. He talked to both horses, using his voice to calm the roan.

The stallion lifted his head and raised his upper lip. From a human, it would be an insult. But Burn laughed—human stink, rabbit flesh, hot fire, scrubbed skin. The stallion began a charge, but Burn slapped his hand against his chaps and the stallion veered off toward the complacent mares.

Eventually the stallion grazed, occasionally lifting his head to watch Burn and the roan. Burn headed down the narrow end of the cañon to his woven fence of twisted juniper and light pine. A single horse had fought the fence and managed to break only a few of the junipers. Burn made quick repairs and went back around the pool into the valley.

He and the roan drifted along the east side, the two sections of fence that had been left unchallenged. During the night the band had endlessly circled the valley close to the walls, shying from the fences. They'd run themselves tired looking to escape, but the fencing had held, and now the mares were grazing or sleeping, letting their foals nurse in peace.

A long hour passed, and the stallion kept a restless check on Burn. Burn stayed away from the water and finally the stallion went to drink, standing for a long time in the shallows, head hanging, eyes closed, a mouthful of cool water held tightly in his mouth.

The mares dozed beside their sleeping foals. The stallion barely moved as Burn guided the roan in between the resting mares. He wanted to cut out the injured colt—the hole in his flank drained a yellow fluid that had crusted down the length of his hind leg. Spooked, the colt could run only four or five strides before drawing up to stand on three legs.

The colt was much like his sire, with a fine head, wide ribs, clean legs, and strong hindquarters. The splash of white across the dark face was startling, an uneven blaze much like the markings of a bright sorrel mare in the herd. She had a wobbly filly at her side now, a dark bay with the same uneven blaze.

The colt watched as Burn came in close, but made no attempt to run. Burn sighed—it might work. Unexpectedly, with ears back, mouth open, the stallion charged, scattering the bachelor herd. The roan bolted, and Burn stayed with the horse even as the roan went to his knees, then came up bucking and squalling. Burn imagined he could hear the stallion's breath, smell the raging hate.

The roan leaped twice, went down again. Burn flew out of the saddle as the roan climbed up and ran. Burn's boot caught the stirrup; he couldn't pull free. The mustang ran two strides, felt Burn's weight, and kicked out, missed, kicked again. The stallion slowed, puzzled by the roan's new shape. Burn hugged his chest and prayed that, without the stallion's pressure, the roan would quit.

Then the stallion screamed and the mustang launched into air. Burn's head and shoulders slammed on the ground, bounced over rock. He groaned, hugged himself closely. The panicked roan ran sideways against Burn's weight. His ribs were hit, his shirt torn, the sheepskin coat shredded. Rocks scraped him raw. A blow to his head and he saw light, tasted copper.

He'd seen a man dragged once, had scraped up the pieces before burying them in a small hole.

He reached for the old Walker Colt, thumbed back the leather thong. He cocked it as the mustang tripped and went down. Burn eased back on the trigger, hopeful for that one moment. The roan heaved up and Burn felt a blow on his side, then, aiming at the mustang's belly, pulled the trigger once, heard the shot smash into flesh, heard the roan scream as he shot until the Walker was empty, and the roan went down.

A hind leg was twisted under the roan's gaping belly. The stench flowed out in a steaming cloud. In a final spasm, the roan's quarters shook and a hind leg flexed, kicked out. Burn felt the hoof pass his face, and knew he'd survived.

CHAPTER NINE

"Souter, I got to talk to the boss."

Souter looked at Davey Hildahl and nodded. "He's up to the house, talking with Miss Katherine." That would fluster the man—nothing else but Katherine Donald got Davey scared. True to form, Hildahl's face turned a bright red. "Anything I should know, Davey?"

Hildahl shook his head. "Maybe the boss'll tell you." That was good enough.

At the house: "Mister Meiklejon, I got something to tell you."

"Well, ah . . . Hildahl, what is it?" The man was still having trouble remembering names. Davey guessed he couldn't blame him. They only had one new name to remember.

"I found that cow Souter sent me looking for." He couldn't get the rest past his tongue. It was almost a betrayal, but he rode for the L Slash and, therefore, for the Englishman, and, as long as he took the pay, he owed his loyalty to the brand. He said: "A fella got some horses up to your summer grass, in

Lightning Valley. Next to that old cottonwood got hit bad two years past."

Meiklejon looked at Davey strangely. He hadn't been that far up on his northern range, had been too busy at the home ranch, ordering bulls through the mail, by God. Doing things Davey didn't know to understand.

"Yes?"

"He got a lot of horses on your grass . . . real wild ones. Figures to catch and brand as many as he can."

Meiklejon seemed to be getting the heart of the matter now. "You mean he is using my graze to feed what he considers his own horses, although they are legally still wild and available to anyone who can brand them?"

Yeah, Davey thought. *Range law says one thing, but this time the bronc's belong to the bad-tempered horse chaser.* He hoped Meiklejon could see merit in the unusual argument. Davey nodded. "There's more to it." He glanced at Miss Katherine. She smiled and he forgot what he was meaning to say.

"Well, Hildahl?"

Davey choked. "Fella got those horses on your grass . . . he's the same one saved your hide this past winter."

Meiklejon stared, then rubbed his face gently. "A small man, very dark, almost rude, but basically a decent fellow?"

Got him right there, Davey thought. *Had to be the same man.* "Yeah, something like that. Name is Burn English, and he's a runt hardcase, and all-'round wild one." Davey risked a glance at Miss Katherine.

"Well, I can't just let him have the grass."

Ah, hell, Davey thought.

"And I can't chase him off. He did save my life, and a great deal of money, and never asked for anything in return."

So the foreigner weren't that much a fool.

"Mister Hildahl, you tell the gentleman he has two weeks on

the grass. That should give him enough time to catch all the wild ones he can, although I still do not understand how he thinks he can manage alone."

That was it. Meiklejon turned with a kind of bow to Miss Katherine, and said: "My dear, where were we?" Davey had been dismissed.

Davey caught and saddled a rough dun. The horse was a sorehead, bucking at every touch of the rein, but the son could hit a high lick through brush and rock and never miss a stride. Davey figured to finish two chores, and so roped out the ancient, Appaloosa mare Souter had told him to get rid of. "She ain't of no use no more . . . take her off and shoot her," he had told Davey. An order Davey hated, but it was kinder than turning her loose to starve.

Burn was sitting up, checking the damage, when Hildahl rode in.

Davey stayed on his dun. The App mare was restless. He had planned to turn her in with the stallion, give her one last chance. He watched the *mesteñero* finger a cut over his eye and saw it needed stitches.

Burn would bet some ribs were cracked, and his chaps were laid out along his legs in strips, plumb worthless now, but they'd saved most of his hide.

Hildahl started talking. "I found that brindle cow a few days back. Standing over a dead calf, close enough to dead herself. I finished the job. Calf had an extra leg. Seen things like that before. I buried the calf real deep. Now I got this mare to get rid of and looks like I need to give you a ride to some place safe."

Burn found it hard to keep the man in focus. The round head and hazel eyes got too close to him, then too far away and the mouth flapped more words, looking pleased and mournful

82

at the same time. Burn shook his head, found it wasn't a good idea.

They watched each other, taking measure. Hildahl grimaced and looked off first. "Told the boss about you. And them mustangs. You got two weeks, then you better get gone." Burn found he couldn't move his head fast, or think much at all. Hildahl plodded along. "Good thing I came by, Mister Mustanger."

"Hell, mister yourself, I don't need your help," Burn fumed, angry at the lanky cowboy.

Hildahl grinned. "Didn't say I'd help, just said it's a good thing I came along. You ain't got a horse now . . . how you plan to catch up those bronc's?"

Burn stood by himself, took two steps, and fell. It was a struggle to get up again. Burn hated showing weakness to any man.

Hildahl surprised him—didn't offer help, but kept talking. "Handsome devil, that stallion. Good mares, too. Best of the wild stock I've seen in a long time. Too bad about the dark colt . . . that leg'll kill him."

Half listening, furious, Burn got to his feet again and shook his fist at the talk as if the gesture could booger off the man's interest in the horses. A whole nest of sore woke up—ribs, shoulders, back, and butt. Only his legs spread wide, and his anger, kept Burn standing. He glared at the remains of his chaps—laid clean off his legs, useless to him now. Rocks could do that to leather. Burn shook his head, careful of his balance.

Hildahl must have stepped off the dun. His fist came into Burn's sight, holding a wad of material. "Here, you might tie off that cut, looks like it could bleed you dry."

Burn looked down, saw that the dirt at his feet was red-spotted. His thigh was wet. He took the bandanna and twisted it above the wound. The rest of the repairs he could make by himself. Hildahl was unusually quiet. Burn wasn't going to say thanks. He walked to the dead mustang, intending to yank his gear free of the carcass. He dropped to his knees, and was unconscious as his face rolled in to the churned dirt.

He woke to Hildahl fussing with him, just as he had feared. Water dripped into his mouth. He swallowed some, then spat out the remaining liquid, anger coming back full force. His first word was "No." Then he asked for the old mare.

"If Meiklejon said for you to get rid of her . . . I'll take her off your hands. Give her a few more weeks, and then turn her loose . . . or shoot her. Depends on how she holds up." It was a stand-off. Burn up now, raging inside as he glared at his rescuer.

Davey recognized that the *mesteñero* would take nothing but the old mare. Good thing he'd brought her along or the man would try roping a mustang on foot, kill himself for sure. He held out the length of rope. "She's all yours, son. I'll be back to bury your carcass along with hers."

Davey's report interested Meiklejon. There was still no real comprehension of a world in which men like the mustanger existed. Meiklejon had no basis for understanding the man's way of living. He deemed Burn English full of false pride, relying on skills that were no longer needed, and determined to retain his calling despite the reality of the world.

Gordon did admire some aspects of the man, and Hildahl and Souter both had asked for an extension to allow the man, injured as he was, time to gather his horses. Gordon gave them his word. Still he was not comfortable with the situation. Finally he sought out Miss Katherine in her kitchen, where she was washing up the last of the blackened iron pans in which she cooked cornbread and fried bacon. He was not in the habit of passing time with her, but a thought was lodged in his mind that he could not shake, and perhaps speaking it out loud to a person he believed capable of understanding might relieve him of its unwanted burden.

Miss Katherine acknowledged his appearance but did not cease her labors.

Gordon started hesitantly. "May I have another cup of coffee? Thank you." It was always best to start any conversation with Katherine Donald on the basis of a request; it seemed to give her a security that mere talk did not offer. "I gather the man has cornered a number of horses on what I understand is my best summer range." He took another sip, let the words settle, then broached what had begun to trouble him. "I understand the horses are a wild band, without any claim of ownership. Since they are held on my land, and are living on my grass, do they already belong to me, and are they worth the effort of taking them?"

Gordon noted the flinch that stopped Katherine Donald, a bare withdrawal of movement easily missed. Then she continued her work, but allowed him the courtesy of a reply. "Mister Meiklejon, I do know that any interference with a *mesteñero* and his horses would gather you more trouble than any sale of the animals would justify. Legally they are yours . . . morally I believe you would have a horrible time owning them. I would leave it alone, Mister Meiklejon. The cost in men and time would not be worth the sale price of whatever was left after the war. And the man would fight a bitter war to keep what's his."

A clear opinion clearly given, Gordon noted. He rose, leaving his cup on the plank table, eager to get on with his journey and be rid of the superfluous thoughts that sometimes nagged him.

The fever wasted two good days. Burn had managed to hobble the mare outside the valley, and to drag his gear off the stinking roan. The rest had been a nightmare of sweat, heat, hunger, and thirst, with constant pain each time he moved in his filthy blankets.

The third day his head was clear. With a great deal of effort he saddled the mare, who rode short but steady. At the edge of the valley, he got down gingerly and tied the mare securely. The red roan lay fifty feet into the valley, and Burn could still smell the rot. He sat down suddenly. Wolves and coyotes and others in their turn had taken what they could of the roan, leaving ribs and hide, a skull, and memories.

He forced himself to focus. The wounded three-year-old was holding that bad leg off the ground. The colt was easy prey for an eager coyote, or for Burn's rope. He rubbed his hand along the side of his face, and winced at the touch. Hell, he needed a horse. He couldn't buy one, couldn't use the dammed mare, so it was the dark colt or nothing. Burn wiped his face again, careful around the new scar, trying to scrub out the mix of thoughts.

First it was a short meal and some sleep rolled up in his stinking blankets again. No fire, so no hot food or coffee. So he could once again smell like the broncos. Less than an hour later he rode back to the wild horses. The mare tied to a tree well away from the fence, he crawled through the rails with rope in hand. He cursed anything that stabbed him—the bark left on a rail or a stone jutting up from the ground. It was a foolhardy thing he was doing. The colt could half kill Burn on a three-legged charge.

Finally he hunkered down less than twenty feet from the colt and took in steady gulps of air, held them, let them out in short puffs. The colt still paid no mind. Infection ran him like it had run Burn—head low, eyes closed, coat unevenly sweating. Burn crooned mindlessly. At first the colt jumped at the strange sounds, then pretended to lip thin grass.

It was a peaceable half hour except when the colt would forget and lower the hind leg to carry weight. He would jerk the leg and stagger. Burn shuddered with him. When it seemed right, Burn stood and fashioned a loop and dropped it over the colt's head, with the rope behind his back. Holding on with both hands, Burn swung the colt around. The colt shook his head, clearly annoyed as Burn tugged more on the rope. The colt moved forward. Burn suspected the horse's intentions, but the colt did nothing but follow Burn erratically. He tied the colt at a low juniper and removed the gate rail before he led the colt outside.

Burn walked around the colt. Aside from the horrible-looking leg, the big youngster was a beauty. Burn realized no wild bronco stood this quietly under human touch. Still there was no sign that any man had tried ownership—no rope burn, no brand, no saddle gall, or spur cuts. Maybe in the doctoring he'd raise some fight, dig some spirit out of the youngster. Astride the red App mare, Burn got the colt to follow with only a few false starts. The mare flagged her tail; the colt arched his neck only for a moment.

Burn dragged the colt into the shallow stream, caught a front hoof, and yanked the colt off balance. The colt knelt and Burn pulled its head back over its barrel until the colt fell. He dug a knife into the wound and drew out yellow pus laced with red as the colt fought and bellowed until Burn clamped a hand over the colt's nose. The colt lay flat in the healing water.

Two days later Burn saddled the colt. When Burn mounted, the colt humped its back and thought to buck, but then didn't bother. The colt even turned left or right when Burn pulled on the rawhide hackamore. Burn couldn't believe what he knew was happening.

The next day Burn headed a small parade to the penned herd, leading the red mare to set her loose in the valley. The old girl galloped off heavily, then stopped to signal interest with her raised tail. Burn laughed. Lame as she was, she'd have a few years before age and the weather wore her down to a pile of bones.

He needed miles on the colt, so he chose a trail and followed it. A good meal, a few bets on a bronco ride, and he'd come back with cash and renewed interest in the mustangs. He'd done this before. His own ribs were sore, but most of the cuts were healed. Burn laughed outright—he must be living a good life.

It was all rock and sandhills where he rode. Red cliffs hung out over weed-filled bowls. Burn let the colt pick its way as a series of cañons went to the left and on the right the land smoothed out and folded into a number of low hills, carrying the pale green of spring grass. The trail dropped off a rim of red sand and widened into a double wagon track.

The town wasn't much. The first building was a livery where a few scrawny horses hung their heads over the fence. The water trough was a carved tree trunk, and the water was green with scum, but Burn figured the colt wouldn't care. He reined up, and, when a man appeared, Burn asked if he could water his horse.

The man was short and wide, wearing loose pants held up by braces. Filthy hands patted a washed shirt the color of the sandy ground. He looked Spanish, with dark hair and skin, the usual moustache. When he spoke, his voice was loud enough that the colt backed a few steps.

"That's a pretty one you ride, *señor*. The name is Melicio Quitano. And, yes, you may water your good horse. It is a shame that leg scars him so . . . such a beautiful animal."

Burn shied from the man's too friendly tone.

"You, too, *señor*, if it is water you wish to drink. For myself, I drink whiskey or beer only. The water is for the animals."

"What's the name of the town, *Señor* Quitano?" Burn asked. "I come in for a few supplies, and looking to see if anyone needs a horse or two broke to ride. I can set almost anything a bronc' can throw."

The hostler pulled at his nose while he studied Burn. It wasn't a friendly face now; he'd been judged like this before. "Ah, *señor*. We do not have many wild horses here. It is mostly sheep, *señor*. José Padilla and his family, they have run sheep here a long time. José, he rides a quiet mule. So, *señor*, there is little need for your . . . talents."

It was judgment on Burn, his size and heart, his very being. He'd heard this before with few variations—"Your kind." Burn felt his belly tighten. The fat man was no different than the rest, quick to judge an Anglo for his wealth. Then he laughed at what he himself was doing.

"He is entire, *señor*. You will use him as a stallion? Does he have the heart to pass on the qualities needed in a good horse?"

Burn told the truth, knowing it would not be believed, but he was already bored. "I saddled him four days ago, and he ain't bucked yet."

Quitano snorted in outrage. "No wonder, *señor*, that you ride the grub line. For you cannot tell such outright lies and expect to be believed. It is easy to see you ride a mustang, *señor*. And they cannot be ridden the way you speak of this one."

Quitano drew in a deep breath, and Burn watched the impressive rise and fall of his girth. As the fat hostler shifted his weight, Burn felt the colt slide under him. It was a woman, tall and severe, walking toward them. Behind her stood a fat and shiny sorrel harnessed to a light wagon.

"*Buenos días, Señor* Quitano." Her accent was perfect. She stopped, looked at Burn. "That is a fine horse. Are you Burn English?"

Sweat trickled down inside Burn's shirt. There was no malice in the woman or her question. She was generous as she smiled at Burn, and he was shamed by his poor manners. He sat on the colt, his battered hat yanked over dusty hair. He'd been better trained but it had been a long time since any of the niceties mattered. He swung down from the colt, held tightly to the reins, and raised his hat.

"Yes ma'am . . . how'd you know?"

Her voice was quick, clear. "Mister Hildahl described you quite well, and he mentioned you were badly injured, and that he'd left the lame mare as your mount. You must be a genius with horses." She extended her hand. "Katherine Donald, *Señor* English."

The feel of her cool palm eased him as he did his best. "Good day, ma'am." The dark colt nudged him at the small of his back and Burn had to step too close to the woman.

The woman studied the colt. "I trust you did not trade the mare for this colt, Mister English. Therefore I am curious as to how you are riding an animal as fine as this one?"

He told her about the mare, choosing his words carefully. She listened with a glint to her eye that let Burn know she was no innocent.

When he finished, she laughed with delight. "I am certain the mare is pleased with your generosity, Mister English."

"Ma'am, I'm catching the wild horses now."

The woman hesitated. "There has been talk of the stallion. Several of the hands have seen him and said how wild he is. You be careful, Mister English. This is not a simple matter."

She was pretty when she talked, with light in her eyes and expression easing her face.

"Ma'am, you seem to know the folks around here. Maybe you got a rancher who'd pay to get bronc's ridden."

She smiled gently. "I saw Eager Briggs with my father not long ago. Eager was leading a big gray brute, just your kind of horse, Mister English."

He scratched at the sore on his arm and rubbed his face,

then ran a hand through his hair.

She didn't let the gestures go without comment. "You are rougher than your horses, Mister English. And despite the wound in your colt's side, I suspect he is healed more than you."

The colt reared, drawing Burn up with him. Burn clung to the reins, letting his weight bring the colt back down. The terror was caused by a gray horse tied to a burro being led by a fat man on an ancient white mule. The gray kicked and squealed, infecting the colt.

The hostler spun his tale while eyeing Burn but addressing Katherine. "Your blessed father sold this gray to *Señor* Meiklejon as a fine ranch horse. *Señor* Meiklejon, he was thrown over the fence on the first jump. He had worn a pair of *vaquero* spurs and did not think about the horse's tender hide. Your father swore the gray was well trained until the spurs tickled him. He has not been ridden since . . . not by any man." Quitano turned to Burn. "*Señor*, if you wish to advertise your skills, here is your chance. You can offer your colt against a ride on the gray. And you will win a new horse, or run up a bill with a *curandero*. Either way, *señor*, you will rescue the town of Quemado from a dull day."

The gray stood close to sixteen hands, and the story was on his hide—scars along the great rib cage, healed tears at the mouth, several brands on shoulder and hip. The gray would do nothing but fight.

The fat man was introduced as Eager Briggs. It was his burro who hauled the gray; it was in his pockets that the betting money was put for safekeeping. When Briggs held out a plump hand, Burn shook it and noted the old man's eyes hard on him. Briggs was old, sloppy, belly hanging over his pants. He led the gray into one of the empty pens while Burn led the colt into another, taking time to put out wispy hay.

A second man joined Briggs, introducing himself as Katherine's father, Edward Donald. He held out his hand and said he'd heard about Burn from a mutual friend, was right glad to meet up with him. Would Burn be interested in wagering a bet on the gray? he asked. Donald was short and tidy, and his delicate hands moved about quickly, touching and patting a man on the shoulder or seizing his arm to make a particular point. He said he'd take the dark colt as payment on the bet.

Burn agreed to the wager with stipulations. "It's the gray against my colt *and* hard coin . . . 'cause that bronc' won't be nothing as a working horse." He faltered for a moment before he said he'd ride the bronco. He hoped no one had heard that break. He wanted no outsider's pity.

As the news went out, the town began showing up in force, with the crowd staying back from the gray's restless movements. No one wanted to get too close to the bronco, yet they were anxious to watch the show.

The hostler opened a round pen where they'd once bucked out a lot of broncos. Now grass grew under the rails and weeds clogged the center where the snubbing post tilted, rotted almost clear through.

Burn stood in the pen, alone but for the gray bronco. He watched the eye show its white edge. He snubbed the gray to the post, threw a saddle blanket over the long head. The gray quivered but stood still. Burn slapped on the saddle, drew up the latigo tightly, testing the gray's tolerance. One front hoof stamped on the weed-packed ground. Burn slipped the rawhide hackamore over the hard ridge across the gray's nose, settled its thick knot under the sensitive chin. When he removed the blanket and touched the gray's neck, the horse barely rolled its eye. He climbed aboard quickly. The gray trembled as Burn caught the stirrups with both feet, drew in the rein to snug the gray's head. He remembered the story about the spurs and touched his own pair to the quivering hide.

Miss Katherine's father had the final word. Even as the gray bronco exploded, Burn could hear the man's voice above the labor of his own breathing.

"That little fellow looks like he might be able to ride."

CHAPTER TEN

Burn cleaned a lump of muck from his mouth and asked for his $10. His lips bled when he spoke, but he didn't care—by God, he'd earned the money. Fear had ridden with him; no one else knew that.

Edward Donald looked right through him. "I don't have the money with me, Mister English. Perhaps I can pay you another time." Burn shook his head, and Donald sighed as if he'd known. "Come to the house, we'll settle there."

The woman's voice was sharp. "Mister English, you have proven your boast. No one in Quemado, or any town around here, will doubt your skills again. But is that horse going to be worth anything?"

Burn wanted to ask what good the horse had been before he bucked it out, but his mouth was too thick. He settled on a grim smile and walked away, taking the gray gelding with him.

He rode the stumbling gray in the wake of Edward Donald's wagon, sorry that the daughter hadn't come with her father. It occurred to him that she'd arrived in Quemado by herself, and had shown little interest in her father's doings. He grunted to himself—business between a man and his family was personal.

The spread was a soddy with a dogtrot to the back, set in a shallow bowl rested against a ridge—a shirt-tail outfit with a sagging barn and fallen fence. Burn saw no cattle, but a sign was carved into a slanted fence post, the Bench D. Could be Donald's brand but, from the look of the post, it could have been lifted from another man's fence line.

"Set, boy, grab a chair, have a drink. You look like you need oiling. That gray took some hide off you." Donald at least knew his range manners. A drink would set right with Burn.

The whiskey scoured its way down and tasted better once it landed. The fat man, Eager Briggs, came up quiet-like, and sat down, took his turn at the bottle, and kept his stare on Burn, until Burn stared back.

Donald had a lot of talk in him, and the whiskey let it roll. "Here, son, take another drink. That Englishman my child works for, now he thinks he can come in and do whatever the hell he pleases and cut us off from water and graze. Hell, son, I've used that land, that water, to fatten my stock. He got no right putting up wire like he is."

The wire talk blinded Burn, and the whiskey made it easier to listen.

"I hope my child didn't put notions in your head about Meiklejon. She's thinking he's better'n her own pa. But I know, and you know, a man uses wire, he's a curse to the free range and us who ride it."

Briggs found a second bottle. Burn thought Donald kept talking after that, but he couldn't figure the words. They sat in the dark, three men on patched chairs, pulled close to an uneven keg serving as a table, sucking on the bottle till it ran dry. Briggs kept his stare on Burn the whole evening's drunk like he was considering a fight. The watchful eyes were almost familiar, but Burn had ridden a wide chunk of earth, seen a lot of faces, and mostly he'd tried not to remember.

At the finish of the second bottle, Burn thought Donald said they might be partners, go up against Meiklejon and his L Slash, show the damned foreigner what ranching was about. Donald gave his solemn word—his share in the partnership would be headquarters, the sod hut, and horses and cattle marked with the Bench D. Burn would catch and ride the broncos, brand,

and sell for profit. Then they could expand, drive Meiklejon and his like from the range.

Burn was drunk, even he had to admit to the fact. It was nighttime, and through the door he saw that shiny horse harnessed to that lady's wagon. Horse was branded L Slash, had to belong to the Englishman. He looked at the woman come in the house. She was tired and dusty, but how could he have thought her plain? She was beautiful, and he best tell her so.

"Mister English, I don't appreciate drunken compliments," Katherine said. "Whatever promises Papa has made to you, do not believe them. Take the hard cash he has given you and ride on before he draws you into one of his schemes."

He stood on legs that wanted to fold up. "Ma'am." The sound was inside his mouth. He wanted to spit, but that wouldn't be polite. "Ma'am," he began again, "I got the money and the gray bronc'. More'n I started out with this afternoon." He removed his hat in what was meant as a gallant gesture and fell down. No hand reached to help him; no female voice asked if he was all right. He climbed up on his own and reset the hat.

She had disappeared, so he staggered outside to where the gray was tied, still saddled. The bronco lurched into him as he tried to mount and the move shoved him into the saddle. Once mounted he touched the gray with his spurs and the bronco made to buck, but was too worn down. Burn gigged the horse into a slow retreat.

He woke in sunlight, threw up before he could roll over and do it proper. He looked through blurred eyes and saw the dark legs of the gray gelding and felt a tug from the leather that was tied to his wrist. A fool's trick, and only because the gray was bucked out was Burn still alive. He stared up at the gray horse and shivered, then climbed to his feet. The gray's flanks were caved in, its eyes half closed. Crusted lather stuck to the gray hide and traces of red were dried on the rib cage. Burn winced, then remembered the terrible power of the fight and knew he'd won the only possible way.

Eventually he reset the rigging and picked up the reins and climbed into the saddle. The gelding still wanted to fight, but Burn held up the powerful head. The gray shook twice before settling into a long trot back into town. No gait of any horse would be smooth enough to stop the explosion going on in Burn's head. He wasn't up to talking as he paid a few coins to Quitano for the dark colt's feed.

He headed back to the valley, and the ride was pure misery. The colt unexpectedly fought being led and the gray tried to take a piece from the colt's hide at every chance. Burn's arm felt two inches longer, and his temper that much shorter when the rough trio regained the quiet of the small camp.

The gray had to be bucked out each morning before it settled to work. It seemed a miracle each time Burn wasn't thrown. He didn't trust the bronco, but it was strong enough to catch the bachelor colts. The dark colt had time to heal; the circle of pink grainy flesh got smaller each day. The colt remained calm and steady, traits certainly not in the gray's makeup, yet Burn knew what the gray would give him, and he didn't trust the colt.

The valley grasses were cropped too short; the mares were foaled out; the stallion leaned down from a frantic need to court and service the harem and fight off any outsider. Burn rode inside the fence each day. The horses watched and kept their distance, but the mares no longer panicked when Burn and the gray rode by.

This day he climbed down, hobbled and side-lined the gray. It was a bright, noisy day in which birds squabbled over new seeds. Burn fitted his back to a sun-warmed rock and shoved the hat back from his face. Where the cuts had healed, he carried an itch to remind him. All else that was left of the wreck was Burn's dreams each night and a few bones scattered between the rocks. He knew he needed to hurry, but the warmed rock felt good and he was tired. A dream beckoned him. A simple house built well enough that a man could bring a woman to it and be proud. A kitchen with water pumped to the sink, a shiny black cook stove, a bed wide enough to hold two people's passion. A few mares and foals, a dark stallion as sire. The dream was a long shot, but it didn't hurt to dream. It only hurt when the dream was stolen.

He knew he had company. He kept his eyes stubbornly closed, but it had to be Davy Hildahl.

" 'Morning to you, English. You thinking 'bout something?"

There was that cheerful note, that easy humor that hid the tough core. Trouble was coming—the woman in Burn's dreams was Miss Katherine Donald.

He opened his eyes. True enough, Davey Hildahl sat a bay horse and his shadow covered all of Burn through the crude fence.

"I brought some grub, English. Nothing needs cooking . . . can't have you changing that smell you been working on." Hildahl waved his hand as if to move something along. "Jerky and biscuits, a few airtights, and a fruitcake Meiklejon had sent from home. Says it's a tradition there. The boys and I say it's poison, but it don't have to be cooked."

Burn crawled through the fence and got on the restless gray.

Hildahl kept talking. "That's a rough bronc', English." There was a bit of silence. "Meiklejon's beginning to think maybe them bronc's you prize are his after all. Custom gives him the right, but you got a head start."

A man wanted what was his. The land—the damned grass—

wasn't the question. That all belonged to Meiklejon. It was claiming the few horses worth catching. Burn raised his eyes to Hildahl.

"Yeah, English, he gave his word and you still got a deadline. But it's closing in and I thought you better know."

Burn shook his head. "He claiming this gray 'cause it eats his grass? He want this rank son-of-a-bitch back under his brand? Couldn't ride the bronc' the first time, now he wants that damned fool back? He that kind a man?"

Hildahl looked from Burn to the gray. "English, that bronc's got him a rep. Dumped every ranny said he could ride. So now you got famous . . . a tough man on a tough horse. Listen to me, he ain't wanting your horses, he's just asking questions on what rights're his."

Burn spat out his temper, knowing it was wrong, but he felt the edge of meanness. "Your boss has been fencing off the springs, Hildahl. Water other folks been using all these years. There's a precedent set by use. He can't change the rules just 'cause he wants to."

Hildahl's face contorted in surprise. "I got schooling, mister. I can read and write and talk proper when I need to. Precedent . . . ain't that big a word." The mustanger's eyes stayed on Hildahl's face. "English, you been talking to Katherine's father. He gets on water and wire and forgets he don't own the land he's squatting on. Owns the brand but that brand ain't on too many hides. It sure surprises me that you got took in."

They watched each other. Burn got squirrelly first.

"You came up here to warn me about something, Hildahl? You gonna tell me, or do I have to poke you in the belly with a tree limb?"

Davey pushed back in his saddle and a grin passed quickly across his face. "You ain't so dumb for a horse chaser. Yeah. I come to tell you Meiklejon's stuck in Albuquerque for another week. That gives you extra time."

"Why tell me this, Hildahl? You ride for the L Slash, you better be loyal to that brand."

Hildahl came back quick. "English, you're the fool." They sat on restless horses, each hearing the other's truth. Hildahl continued: "I seen you with the wild stock, watched you saddle and ride that colt. Yeah, I been up here before, and I'm telling you now . . . you've earned those bronc's, and Meiklejon knows it. But I don't want him making a mistake we all suffer for."

Burn opened his mouth and out jumped his plans. "There're a few mares I want, and some of the bachelor colts. Then Meiklejon can have the rest. Hope he knows to let them run. I just want the few I've got marked."

"You better be certain sure that brand's registered in New Mexico. Otherwise, the boss'll have right to take the sorry bronc's."

Burn got mad. "You ride back and tell Meiklejon the mustangs are mine. I ain't stealing nothing from him can't grow back on its own."

"English, you can't do all this alone. If you was to ask, I'd stay to help. You can't rope and brand what you want in the time left."

Burn wiped his mouth, tasted cotton wool. He couldn't look straight at Davey. "I ain't asked for help. I don't need it. I got the gray and a good rope. You'd be in the way." He looked away, giving Hildahl room to back off.

"What bronc's you planning to own?" Hildahl asked. "So if Meiklejon sends a crew, I can slip the bronc's free. 'Bout all I can do. You ain't even set up a pen. Those bronc's'll run you and the gray flat 'fore you're done."

An honest answer didn't cost much. "Three mares. That sorrel with the off hind stocking . . . the brown colt she's trailing. The dun mare with the dun filly, and the solid red mare with that palomino colt. Figure the filly's not from the bay stallion, so that'll give me four brood mares and a few to sell. Some of the colts, too."

"Can't fault the choices, Burn. But that stallion's going to hate you taking his best mares. Planning on the colt as a sire?"

Burn shook himself, listening to the easy words. It felt almost right to be setting on the gray and talking about horses with Hildahl. Talking to a half stranger who listened and nodded and all the time worked for the enemy. He weren't bright, Burn thought, all because a man asked a few damned fool questions. Damn Davey Hildahl.

Hildahl continued like nothing was wrong. "Since you got good taste in horseflesh, got a man you need to know 'bout. Name's Jack Holden. A handsome kind of fellow, smiles a lot. Always got him a good stepping, pretty mount that don't carry his brand. He can rope out a horse or point a gun, and smile while he's stealing you blind."

Burn stared at Davey. "We've met. Gent tried to steal my roan and I changed his mind."

The two men watched each other, full of private thoughts.

"Remember, English, I'll help . . . if you want."

Burn turned the gray and let it drift toward camp. But then he brought the bronco around, reined in next to Davey's bay. "Thanks for the offer, Hildahl . . . Davey."

Burn guided the gray to the high fence, kneed the horse into the rail gate, and leaned over to pull a few rails loose. Reining the gray back several strides, he let the bronco's head free, touched the gray with his spurs. The big gelding took three strides, jumped the gate, was hauled up in a stop, spun around, and came back to the fence. Facing Hildahl over the lowered rails, Burn leaned down and slipped a pole in place, caught another rail. The end of this pole skidded on the gray's shoulder and the horse leaped sideways, started pitching. Half out of the saddle, Burn flipped the end of the pole into place.

Davey hadn't moved. "Maybe you can catch and brand them, English, after all. Any man rides that way, maybe he can." He raised a hand in salute, and Burn saluted in turn.

It took three days to fence off the water. The horses scattered on the first day and weren't much trouble, but, toward the end of that third day, they came in driven by thirst. Burn was counting on that need. The morning of the fourth day, the band pressed against the fence, whickering and calling. Occasionally the stallion would stare at Burn as if knowing the horses' suffering was a human's fault.

With the last rail in place, Burn built his fire and laid out a running iron. He'd use Donald's Bench D since he didn't have a brand registered in New Mexico. Even Hildahl said the brand was good, and Donald had given his word in the company of another man. Donald didn't scare him. He'd hold the stock at the man's place, as agreed. Payment of one colt should be enough for Donald.

When he dropped the rails and let the horses in to water, it was the mares who spilled around the raging stallion. Burn kept the gray bronco well away from the milling horses. He watched the mares drink, their foals pressing tiny muzzles into the suspicious liquid, taking only small laps with baby-pink tongues and then raising their heads in mimicry of their sire.

He gave them a last hour of peace, and, when they were waterlogged and sleepy, Burn rode the gray among them. Even the stallion showed the effect of Burn's campaigning—while the horse raised his head and shook it, he made no real threatening move. Too tired, too filled with water, and already used to Burn's presence, the mares barely lifted their heads to watch as their foals stretched out on the grass, filled bellies rising and shaking with each breath.

The dun was dozing over her sleeping filly when the gray

ambled up and Burn dropped the rope over her head where it snugged around her neck. The mare reared and the filly staggered as the stallion charged. Burn slapped the dark head with his hat and the big horse stopped abruptly, shook his head, but did not challenge Burn again.

Choking down the mare was ugly. Burn flipped a loop around her front legs and laid her sideways with a hind leg tied up. The mare sighed and quit fighting. It was even uglier when he pressed the crude brand on her flank; she twitched and cried but couldn't get up. Burn smelled the stink, and shuddered. Back on the gray, he leaned down and freed the mare, having to slap her on the rump before she would get up. The mare stood slowly. The foal came whickering and nuzzling, first her mama's head and shoulder, then to the warm bag where she settled in to nurse.

Burn waited to dredge up enough strength before roping out the red mare. The stallion paid no attention at all. The mare fought harder than the dun, even savaged the tired gray, but Burn's hat worked its miracle and the mare sat back on her haunches, where Burn caught a front leg and brought her down.

When he caught up the third mare, the bright sorrel with the off hind stocking, he found his hands trembled as much as the mare's heart pounded. The gray was barely capable of holding the sorrel while Burn tangled her in the rope and threw her. The new brand was faint and wavering, but it would do.

It was near dark. Burn stood at the gray's side. He grabbed for the stirrup and the big gray quivered between its ribs where the tired heart pounded. He knew the gray would give out under much more work. So he led the horse to the pole fence, where it took five tries before he could reach the top pole and slide it free. When the last pole was added to the untidy pile on the ground, Burn led the gray through. Next he had to put the fence back up. He leaned all his weight on the fence once it was rebuilt. He needed two hands to pull himself aboard the gray that staggered under Burn's slight weight.

He'd do the bachelors tomorrow. As the gray labored uphill, Burn held himself to the saddle and fought open his eyes, struggling with an immediate need for sleep. Tomorrow, he'd do the colts, tomorrow. Right now he plain didn't care.

The bay colt woke him well after daylight. Burn rolled over and grabbed for his Spencer, sat up, looking for the trouble. The colt and the tired gray were staring along the east side of the valley.

Burn grabbed his gear and slapped it on the gray. When he drew up the *cincha,* the gray went to its knees. Burn patted the crusted neck. When this was done, he'd turn the outlaw loose. With Burn aboard, the gray labored into a downhill run, sliding to a ragged stop near the east gate. It opened directly where the approaching riders would appear.

Burn lowered half the rails, jumped the gray in, feeling the hind legs scrape the rails. He spun the gray around and reset the rails. He rawhided the top rail, spat on the hide for luck. Hell, he needed everything he could get.

He whipped the gray into a run across the valley, uphill to the west gate, where the rails were lashed tightly. He cursed his own thoroughness as he cut through the thongs, dropped rails as fast as he could. And he cursed himself for not having branded the colts yesterday. The gray staggered back to the water hole, and the stallion challenged them over the fence. Here it was easier to cut the rawhide, drop the rails. The band of mares slowly came out, walking at first, then a trot, and finally into a lope.

Burn spurred the gray, wondering about the depth to the horse as it ran past the stallion and scattered the mares. The mares circled, slowed; some of the more curious started toward the hole in their prison wall. Burn let the gray come to a jog while keeping to the back of the band, yelling and slapping his hand on his leg when a mare stopped to graze.

He reined in, listening for what he knew was coming. The stallion made several passes in front of the gate before the first mare ducked around him and escaped. The rest of the band followed, leaping the downed rails, disappearing through the natural break in the rock. The stallion turned on the bachelor colts and savaged them, furious that they would dare crowd him.

The first rifle shot came as the stallion leaped the poles. The colts milled in confusion at the break, distracted by the stallion's charge, terrified by the rifle fire. Burn reined the gray around, looked across the valley. Two men were working together on the rails. A third sat on his horse, holding the other's mounts. A fourth man held the rifle. He raised it again, and fired.

Burn saw the explosion of grass fifty feet short of him and the gray. He let the gray turn, catching sight of the panicked colts running the rock. More shots echoed behind Burn, and he felt the gray leap forward. If all the horses escaped, Meiklejon would have no more claim to them.

Burn rubbed his dry eyes, thinking of the dark bay colt, hobbled and helpless at camp. He had almost turned back when one of the frantic colts hit the fence. He heard the rail snap, heard the colt scream. Burn jammed his spurs into the gray.

Now the pack of four men rode close together. Then they slowed down and drew into a circle.

The gray bronco eased back. Burn drew out his old Spencer and fired, aiming carelessly. He didn't care if he hit a man—hoped he didn't kill a horse. The shot set the gray into a bucking fit, pushing the bachelor colts through the open fence. Two of the colts went down. Burn pummeled the gray, and the big horse shuddered into a gallop, not hesitating at the tangled rail, but jumping, landing, almost losing Burn. The mustanger kicked and yelled and the horse veered toward a patch of bright grass seen through the pines.

Burn saw the dirt ahead of him and to the left kick up in a thick puff. He slammed the gray hard with his spurs and the horse jumped. Two shots in quick succession, even more off target. Burn stood in the stirrups, lifted his hat, and hollered. When he looked back, one of the riders was out ahead of the rest. A skinny hand on a big-running bay. *Davey Hildahl.* Burn's throat closed. A shot kicked up near the laboring gray. Damn Hildahl for shooting at a friend.

The colts scattered through the pines. The gray staggered between the trees. Burn's right leg caught a branch, and he slid in the saddle, grabbed the gray's mane, and hung on. A clearing showed—sunlight framing high grass. Burn could hear nothing but the outlaw's harsh breathing.

Ahead, two of the bachelor colts went down. A third disappeared among the dark trees. Burn tried to slow the gray, but the gelding was numbed to the bit. The wire came up fast. The horse hit it chest high and rolled. Wire wrapped around its front legs—wire twisted high above torn hocks. The deep chest was opened. The gray rolled again, hind legs cut to the bone, tendon and muscle exposed. A single wire sliced the gray's windpipe.

The wire tangled around Burn amidst the thrashing legs. Burn's shoulders were pared, his neck opened. He clawed at the strangling wire. Blood sprayed from the gray's wounds, blotting the gray's soaked hide. The horse shuddered. A hind leg kicked back in reflex. Dark blood poured from the gaping throat wound. The gray coughed, blood spewing through bared teeth.

Burn lay tied to the gray carcass. He looked up through the tall pines to the blue sky. He heard the gray die, closed his own eyes, and felt nothing.

★ ★ ★ ★ ★

Davey Hildahl

★ ★ ★ ★ ★

CHAPTER ELEVEN

Davey yelled at the mustanger as the big gray jumped the fence rail. He yelled a warning about the wire that stretched through the pines, cutting off escape. As he called out, he knew English couldn't hear him, probably wouldn't listen. Still he raced ahead of the rest—Meiklejon and Souter, and the kid, Red Pierson. He drove the bay through rocks, across the churned ground. Davey held to his Winchester and hoped for a miracle.

He knew when the bay skidded and stopped. Davey sighted the Winchester and fired. The bullet's heavy *thump* startled him and he came off the nervous bay, found he was talking to himself as he walked around the carnage. Talking gave him false courage for what had to come next.

He walked past the dead gray bronco to a mustang caught up in the torn wire. He shot the colt, directly into the brain. The colt sagged in the wire trap. It was all Davey could do to stand. The gray was more than likely dead when Davey's bullet hit it, bled dry from terrible wounds. Davey walked back, each step digging into the pine-needle earth. Raw pine couldn't cover the stink of blood.

The slight body was torn, covered with pine needles and clods of dirt; flesh showed through fragments of cloth; blood shimmered in pools at the man's neck, along his arms. Davey forced himself to kneel and close the obscene eyes. Those eyes blinked, shut, opened again. Filled with dirt and more blood, focusing on Davey's face. The lips opened, tried to mouth words. Davey leaned in, shaking from the stench.

Then: ". . . Why . . . ?"

Davey defended himself. "I tried to warn you, English . . . 'bout the wire." Here he shivered. "Tried to catch you before . . . this." No more words; instead he sat back on his heels and swallowed hard. Helpless, the first time since he'd grown up. Never seen anything like this.

The mustanger's eyes closed, and his small frame convulsed into the scarred ground.

Then Meiklejon and Souter and the kid rode up. Even Meiklejon was quiet. No man could see this wreck and be untouched, no man Davey would ever work for or call friend. Meiklejon flinched as English's harsh eyes opened, staring at his accusers. Souter told Red to drop a rope on the gray's head. The boy leaned over the side of his sorrel and vomited, then wiped his mouth, uncoiled his rope, and did as Souter told him. Souter caught the hind legs and backed his coyote dun, signaling to Pierson to back his sorrel.

Davey held English's head as the bulk was pulled off him. Those eyes fastened on Davey, forced him to stay calm. Davey used a bandanna to wipe the *mesteñero*'s face, revealing no cuts—the blood must have come from the horse. English didn't look bad, until his right hand picked at Davey's sleeve and Davey saw the deep tear across the inside of the hand up to the elbow. Blood thickened, began to drip, and Davey heard a sound, looked up; it was Meiklejon. Man's mouth was open, his eyes blank.

Davey spoke in fury, damning the Englishman. "This is what your wire does! Kills what it touches, that wire . . . look what it done." The voice came from inside where he rarely ventured. Burn English was a good man, and he was dying.

Meiklejon choked as he tried to explain. "Mister Hildahl, this is indeed terrible, I agree. But he ran from us when we came only to talk. I am truly sorry, Mister Hildahl. What can I do?"

Davey began to straighten out Burn's twisted legs. The man groaned lightly, and Davey bit his lower lip. He watched his own hand reach out to brush at the stained front of Burn's shirt and saw blood smear his hand, saw the bleeding spread quickly across the one clean piece of material on the shirt, then drip down along the ribs and soak into the ground. *Mesteñero* blood. It was everywhere now, bubbling out of each cut and tear.

His palm was red with another man's life. He wiped that hand carefully on his pant leg, took a closer look. A long tear on the man's neck spilled blood. Davey wadded up a bandanna and pressed it against the wound. English's mouth lifted in what could be called a grin. Davey grinned back, awed by the force left in the mustanger.

Gayle Souter kneeled next to Davey and inspected the injuries. He ignored Meiklejon. "Hildahl, rig a travois. Miss Katherine will know what to do."

Davey looked up, caught the edge of Souter's pale blue eyes. They'd both seen wrecks not this bad, and still the man had died.

"Mister Souter, I will ride in ahead to tell Miss Katherine and send a man to bring back the doctor."

Davey watched the old man tell the boss to get riding—"Hurry dammit."—without ever taking his eyes from English.

As Red gathered tree limbs and cut a rope to fashion a travois, Burn lay with his head resting on Davey's arm. Sliding him onto the travois was brutal. Covered with Davey's canvas jacket and Red's torn sheepskin, lying on Souter's old coat and his own hide jacket, English stayed awake for the entire trip, his eyes studying a world he might leave. Souter's big coyote dun carried most of the travois's weight. Souter rode the boy's mount and Red doubled behind him. Souter kept looking straight ahead, refusing to glance at Davey or stare down at the fragile body.

Davey thought too much in the silence. Burn English was important and he didn't know why. He'd never thought much before why one person was a friend, another was just someone to know. He couldn't bear riding and thinking, so he climbed off his horse and walked beside the travois.

Souter spoke back at Davey. "Hildahl, get on your bronc'. You ain't doin' the man no good walkin' and lookin' like a mourner come early to the buryin'." A long speech for Souter.

Davey remounted his bay. He pinched his nose, rubbed his eyes. Worry bit into him. He was good at taking orders but not so good on making his own decisions. Maybe he'd made a mistake, maybe warning English was what had got the man riled up and running. If English hadn't known, maybe he wouldn't have gone with the horses. And now he wouldn't be riding a pole bed.

The procession stopped at a big pine blocking the trail. At Souter's orders Davey roped and dragged the tree clear. The *mesteñero*'s eyes were open, and, Davey swore to himself, the man's gaze looked clear. The son was pure iron. When the eyes blinked rapidly as Davey rode back, he got down to listen.

The cut across English's throat had swollen and leaked fluid. Each time the jaw worked and the light eyes blinked faster, Davey swore he could see the pain. But the man was determined, so Davey paid attention. Nothing between him and this mustanger was easy.

"Bay colt." English got out those two words and the veins on his neck throbbed a deep blue, his mouth pulled white around the drawn lips. Then: "Colt hobbled . . . turn . . . loose."

So he'd caught at least one. A colt.

"Hildahl . . . colt needs branding." A long wait here, so Davey thought maybe that was all. "Use Donald's brand." Then a deep, rough breath. "Dark bay, like his pappy."

Ah, Davey thought, *that colt.*

A hand on his wrist, no weight or strength, only the warmth of skin, the light heft of bone. He looked down at scarred knuckles, a shallow cut drawn over past scars. There was a hint, a pushing. English wanted more. One word.

"Please."

The eyes closed, and Davey had the odd notion the single word was rough passage. He nodded. But he was promising an unconscious man.

He looked up to see Gayle Souter, his mouth drawn in that ugly line. Davey let his hand rest on English's forehead, felt the dry skin, a pulse vaguely working at each temple. Then he made the mistake of lifting the coat off English's belly. He gagged, swallowed. Pools glistened in the hollow beneath the rib cage; the coat had soaked up a whole lot of the blood but more kept coming. Fresh blood. Davey pressed the coat back in place and looked up pleadingly at Souter.

The old man wiped his jaw with one shaking hand. He couldn't meet Davey's stare.

When the ranch was in sight, Souter sent Davey to Miss Katherine, waiting on the steps. Bit Haven had gone for the doc, she said calmly. And she'd already started water to boil, had bandages laid out in the small back room. All that was needed was the patient.

Davey tied up the bay, stood close to Miss Katherine, and found it to be hard breathing for a different reason.

Red slid off the back of his horse and Souter took the reins to his coyote dun and guided the travois up to the steps. Miss Katherine was quick to draw back the coats and look for herself. Three coats laid on the man, all three thick with blood. She dropped them one by one in the dust and they made a wet sound. Red got sick again. No one noticed.

Miss Katherine made crooning sounds as she touched her

patient. Red and Davey lifted Burn from the travois and carried him into the house, to the back room. Davey knew they carried too light a burden; English didn't weigh enough to live, even wrapped in clothing and wearing boots. Davey imagined him on a bucking horse, instead of drowning in blood.

Canvas covered the mattress, and Red and Davey laid the mustanger there. Red looked over to Davey. He was stained down the front of his shirt, and when he raised his hands, they were bloody. Dried flakes rolled off as he rubbed his hands along his filthy pants.

"Get going, Red. Don't want you going down in here. There ain't room." It wasn't much, not really a joke, but a few words to leave the boy something.

Red nodded once, gulped hard, and left the room on his own two feet.

Good kid, Davey thought absently, *might make a hell of a hand.* "Strip him."

It took a woman to be this practical, Davey thought as he began the task. The gear was rags and easily peeled off. Davey blushed when he got to the combinations, for Miss Katherine was looking over his shoulder. His fingers became impossibly clumsy, and she pushed him on the shoulder, but he refused to quit.

"I've seen a man naked before, Mister Hildahl. There are no surprises."

A bit of cloth was stuck to flesh, and Davey shuddered as he yanked it clear. Miss Katherine shifted in to work next to Davey with a bowl of hot water and clean cloths. It was a slow and ugly process. There wasn't much to English, mostly skin and bone, and most of that torn and marked with old battles long forgotten. As he glanced at the *mesteñero*'s face, inspected the thin nose and closed eyes, then moved to the large-jointed hands heavy in contrast to the narrow body, he wondered what kept the man alive.

He averted his eyes when Miss Katherine removed the last of the combinations. Davey'd never seen the human body laid out bare, never had tended an injured man, never had much doings with illness or dying. He had to look away from Burn English, but saw the effect on Miss Katherine. Her eyes were shadowed, her mouth tight, still she washed and rinsed and wiped, then had Davey get more hot water, never looking up from the work. Her hands were gentle on English, across his chest, down his belly, and over his groin. Davey's head ached. He went for more water, furious at himself, jealous of a dead man.

When he returned, English was still bleeding. Past the great number of minor scratches, there were two major wounds. One sliced diagonally across the belly, exposing gut and rib. The other went from the right leg, above the knee, in a long wrap to the top of the rump. The worst of that was inside the thigh, high up where it bled occasionally. Miss Katherine had tied a cloth over the cut, but there wasn't much to be done with the belly wound as it kept bleeding.

A faint blue ringed English's mouth and the fine skin under his closed eyes was the same milky-blue. Davey sighed and Miss Katherine's head came up. Tears softened her gaze as she stared past Davey; her hand rose clutching a bloody cloth.

"He'll bleed to death from that terrible hole." Her voice was raspy. Davey flinched. "We're going to lose him. I can't stop the blood!" Hysteria was in the last words and she clamped her mouth shut.

Davey ran to the kitchen and got a sack of flour, hurried back to the small room, and dumped half the bag into English's belly. The wound disappeared in white powder, then turned pink, finally a thicker, darker red. He spilled more flour until the bleeding stopped. Davey sagged.

Miss Katherine touched Davey's hand. "The leg, Davey. Help me."

They rolled the body over and she supported English's head while Davey poured flour into the raw haunch. It turned ugly as the blood thickened into a muddy paste. They let the body roll back on its own.

Miss Katherine stared at the man laid out on the narrow bed. Davey fled from the ranch house, stopped, leaned against a wall, and swallowed twice to keep from fainting. *Keep busy, keep moving* was all he could recite through his fears; he thought of Red throwing up. *Keep busy, dammit.*

At the water trough, he worked the hand pump and shucked off the filthy shirt, bent under the pump, scrubbing hands and arms and chest until he felt almost clean. Endlessly he spat and drank and washed his hands, but when he opened his eyes, new blood stained the knuckles and the creases along his wrist. If he closed his eyes, he saw Miss Katherine's face, and the still form of Burn English.

A weight settling on his bare shoulders made Davey step back until he saw it was Gayle Souter, speaking almost soundlessly like Davey was a spooked bronco. "Son, you ride up to that camp. Seems to me you made a promise. You best keep it." Then Souter turned away.

Davey went back to washing. His hands were still bloody. When the cold got to him, he walked, stiff-legged, to the bunkhouse where Red sat on the edge of his thin mattress. Still shamed by his weakness, Red asked: "He gonna live, Davey?" The boy did a man's work, but in truth he was only a boy.

Davey touched a hand to his own neck, his belly, and chest. "Don't know, Red. Won't know till the doc comes." It wasn't much to go on and the boy ached for some small truth. "He's alive now." Having said all he could, Davey turned to digging through his war bag for a clean shirt, a pair of pants. When he stood up to dress, he was alone. And when he got outside, buttoning up a canvas coat, a big sorrel gelding, saddled with Davey's rig, was waiting. A blanket roll and empty saddlebags were tied on. Another horse stood close by with halter and lead.

Red Pierson was there to hand the lead up when Davey mounted. Davey felt old, as though he had seen too much. He gulped and shuddered, rode out not saying thanks or see you in a few days.

Gayle Souter raised a hand in half salute. Red drifted in to stand near Souter. They watched, and said nothing.

Davey wished he could explain this to Meiklejon, wished he could set the man down and show him Souter and Red and even English. It was more than a man could talk out, more than a cow pusher could put into words. They knew the facts of money, the reasons for the wire. But more than that, a way of life was disappearing and those like English would not make the change.

Davey gigged the sorrel into a lope and felt the haltered horse set back on the line. The sun began a sliding drift behind Cat Mountain and he welcomed the shadows.

Chapter Twelve

His hands trembled so he forced the instrument down and pushed back from the table that served as his writing desk. In the future he would import a proper desk, but, until life included a defined income, he would utilize what was available from Littlefield's meager collection.

Such idle thoughts were meant to cover the turmoil and obviously the effort was not enough to prevent panic from settling in. He was scared. This terrible accident was from his decision; he had had the wire strung, he had made those comments, out of curiosity, about the possibility of his being the rightful owner of the horses. Through all this he had discounted the mus-

117

tanger's fierce temper.

He went into the kitchen to find it cold and empty. No remains of a cooking fire, no signs of a meal in interrupted preparation. Lighting an oil lamp, he carried it to the back room, where he intended to peek in and see for himself how the patient was doing. Perhaps the doctor was already in attendance. Miss Katherine would be found there, silent and contained, waiting for either life or death. Her vigil was a mute reminder of Gordon Meiklejon's failings.

Davey let the sorrel pick its way. There weren't many folks in his life he'd trusted, but he knew and liked the mustanger, and he trusted Miss Katherine. Thirty-one years old yesterday, and no ties except to the brand. Worked since he could climb into a saddle alone, like most of the men he rode with. Youngsters thrown into the world and meant to live or die by chance or fortune.

He had no complaints—the cook fed well, the foreman was solid. The bunkhouse didn't leak much and a man rarely woke up with snow covering his feet. Miss Katherine was the only problem, and now it was Burn English added to the list. They both made Davey take a good look at himself, and the truth was bitter. He was a bony, long-legged son-of-a-bitch. Like all his parts didn't fit together. He admired the compact men who were quick on their feet, easy in the saddle, and easy talking with Miss Katherine and other ranch women.

It was one-sided love for him and Miss Katherine. He could look in the cracked bit of glass that served as a mirror and see the round face with its shapeless nose, the brown puppy eyes, the blond hair that fell in his eyes or stuck to his skull. Man in his dreams didn't look like that. The man he'd like to be would have her fall in love with him. Not so with the real Davey Hildahl.

English was quick in his movements. He shamed Davey by his handling of the broncos, and he raised an instinctive jealousy by his stubbornness. Davey would like to feel that strongly about something, but, other than Miss Katherine, nothing was worth the effort. To English, those broncos were everything, to Davey they were horses. Thoughts confused a man, he figured.

It was pitch black now, but the sorrel stuck to the faint trail and Davey let the horse do its job. That's all he asked—to do his job and live out his life. He'd ridden this trail too often lately. Maybe if he hadn't come up this way looking for a stray brindle cow, none of this would have happened.

The sorrel nickered and Davey heard the colt before he saw him. Heard the odd *thump* of a horse traveling on hobbles. Davey climbed down and took care of his own horse before he approached the colt. It was a mustang with little experience of strangers. Yet the colt humped up to Davey and stuck out its nose, snuffled at Davey's hand, and then nipped his arm. Evidently the colt was glad for company, as it stayed near camp and watched Davey set up a few comforts. Surprisingly the colt did not wander over to the sorrel gelding, now hobbled and chewing grass.

There was a promise Davey needed to keep; he was tired but the promise had been made. So he laid a cinch ring in a new fire, an act against the law but handy when an off-brand had to be drawn. As the ring heated, Davey played in the dirt with a stick, tracing out Edward Donald's mark. He hated this, putting that sign on the colt, but it was a promise.

He was pushed from behind, and, looking back, saw the lively eyes and pricked ears of the dark colt. Hard to believe this was a slick mustang, and entire. But English said the colt was caught wild, and, as Davey made an inspection trip around the horse, he saw no sign of previous ownership. English must be some magician with the broncos, to keep this colt friendly and will-

119

ing, and already saddled. No spur marks on the dark sides, no tears or cuts at the muzzle. Some kind of magic.

He admired the colt and wondered how he would throw and brand it. It was too easy. He slipped a short rope around a hind leg and yanked, and the hobbled colt fell. Davey roped up the legs and laid on the brand. He'd given his word. He undid the hobbles first, then the leg ropes, and let the colt up. The mustang snapped at its scorched flank, struck out at Davey, and then charged the Meiklejon horses before bolting into the dark. It was just as well English hadn't branded the colt.

He had time to cook up beans and boil coffee. He ate a sour meal before rolling up to sleep.

In the morning he woke wrestling with nightmares. He hustled and it didn't take long to gather English's few belongings, pack them on the led horse. Davey swung up on the sorrel, in no great hurry.

He took the west fork, which went the long side of Lightning Valley before opening to the Quemado trail. He tracked left toward the bright strip of grass seen through a stand of tall pine. At the wire fence he got down, tied his horses real tight.

A mustang lay with its skull wrapped in wire. Davey pulled gear from the gray outlaw's hide. The ground around both horses was dark in too many patches, and Davey fought to do the chore, to see nothing else. He'd done ugly chores before, but none of them stuck deep like this one.

The gear went on the led horse, and for a moment Davey let his fingers slip over the saddle leather. Old, patched, well-tended, and solid. The latigos were new, the *cincha* woven with gray hairs and pine needles. The bridle was a broken ring bit and long-plaited reins. Davey wondered how English ever rode the gray with such a rig. Even the blankets were worn, mended by a craftsman's hand. The gear told English's story.

★ ★ ★ ★ ★

Katherine watched the doctor climb in his buggy and hurry along. Had other patients he said, and was still angry with Mr. Meiklejon's messenger, who had bullied and threatened the good doctor into leaving a sick man to come to the L Slash. The doctor admitted to Katherine that he did not know how English had survived.

The belly wound was infected, he said, although the liberally applied flour had been the only remedy for uncontrolled bleeding. If the patient were not on the verge of starvation, then he might hold out some encouragement. As it stood, there was little hope.

With instructions to keep the wound clean, the man quiet, so the bleeding would not restart, the doctor drove away, to deliver a baby ten miles downcañon and then patch up a driver who got drunk and shot himself in the foot. "Pray, Miss Katherine. Like I am certain you have been praying. For it will take a miracle."

Katherine did not have to be told about infection. Bathing him was one thing she could do. So she washed his face and hands with cool water, and wiped at the edges of the belly wound, even gently sponging along the deep cut on the leg and buttocks where she could reach. As she gingerly manipulated him, the mustanger seemed to help. His body twitched, an arm rolled out of the way. It was impossible, but she was certain, as she washed his face again, that he touched his tongue to the side of his mouth where she laid the damp cloth, and even once tried to speak. All of this was her imagination, yet she believed he was aware of her presence.

She fell asleep in the rocking chair and didn't see the closed eyes open, the head move against the suffocating pillow. The feverish eyes searched until they found Katherine in her chair.

Then the head dropped back into its cradle, using the last of a dimming energy.

The doc had come and gone when Davey returned. No one was in the ranch yard, so Davey put up his two mounts and hung English's gear from the stable rafters, stuffing the few clothes and camp gear into a burlap sack that he stored in a tin-lined chest. Mice around here would eat almost anything.

He knocked at the kitchen door. No one answered, so he pushed in, sure that English was dead. He was quiet as he walked back to the small room. She was there, curled in her familiar rocker, hair fanned over the chair railing and around her face, reaching her shoulder. Davey knelt beside her, let his fingers reach toward but not touch her. He couldn't believe the hair's rich color—light from a ray of sun streaked the long threads. His breath caught in his throat; he pulled back, stood up slowly.

On another impulse he put his fingers to English's jaw, near the joining with his neck. He didn't know why it was important the man lived. Everything died, some sooner and harder than others. But he wanted this one man to live. Davey was tired of being the philosopher; he counted Burn English a friend.

His hand placed on Burn's shoulder felt bone, not flesh. The face and hands were burned from weather, making English look more Indian than anything else. The eyes opened. Davey's fingers were sticky from the man's fever. Those eyes stared without blinking, then closed, and Davey let out a big gulp.

"He's asleep, Davey. Doctor Lockhart left a bottle of laudanum and said to use it liberally, as any thrashing would open the wounds. He also said to spoon broth into Mister English whenever possible. He's much too thin." She let her head sink back on the rocker's support. "But we know that, don't we. His chances aren't good. Lockhart said without your quick acting with the flour, he would be dead now." She stuttered on the next words. "Thank you."

A vein throbbed in Davey's temple and he wanted to rub it but was afraid to stop her talking.

"I'll fix you a meal, Davey. He'll sleep a while. We need to get you fed." It wasn't much, but she had spoken his name.

Time slowed. A week passed since they had brought in the *mesteñero* and he was still alive. Meiklejon didn't come out of his room much. Souter gave the orders as usual, but there was no shadow of the boss behind him. Davey figured the man was carrying some big guilt over the accident.

Souter told Davey to harness up a team and go to Datil for the Socorro supplies. He picked a team of good sorrels, part draft, part mustang, harder than hell to drive, but tireless, steady travelers once they got lined out. It was a long stretch between the ranch and Datil by wagon road, about twenty extra miles. Souter gave the job to Davey to get him off the ranch before he started up more fights.

Just yesterday the doc had swung past, come in from near Omega where a woman had lost her husband and two children to the smallpox. Doc had washed up well before he went in to see English. Wounds were septic, Lockhart said. Badly infected— couldn't be helped—couldn't be treated except to wash them with heated water, use laudanum to dull the pain, and keep hoping for the best. The belly wound was worse, the smell enough to make a strong man puke. The doc was bitter, dark-tempered when he asked did Davey have another trick like the flour to save English's life. Then the doc stared down at Burn, shook his head. Spoke his mind to his patient.

"Son, I don't know what good we've done you. Your suffering ain't fair, boy, and for that I'm sorry." Brutal words that laid on more guilt.

Before he left, Lockhart put a bigger bottle of laudanum on the table. Spoke directly to Miss Katherine with a special slowness. "Be careful, miss. Too big a dose can kill him, weak as he is."

When the doc was gone, Souter had taken charge. He sent Red for a *curandera,* wife to Enselmo Ortega, a sheepherder in Quemado. She'd come to help and she'd come with her own ideas. She was going to use plants from the land, she said. Sage and purple coneflower. It was only after English had his belly wrapped and packed with the herbs, and smelled decent, that Davey caught up the sorrel team and left on Souter's errand.

He felt the team's sudden tiredness through the lines and let them come to a walk. They'd reached the base of the mountains, a long way still from Datil. This stretch of the road was sided with pine and some fir, scatterings of meadows where he imagined deer would come in at dawn to feed. It was too peaceful, tempting a man to draw the team off the road, unhitch, and let the tired horses graze while he rested his back at a tall tree, chewed a bit of grass himself, and tried to make sense of the past weeks and the endless raw anger raging within him. Instead, Davey drove on, mindless and numb.

He came out of his self-pity once when a dark colt with a ragged white scar appeared on a ridge, to the side of the team. The colt whinnied. Davey stopped the team and the off-sorrel whinnied back. It was the *mesteñero*'s orphan mustang—maybe he was lonesome for company and Davey could rope him, bring him in for English to see.

The colt snorted, lowered his head, then flicked his tail and was gone. Davey hoped it wasn't a bad sign.

CHAPTER THIRTEEN

The supplies were piled up outside the small hut that served as a sometimes post office. It was well past dark when Davey got in, and he loaded up alone, tacked a note to the door saying *Thanks* to the driver and that the L Slash had what they needed. He turned the now docile team around, headed once more for home.

He had to stop around three in the morning, by his crude reckoning. It was god-awful dark. His eyes burned, but mostly the team needed a drink and a few minutes rest and some grass, before they tackled the long uphill pull to the L Slash cut-off. It wasn't a long trip home in miles, no more than five or so, but whatever Meiklejon had ordered was heavy, and Davey could read that the team was working too hard at each small rise.

So he slipped their bits and let them graze a half hour while he built a smoke and leaned on a wheel, knowing if he laid down or even sat with his back up against something solid, he'd sleep and be even more late getting in.

By the time he reached headquarters, Davey was nodding over the lines as the team set a good trot, eager for a nosebag of oats and a roll in the corral dust.

There was little change in Burn English except he was sleeping better, or so Miss Katherine said. The room smelled of the grassy plains now that *Señora* Ortega had her hand in the medicines.

Each day he could, Davey poked his head inside the sick room or asked Miss Katherine for news, in the kitchen. The crew was busy gathering spring calves, driving steers out of the hills and draws. A sick man was poor excuse for conversation when wrecks and mountain cats and the tracks of big grizzlies and losses from the rustlers were the more usual bunkhouse gossip. Most of the talk was about rustlers; someone close to home was stealing from the neighbors.

Finally Davey presented himself at the kitchen door, well after the big Sunday meal. Meiklejon tried to stop him, but

Miss Katherine showed up and settled the matter, as she often did.

"Ah, Mister Hildahl, you've come for your usual visit."

Davey squeezed past the boss, who stared into the distance as if Davey didn't exist.

She left him in the small room, alone except for the patient lying on the narrow bed. The room was dark and smelled sweet with the herbs and an undertaste of something putrid. Davey's eyes watered, but he didn't rub them; he knew from experience that only made the itch worse. It was the voice that galvanized him out of his trance.

"Who's there?"

A weak voice Davey hadn't heard for a long time. He grunted: "It's me, Davey, come for a Sunday visit. Wanted to tell you I saw your colt a few days back. That leg healed fine . . . no limp and only a few white hairs. He's looking right good for a durned mustang."

"Did you brand him?" English's hand came up, grabbed Davey's wrist, and, even half dead, there was strength in the smaller man. Davey was pulled close, so all he could see was the violent twisting of English's features. "Did you brand him?"

Davey nodded as he pulled his hand free. "Yeah, and cut him loose of the hobbles."

English was slow to hear the words. He coughed and slid both hands over his belly and shut his eyes. "How long I been here? Where . . . you brand that colt?" Then the hand got Davey again, but most of the strength was gone.

Davey pulled up a chair and sat, let the hand cling to him. He thought of Miss Katherine sitting in the same chair through the long nights and days, dozing while she waited for Burn English to choose. Now Davey tried his own brand of comforting. "English, you rest. Let me tell you, and you listen, 'stead of pushing and making me mad." He watched the drawn face, shadowed by a thin, dark beard, the eyes sunken deep into the bony skull. Usually lit with fire, the eyes were soft, downright friendly. Man must be weak as a new calf to show emotion. Davey wondered, as he did sometimes, what got the mustanger this far, what grew the fire and rage inside him.

English nodded, all strength used up, and Davey did the talking. "You been here more'n two weeks now. She's been tending you with a Mex woman. She got you smelling good . . . first time for you, I bet. Kinda like grass after a good rain. Beats that mustang stink you favor." English's face tightened and Davey decided it wasn't right teasing a sick man.

"Got a hole in your belly and a cut cross your right leg goes up to your backside. Your neck got scratched some, but it's clean now. Hands're cut up, too, but they're almost healed. Hell, you ain't much worse than you been running the brush on a half-broke bronc'."

English surprised him; nothing new in that. "Yeah, my gut." The man let it rest while he took in air. "Feel it . . . sleeping. Fire inside my bones." That was a truth near as anyone could speak.

Davey rested his arms across his chest, hunched over. English's words dug deep.

"Davey?" Too soft, Davey leaned over, close to the man's mouth. "Saw things . . . heard voices. Like I wasn't here." Rested again, struggled for air. Davey wiped his friend's wet face. "Where I was goin' . . . good enough. Strange . . . hearing about your own dying."

Like any lonesome man, English talked his own brand of talk. But not now, these were clear and precise pictures that shivered along Davey's spine.

"Light, Davey. I could lie down and rest and not hurt. That was the promise."

English quit then, sagging deep into the mattress until Davey knew he would disappear. The fiery eyes closed, the large bony hands, covered with half-healed scarring, lay fragile on the stained blanket. Davey got up and walked to the door, glancing back at the cot and the exposed figure. He hoped that English would come awake his cantankerous self, and forget the voices, the light, and then maybe Davey would return for a visit.

Gordon Meiklejon thought he'd tipped the young man quite well, and was surprised at the look on the boy's wind-burned face. This messenger had brought the news that a great, snorting bull was arriving in Socorro, with Meiklejon's name stapled to the entire railroad car in which the bull rode in its solitary glory. A trip to Socorro was in the making. Miss Katherine had her long list of needed supplies; it was mid-May and the winter reserves were depleted.

Gayle Souter drove the wagon, pulled by a sorrel team, and Red Pierson rode with the foreman. Gordon was pleased with himself; he knew most of the men's names by now. Pierson was a stout youngster who followed orders, yet could think for himself, if needed. This, Souter had repeatedly told Gordon, was a necessity in any good hand.

The season was late to be putting the bull to the L Slash cows. Timed delivery of the calf crop was important to maximize their growth before the all-important fall gather, according to Meiklejohn's schedule. But this was an experiment, and the bull's first harem would be herded with him to the pasture north of the ranch.

It was much easier ruminating over the matters of Edinburgh Supreme and his ladies than to consider the chaos at the ranch. The unwanted patient remained, better now but not yet well, and Miss Katherine showed the effects of his stay. The woman was drawn thin, and barely spoke even to her obvious favorite, Davey Hildahl. Hildahl was another matter entirely. Meiklejon refused to dwell on what he saw in the man's eyes.

When the procession arrived in Socorro, they first visited the rail yard where the magnificent Red Durham stood in its reinforced pen. The bull swayed impassively, chewing massive amounts of old hay, occasionally blowing long strings of mucus from its nostrils, bellowing, eyes closed, head back, as if proclaiming its potency to an indifferent world.

Well satisfied with the purchase, Gordon waited while Souter took a closer look. Gordon watched his foreman—would Souter find the generosity to admit that Gordon had done the right thing in buying this animal? Souter took his time, but finally said it was a magnificent beast, indeed. Ought to make quite a change with the range cattle they were now running.

Later, when he was settled in his room at the Southern, Gordon realized the crafty old foreman had not said anything approving Gordon's choice. For that maneuver, Gordon smiled to himself, delighted with Souter's gambit.

Souter set Red to putting up the horses at Billy's livery while he returned to the rail yard and the Red Durham bull. If he went into Billy's, there'd be drinking and cursing and stories to swap with his old friend. Let Red deal with the hostler's sour nature. But first he paid Red some of what the ranch owed him, warning the boy to keep out of trouble, especially to stay away from the liquor. "This ain't a night on the town, son. We got hard work tomorrow and you best be ready. Find yourself a nice girl and talk to her, maybe buy you both a piece of pie." He watched Red's face, read the embarrassed anger, and grinned. Some things never changed.

Souter cursed his own self. It was having the *mesteñero* on the ranch that had gotten to him, like he had gotten to the rest of the men. Meiklejon showed signs of the strain, but it was Davey's hurt that hung on. Souter could almost see Davey coming to a wrong conclusion about blame and guilt. It was a wrong conclusion, but no one could tell Davey. The truth was that, whatever drove Burn English, it was the *mesteñero* who had sent the herd into the wire. It had been him and no one else, not Davey, not Meiklejon, that had acted in haste and killed the horses, and maybe himself.

Souter rested a boot on the bottom rung of the fence and the red bull turned its enormous head, shook it violently against the spring gnats, and glared at Souter out of fiery eyes. *Ugly son, but if that sac of his were any hint of potency, let the cows line up and put the ugly son to them.* Souter wasn't going to give his approval in any way Meiklejon would understand yet, but if the fancy red bull did its job and the calves carried that bulk of meat and bone, then Gayle Souter wouldn't mind playing nursemaid to a slow-moving, mean-tempered son-of-a-bitch like Edinburgh Supreme.

He sighed, spat, and watched dust rise and settle. *Damned dry too soon. Always too dry or too damned wet . . . full of too much and too little.* Souter hoped he had learned something in his fifty plus years, and change was part of that learning. He didn't like the wire fence, but it was here, cutting off the range, and none of the change would go away, so he might as well stare at the ugly red bull and pretend he liked what he saw. At least until Edinburgh Supreme proved his worthlessness. *Or sired a whole herd of ugly, fat, red sons-a-bitchin' steak-carryin' offspring.*

Constant work kept Davey tired, almost let him sleep. Red-hazed anger followed him while he worked. He and two hands restrung the broken wire in the valley. Davey started calling it Skull Valley for the piles of bones. Remains of meat and hide still clung to the skulls, but the wire had been re-stretched and the rest of the ten sections had gotten fenced. It had taken more than a month of hard work and a lot of knuckle hide and cursing to get the job done.

Right now Red, Davey, and Souter were trailing after the bull—had a name to go along with his fancy pedigree, Edinburgh Supreme. Davey thought naming a bull was dumb. They got born, serviced their cows, and died from old age or a deep wound, and a new bull took over the job. It was the nature of animals, and naming them didn't make them into anything more than what they were.

He was content to ride drag. The selected cows moved too quickly sometimes, kept the boys busy. But old Supreme, he walked like each step declared his majesty. Watching that heavy rump spring up and down could make a man think on all those future steaks. Ahead, Meiklejon rode his easy-gaited grullo. Souter hung to the left, out of the dust but ready for trouble.

Riding in the wake of those massive hindquarters, Davey let his thoughts wander. Summer would fill out early spring's promise—hot, dry, dusty. About usual for these mountains. Davey watched the great motion of the bull, and wondered where English's horses watered now. The ten sections they'd fenced off included that watering hole. But Davey didn't think the band would go back to their old prison.

English was still to the ranch—weak, pale, even thinner if possible, but alive. Didn't talk much, walked half bent. At least Miss Katherine no longer had a grim set to her. She even teased Davey about small things, and he'd enjoyed her laugh. She trusted him, looked to him for help. Maybe English's accident held something of value after all.

He thought about the mares. Maybe they had figured out the wire. Maybe they were all right. But with the dry winds, little rain, no storms to fill up the streams and gullies, the water hole would look awful good. Maybe they'd moved on. The dark stallion now leery of these mountains . . . maybe they'd gone where no wire crossed their tracks.

Davey knew he was thinking wishes and not facts. Horses

were just that, horses, and the stallion would see water across a fence and hang around, wanting a drink. The foals would weaken as their mammy's milk dried up. The mares would turn ribby and poor.

He'd heard Meiklejon's talk about the "necessity of preserving the bloodlines" and he hated the man for his callous misunderstanding. An animal that couldn't survive the range without help had no business eating and shitting and sleeping and growing. It made no sense to breed hot-house stock. Not in southwest New Mexico.

They guided the bull and its harem up the west side of the valley, not wanting to risk Supreme's tender hoofs on the hard rock and flinty ground of the eastern trail. So they had to ride past the depression where the scattered bones and the new wire blended together, leaving Davey to keep score. He choused the bull into a labored trot, saw the huge sac swinging between the distended hind legs.

Souter's pale eyes said everything, and Davey reined in his bay, letting the bull come back to a walk. Souter knew. Souter counted the bones, hated the wire, but they both took the man's wages, they owed him their loyalty.

They entered the valley between high wooden posts once laced with thin railings that had now tumbled down the steep slopes. The cows scattered easily in the valley. The bull took its great ponderous time making the downhill trail, and finally stood, raising its head and bellowing an announcement of its evident intent.

Davey laughed, and Souter joined in. Meiklejon looked on disapprovingly.

After the cattle were scattered, Souter asked, too politely, if Davey would stay on a few days, keep track of the bull, and an eye out for rustlers. Jack Holden, in particular. Someone had been getting greedy. Holden had to be part of it. Davey said he didn't much care. So Souter pulled out his good Winchester, handed it over to Davey with a pouch full of bullets. Guarding Edinburgh Supreme was serious business.

The L Slash crew rode home in the dark, Meiklejon comfortable on his pacing grullo. Once they were gone, Davey made short camp in a pocket of trees near the water hole. In the morning he made a fire, using the rotting poles as fuel, finding them easy to break. He put coffee to boil, opened up a can of beans Souter had left him. He liked the morning silence; he liked knowing he was the only man in the wide valley.

Finally he walked to the rock ledge, to the natural gaps and wire fence. He touched the burrs that raised hell with flesh. Their pricks were a harsh reminder. He looked along the wire's endless stretch, saw it disappear far ahead of him, and the new day's glory was spoiled.

Davey wondered what Miss Katherine was doing right then—getting up and boiling coffee, tending to her patient before she got to the morning chores. His throat closed and it got hard to breathe. Davey knew he was jealous of a no-account horse chaser who saw Miss Katherine each morning, while Davey was stuck in a high meadow with a bunch of female bovines and a bull too dumb to know what to do with their willing flesh. He wasn't pleased with himself, thinking so of Miss Katherine. She was a good woman and he had no right to his thoughts, except he wanted Miss Katherine all to himself, to love her and be loved by her in return.

Midday he got restless, bored with watching the bull follow one or two cows, and he saddled up. He headed his bay out of the fence and up toward the far end of the valley, where it turned to desert, where the old fence marked a line.

The bay climbed the rimrock and stood next to the wood fence. Below, a small band of wild horses saw Davey and turned to run from him. They'd been close to the wire fence, heads hanging, tails moving slowly to distract the flies.

Davey counted as the band moved out—three mares with long-legged foals, three mares carrying Edward Donald's brand. They showed the effect of the dry spring and early summer— their ribs stood out, their coats dulled. The idea came to Davey.

He put the bay into a lope across the sandy ground to the edge of the wire fence. There he climbed down and pulled out the staples holding the wire and laid down three sections, covering the dammed barbs with rotting pine and rocks, some juniper boughs.

The mares slowed, turned around, judging him with tired eyes. He wondered about the dark bay stallion, how these mares had gotten loose. Back on his bay, he let the horse walk toward the mares. They watched him warily. He watched them in return. Then they bolted from Davey, away from the fenced-in water. Davey kept the bay at a distance. They settled into a loose trot until it was dark, and then the mares walked on, north, into the desert. There was enough light by the low moon and stars to keep Davey on their trail. They were mustangs, and a few hours, even a day or so, wouldn't wear them down. This was the heart that couldn't be bred into a horse; it was born natural, kept alive by active enemies, the weak culled out before their first full year.

The mares wouldn't let Davey get around them, but he kept walking, trotting sometimes, enough to keep himself from dozing in the saddle. As the sun rose, Davey saw the distant spire of Escondido Mountain. He reined in the bay, enjoyed the view, thought of the day's coming heat. The mares stopped willingly, the foals dropped to the dirt and stretched out to sleep. Davey let them rest. His conscience fretted at what he was doing, but he still felt it was right.

He left the bay drift around the mares, to be ahead of them. After a half hour or so, he clucked to the mares. The foals clambered up at a signal from their mamas. The small band went in an orderly procession, Davey bringing up the rear. He herded them back to the wide end of the valley, where they barely stopped to snort and blow at the fallen wood fence rails. Heads high, tails flagging, the mares had scented water.

This time, when they came to the fence line, they jumped where Davey had laid the wire down, and broke into a slow lope toward the inviting water. Davey let them go, watched with pleasure as they stepped gingerly to the pool's edge, stuck their heads deeply in the water, and drank quickly, raising their heads to check for possible danger.

He let them finish their drink before he got back to work. As soon as he raised the first strand of wire, the band spooked and went into the narrow cañon. They were headed into the fenced ten sections, and the company of Edinburgh Supreme.

He could truthfully report that he had checked the fence, seen to the bull, and that all was well. And he'd find the right time to tell English about the mares. It was English's business; let Meiklejon think what he would about his imported stock, these mustangs deserved their chance.

He stayed till his beans were gone. The bull had figured out how to court his ladies, for he was puffing and wheezing and eyeing Davey and his bronco. The bull made Davey laugh. Might be a slow learner, but the son-of-a-gun was ready to mount almost anything now. Davey headed south, in no hurry to return to the L Slash.

He got in at dusk, and the men nodded to him as they put up their day horses and cleaned off some of the dirt before they went for the night meal. Davey was slow stripping off the dusty bay, uneasy about speaking the first words he'd said to more than wind and animals in several days.

Gayle Souter found him as the rest went to eat. Souter made a lot of noise coming up to Davey; the old man understood about being in the brush too long. "We'll get some fancy calves next spring from that big old boy, if he knows what to do." There was an unasked question waiting.

Davey obliged. "He got it sorted out."

Souter grinned, nodded to Davey. "You have to teach him much?" Closest the old man ever got to a joke. "Davey, you see them horses of English's? I saw he'd branded a few mares, and Bit says he saw a dark colt carryin' a fresh Bench D. Now we got more trouble. Mister Donald says he got a band of mares started and wants the boss to unfence the springs. Figured you might have seen these mares up to where they've been runnin'. Fact is you might be the only one knows where they're grazin' right now."

"I seen the mares." That was the truth.

"How they lookin'?" Souter was playing along.

"Thin . . . kind of poor. Felt sorry for them." Then Davey paused, felt a grin half start on his face, one he couldn't keep in. They each held quiet a moment. Davey thought of Edward Donald, refusing to consider the man's interest legitimate.

Then Souter set the deal. "Let's go get us a meal. If those rannies've left us more than a bean or a half slice of meat."

Chapter Fourteen

Davey worked easy chores the next day, mending two halters, plaiting repairs in a long rope, tacking shoes on a new horse, and lacing rails back into a rarely used corral. Simple things that left him with time in mid-afternoon to go back to the kitchen for a cup of coffee, and a visit with Miss Katherine.

Burn English sat at the table. The man looked up, had to see Davey, but nothing showed in the spare face, no pleasure or pain. He remained intent on the difficulties of bringing a loaded spoon from the plate to his mouth. Davey watched—only half the food made the trip.

"It's right good to see you up, *amigo.*"

The eyes stared, blinked once, and then nothing. Like talking to a pint-sized wooden doll. Miss Katherine moved across the kitchen to stand by her patient and translate. "Davey, sometimes it's still bad . . . but he's bound to try. You understand."

Davey wasn't taken with the intimacy. "Yes'm. Just wanted to tell him the mares are all right. Saw them yesterday in fact."

English grunted, and laid one hand on the table.

Davey stared. The fingers were long and badly scarred, the wrist thick, the nails a dirty grey.

English had only one thought. "The colt?"

"Saw him, too. He looks good."

English closed his eyes. Davey touched the man on his back, shaming himself with the gesture. Miss Katherine said nothing; they were trapped in an unnatural quiet.

Mid-morning the next day, Miss Katherine came looking for Davey. Her hair was plaited under a brown bandanna and she held a wicked-looking wire wisp in one hand. Davey flinched. Sometimes she came after one of the hands with that thing, asking him to take swipes at the heavy rugs Meiklejon favored. As much as Davey idolized Miss Katherine, he didn't want any part of that particular chore.

But she smiled and said that there were spools of wire waiting in Socorro, and Meiklejon wanted Davey to go get them. According to her, Meiklejon felt Davey was the least likely of his men to get into mischief that far from the ranch and on his lonesome. She handed Davey an envelope with cash, for the wire she said. She didn't ask him to wallop those rugs, and he realized he would almost have enjoyed the task, being near her, instead of having to leave on his own.

At the corrals he looked over the stock. A pair of flashy bays chewed on their hay and pretended to spook when Davey leaned on the railings. They were all style and speed and not much for strength. Barbed wire weighed a lot, Davey mused, chewing on his own bit of stemmy hay. So he checked the big sorrel, paired now with a smaller mealy bay. The other sorrel had pulled up lame on an infected hoof, was stalled in the barn, the hoof poulticed and wrapped in burlap. Souter was against the effort but Davey thought he could rescue the old son.

The untried bay snorted. It was no more than sixty miles to Socorro; the mealy bay would do just fine. The team was harnessed and ready by noon, and Davey spent the first few miles keeping the unbalanced team to a steady trot, trying to get a handle on the different horses, a horseman's exercise to occupy his wandering mind.

The sorrel gelding was stubborn but willing. The mealy bay had Davey stumped. At times the good-looking bronco would step up to the collar and pull hard and fast enough so that the sorrel almost loped to keep up. Then just as suddenly the bay would slack off and leave the winded sorrel to pull the whole shebang.

Davey drove into the night, finally reining in to make cold camp. The team got a bait of grain; Davey got the usual tortilla and cold beans. By early morning they'd reached the plains and Davey had decided the mealy bay wasn't harness broke at all, and that, by God, Mr. Meiklejon would have a well-broke bronco by the return trip. Must have come from Donald or Quitano. Around horses, Meiklejon would never learn.

He held in the team and rubbed his eyes against the glare of the white sand and grass. He was thinking it was too bad he hadn't put up more supplies when leaving the ranch, like another canteen of water and some decent food. The bay kept jerking the sorrel, and Davey's hands and temper were raw from guiding the miserable team. When they came up to water in the Gallinas Mountains, Davey let the team drink their fill, then walked them by hand, slipped their bits, and let them graze for an hour. It wasn't going to be a turn-around trip.

While the horses grazed, Davey napped. It was the squeal of the mealy bay that woke him from a sound sleep. He came up with his hand to his rifle, laid close by just in case. An old man sat a bony white mule. The bay and the sorrel squirreled around, threatening the mule and wasting energy. The old man watched as Davey came full awake.

"Son, I got me a broke leg . . . be riding to the doc in Socorro. Be a sight easier on me iffen I can catch a ride with you in that wagon." Here the old-timer briefly ran out of breath, before he began again. "*Curandero* up to Quemado, he says the leg's gone rotten and he can't do nothing more with it."

The man was over sixty, and the mule he rode looked close to that. But taking in the calm eyes and seamed face, Davey had no doubt the old man could make the trip, broken leg and all. He had some doubts about the mule.

"Sure enough, old-timer. Let me harness up and I'll get you settled. These bronc's've had enough grass."

The old man stayed put on the mule while Davey worked with the team. The sorrel and the mealy bay showed temper when he tried backing them into the traces and Davey cursed both animals as they kicked and stepped over the lines.

The old man allowed it could be the mule. "Horses don't take to Bert, he's some contrary and they know it. Get me in the wagon, and turn the old son loose. Bert won't follow and he won't worry 'bout being left alone. And no honest, respecting thief would try to steal him. By the time this leg gets set and wrapped, old Bert'll be filled with this here good grass, and ready to carry me home."

The white mule wandered out of sight. The team backed up right smart and stood while Davey finished his work. Only the team breathing in unison and the fat old man's wheezing broke up the daytime sounds. Davey climbed in, pushed a place for himself against the old man's bulk, and picked up the lines, talking to the bay and the sorrel as they moved as a team, eager to be gone from the white mule's miserable being.

The old man spoke up finally. "The name's Eager Briggs. I seen you . . . working for that Englishman to the L Slash. He ain't so bad, for a foreigner. I knew old Littlefield. Your Englishman, he's right 'bout the wire. I don't much like it myself, too old for that. Dangerous, spiteful stuff. But it's the only way now. Open range's gone, too many folks crowding in."

Davey listened to the old man and was reluctant to think him right. But now that Briggs had got his mouth open, he didn't stop. "You be Davey Hildahl . . . come over from Arizona. With a reputation behind you that you swung a wide loop, hired out your gun. Got ridden out of good country 'cause folks didn't trust your name."

These were words for fighting, but Davey didn't bother. An old man earned some few privileges, and talk was one of them.

Briggs shook his head, a sour smell coming from him. "Ain't easy to understand, you being the peaceful one to the L Slash."

These words were a steel trap, closing in on Davey. He'd thought that time in Arizona long gone. It had been close to three years since he'd left. He'd never killed a man, never even let off a shot. Just rode with the wrong bunch. Now an old man with a broken leg was recalling all the supposed truths. He grinned, and shook the lines to the slowing team.

Briggs rambled on. "Son, I come up from Texas. Too many years ago to make a difference. And I come up the same way you did, from over west. Had a sheriff after me, asking questions 'bout what I knowed and seen. What I did. No one else to blame but my youth, son, and my greed. Now I got over that, like you done . . . it seems to me."

Davey said the first thing that came to mind. "How'd you

break that leg? It don't look pretty, and it sure don't smell recent."

Eager Briggs smiled, and that wasn't a pretty sight, either. Few teeth, and the wrinkled face folded up in layers of fat and grease. "Mule kicked me, 'course. Kicked me before, but this's the first time it took. Broke the leg bone clear through and I set it, then the durned mule went and kicked me again. More'n I could set this time. *Curandero* said I waited too long . . . herbs ain't strong enough. Need a doc, he said. So I's headed to So-corro."

Two miles of silence, with Davey hoping the worst of the revelations were done. Then the old man began talking about things too close to Davey's mind.

"I seen that *mesteñero* you got to the L Slash. I seen him before." Then he changed direction. "You know, I rode out of places years back 'cause they was stringing that wire. Rode out o' Kansas in 'Seventy-Seven. They was putting up wire faster'n my buckskin could pace a mile. Had a talk once with a man, setting on his land and guarding it with a musket. Black powder it was, big enough to stop a whole family o' grizzlies."

Davey was only half listening, so tired he could barely see through swollen eyes, but, at least, the team was pulling half decently now, the mealy bay doing his share. Eager Briggs's words became a lullaby. Until Briggs got back to a bitter name. Then Davey came up awake.

"Yes, sir, I seen that *mesteñero* before. Thought so the night he and Donald, they got to drinking, and ole Donald he got to talking. *Mesteñero* did some bragging of his own 'bout where he'd been, where he'd come from. Yes, sir, I knowed that boy when he was a young 'un."

Davey's head snapped up, but Briggs talked on like he never knew Davey had almost been asleep. "Down in Texas, when he was a button. He was working 'longside his pa, fighting with his two sisters. Had him a pretty ma, real pretty." Here the old man sighed, the explosion of hot breath stunning Davey. "It was right sad."

Davey looked over. His passenger was wiping tears from his eyes, then pulling at his long, reddened nose and mumbling something from the folds of his mouth. "Yes, sir, he looked just like his pa back then. Eyes and such, that black hair. Now men used to say John English was part Indian. I never believed it, so I asked John, plain as could be. And he said his family was Welsh, come from a long line o' these Welsh . . . a thick-headed lot he called them. He laughed, said his boy was like him at that age. He was a tough one, John English. Big son, more'n six feet, and only got one arm, lost it in that damned war."

"Burn English is a runt, Mister Briggs. You're thinking about someone else you knew . . . said it was a long time ago."

Briggs shook, like maybe he was laughing, instead of crying. "There's more to it, son. Sorry, I was there when it happened." He choked off, wiped his eyes, and then the corners of his mouth, and Davey was glad he didn't have to be staring at Eager Briggs all this time.

"It took the whole family. The boy got terrible sick with the fever. He lived, but never grew much after. Couldn't have been more'n thirteen when he got sick. Big as he is now . . . never got much bigger. He was a tough one, that boy. After his folks. . . . He worked horses and kept to himself. Local ranchers hired him. Not like his pa, friendly and such. Took me in one time I was poorly. His ma . . . she was a pretty thing. He ain't much like neither of them . . . they was good people, though, and they taught their boy well."

Davey thought of English. What Briggs was saying, it all made sense.

"Yes, sir, heard tell of the boy after that. Shot two men for stealing his bronc'. Got shot hisself, but went after the bastards.

He were only a kid, but that pistol made him full-sized. Killed one man in a *cantina*, other died later. Boy disappeared. Guess he thought the law wanted him."

Maybe that was what Davey felt—a kinship, from looking over his shoulder. Kept a man lonesome and even downright unfriendly.

Eager Briggs rubbed the leg that was broke, above the knee, squeezing the swollen flesh. The wattles along his sagging jaw flipped sideways and made Davey think of an old rooster. He clucked to the team, found his mouth dried out. His eyes burned and were sore.

He stopped at the doc's office. It was dusk and Davey was tired. Briggs came partway around to Davey's side to deliver a final opinion. "You watch . . . Mister Donald's going to make a try for those mares. There'll be hell to breakfast when that boy finds out. Donald ain't got the heart to keep his word. He don't know the English boy like I do. Them Englishes fight for what's theirs." The old man rubbed his damp, toothless mouth before spitting out the rest of his thinking. "You pay attention, Davey. That boy killed two men when he was sixteen, for taking one horse. You think much of him, you'll keep watch, keep him outta the same trouble here. Go 'long now, I got me a doc to see."

Chapter Fifteen

Davey put the team up at the livery, careful of Billy McPhee's temper and the mealy bay's heels. He made a deal with Billy to bed down in the hay; in exchange he gave up his matches and would feed out come morning. Finally he checked in at Miller's General Mercantile, telling Miller he'd be back early the next morning.

That left getting a meal, for his belly was snapping his backbone. On that errand he passed Dr. Lockhart's office and saw a light, and, without thinking, he knocked hard. The doctor brought him into a bright room stinking of spoiled meat and disinfectant and Eager Briggs, who had his leg propped in a chair and was chewing a chicken leg big enough to feed three men. Briggs sucked on the skin, smacked his lips, and made a great show of enjoyment. Davey was pleased enough to see the old man wrapped in clean bandages. He said "Good Night" to the two men, but Briggs wouldn't let him go.

"Son, you set and eat. I already told doc how you brung me in when that blessed mule was making my life a pure misery. Doc's willing to share out more o' this chicken while you tell him how our friend English fares."

Lockhart nodded. "Good of you to help, Davey. Heard you boys been busy this summer. How's our patient doing? Wouldn't have given him a chance, two months past. A tough one for all there's so little to him. Cured buffalo hide and nails. Men like him, they're hard to kill."

Davey winced at the word "kill", thinking too clearly on Briggs's earlier comments. That chicken was beginning to smell awful good as he answered Lockhart. "Doc, he's walking, but not talking much. He's wasted down to 'most nothing. If iron nails hold him together, they's sure as hell gone rusty."

Lockhart nodded absently and passed Davey a chicken wing, a plate with two slices of stale bread, a mess of *refritos*, and green chile. Davey ate under the doc's watchful eye, feeling bribed for more talk about English with a second helping of the chicken. But he had nothing more to say, at least not about the mustanger.

At the livery stable, Billy wasn't around to bother a man with all his unsaid words. Davey burrowed into soft hay. The horses stamped and snorted, so he wasn't alone. He could forget all he'd left behind at the L Slash, and he slept hard, woke in exactly the same place where he'd lay down.

Past sunrise he had the team harnessed and standing in front of Miller's. It was a waste of a good new day. Miller arrived at 7:30 to unlock the doors. With the sun already past the false fronts and shining into the street, Davey was fretting, anxious for the wire to get loaded, so he could get out of Socorro.

Before he settled in the wagon, he bent down and picked up a handful of rocks, some no more than the size of beans. He put them in a pile by his boot, then sucked on bitter coffee while Miller and his boy loaded the wagon. When they were done, Davey, lines in his hands, picked up the whip and nodded to Miller and his boy. The kid was growing; Davey remarked on that fact. Miller nodded, the kid turned red, and Davey started up the team.

The mealy bay hadn't improved with feed and a stall for the night. The horse plain refused to pull, so Davey tickled it along the ribs with the whip, then threw one of the small rocks at the bay quarters, to convince the horse that pulling was easier than Davey's temper. The bay leaped forward, and for two miles or more the sorrel was in agreement on Davey's choice of speed. Full-out bolt, heads high, tails slapping in Davey's face. He kept the lines soft and let the pair run. When the heat and sun got to them, and they wanted to slow, Davey wouldn't let them and the bay went to sulling. Davey used more of his rock supply to keep the bay moving, and once he hit the sorrel by mistake. The gelding looked back at Davey, clearly annoyed. Davey tipped his hat, and the sorrel nodded like it understood. Then the big horse bit the mealy bay on the underside of its neck, and the horse squealed, tried to bite back. Davey's whip got between them and caught the bay hard on the lip. The bay surged forward, then settled into working. The rest of the trip was easy.

Davey saw the white shine of the San Agustin plains in the distance as they started down the slow hill past the Gallinas Mountains, but then the team snorted and shied from a carcass.

145

The hide was white, the flesh half eaten, sinew and bone stretched out, only the thin mane and tail remaining. So the old man lost his mule like he wanted.

He pushed the team till the sorrel up and quit on him. Davey calmed down when he saw the thick white lather between the heavy draft legs, the ribs bellowing up and down to get in more air, and knew he'd been too bent on hurrying. He got out of the wagon, but not before looking around, and walked a mile or two himself, in penance. No self-respecting cowpoke would be seen walking alongside two respectable broncos.

The team dragged him in just before dawn. Every light was on in the house and the men were spread out in the yard. Bare feet, naked chests wrapped in blankets, and not one hat on a head in sight. Their attention was on Burn English in the center—half naked, in loose-fitting drawers, and a thick bandage wrapped across his belly. The men stood watching quietly.

Davey hauled in the team and wrapped their lines around the whip and climbed down very carefully. The team felt his weight move and pulled forward to stop at the corral, waiting expectantly for nothing.

Red Pierson tried to mouth something, but English raised his arms. Red dropped his head, and then Davey saw why. English carried a fancy rifle that Davey recognized from Meiklejon's collection. A real monster weapon that would put a hole the size of a city hotel through any man trying to get within arm distance of a mighty riled mustanger.

Then Miss Katherine came out, her hair loose and flowing, with a dark wool shawl around her shoulders. Her face turned as white as her gown. English moved at the sound of her voice, but that god-awful weapon stayed steady in his hands. Davey, like the rest of the gathered men, didn't twitch or chance a sigh. Her voice held concern. English's hands shuddered and he moved closer to the light. Ugly, blooded eyes a pale fire. Davey raised his hands, took a half step, drawing English's attention from the woman.

"Hell, I like being noticed, same as any fellow, but this reception's kind of much, don't you boys think?"

No one spoke, but English frowned and the big rifle moved a bit, a few inches to the left of Davey's gut.

Davey addressed English, saying: "Howdy. Weren't it cold? How 'bout giving me that rifle? Looks heavy . . . more'n one man can hold."

Nothing seemed to go through those eyes; they held to Davey, but did not see him.

Then there was a slow change, a shift, as Miss Katherine came in next to Davey. English staggered. Davey saw Red begin to reach out. He shook his head, hoping the kid would get the message. English seemed finally to see Davey, so he asked for the rifle again and it was given up with no effort. Davey took the rifle as well as a deep breath. *God, what a monster, it could kill a buffalo from a half-mile stand.*

English's eyes locked on the woman's mouth, as if by seeing those lips he could understand the words that had been spoken. For it was obvious, the man was out on his feet. Davey wondered what had gotten English riled.

He saw the beginning of English's collapse before any of them. The frail body shivered, then the wild face drifted from watching Miss Katherine to seeking out Davey. The strangest eyes Davey had ever seen—a pale green shimmer, even in the dawn light, the black rim struck off sparks, the white threaded with bloody lines as the black lashes laid a shadow on close bone.

Red Pierson remained. The others were gone. English's hands reached Davey and their heat had the feel of dying. Davey's belly turned over on him and he choked down, swallowed. A hand touched his face, a feather's touch. Two fingers swept his jaw and English tried to grin.

"Need to shave, Hildahl. Look like a damned *mesteñero.*"

Davey grabbed for him as the man let go. Red caught an arm as Davey slid his hands beneath the man's shoulders and kept him from falling. It was tough on Red to carry English back to the house, to see how bad off a man could be and still live. Pierson had to leave once they got English laid out on his narrow bed like a new corpse. Davey didn't blame the kid.

Davey found Miss Katherine in the kitchen, holding a white cup to her mouth, sipping noisily, watching Davey over the cup's rim. She said: "My father came here late this evening . . . to argue with everyone. Father took it to Mister Meiklejon, laid it out . . . all about the wire and the brand being registered to Edward Donald and not Burn English, not Gordon Meiklejon, and that no man had the right to take anything from him." She took more of the coffee, motioned to Davey to do the same. He raised the cup to his lips, found there was brandy in the coffee, and took a large swallow, gulping down the heat and letting it calm him. "My father is despicable. When he was gone . . . after Mister Meiklejon had Mister Souter and Stan Brewitt remove him forcibly . . . I talked with Burn. I thought he understood. Then, after we all had gone to bed, I heard this terrible noise, and when I got outside. . . . Thank you, Davey, for helping. I don't know how else this would have been resolved. My father has made Burn sick again, just when he was beginning to heal." Her eyes clouded, and she pulled the wool shawl closer to her chin. "There are times when I actually hate my father, Davey. Do you think I will be forgiven for that?"

There wasn't much Davey could say. He tipped his hat, backed out of the kitchen, and walked to where Red was busy unharnessing the team and trying to dodge the mealy bay's hind hoofs. Davey helped, absently thanking the kid for knowing what needed to be done.

"Davey . . . Mister Hildahl? What's wrong with him? He looks like he's crazy, like he's got to kill someone." The boy wasn't dumb.

"Red, he's crazy from the pain. Bad fever runs a mind in circles, keeps a man from knowing right from wrong or enemy from friend." Davey hoped that was enough for the boy, hoped he'd leave now and let Davey get some sleep. Red finished with the harness, then he was gone. Davey looked at the bank of hay. This time he'd sleep in the bunkhouse, in an honest-to-god bed, or at least something shaped like one.

It was time for the fall chores and chasing rustlers. Davey and old Souter suspected it was Jack Holden gone sour, and so did the law at Silver City, one Ben Stradley. Daily Holden was seen running off some man's best steers. He was in a bar drinking way over by Mangas, then at Red Hill chasing a dozen cows, and down to Old Horse Springs stealing broncos out of a rancher's corral while the man was eating supper. And to Gutierrez- ville, which no one gave much account to. Gutierrez-ville was mostly sheepherder families and some day riders.

Souter grinned and said outright that no one man could be all the places Jack Holden had been seen, and his orders were to chase rustlers, not ghosts. Davey headed up Stan Brewitt and a new man named Spot, and they went tracking and trailing, following so many split tracks they were seeing double in their sleep. They came on a few camps that were left suddenly—fire smoking, ground warm where the grass was flattened. Even so, they didn't catch an outlaw and they lost maybe twenty cows and calves, and a few broncos. Word was Son Liddell's horse pasture had got like a bank—Holden taking out so many of the horses, leaving a worn down bronco in return.

Davey didn't care. He was willing to take his small crew back to the L Slash headquarters, glad to get off the grullo he rode, stretch his legs, and maybe get a glimpse of Miss Katherine. He hadn't seen her, literally, in a month of Sundays. Hadn't seen Burn English, either. Maybe that didn't matter, but he was curious about the man.

So he put up his weary horse and crossed to the main house, to get himself a cup of coffee. He'd been out a month and was thinking about a day in town, maybe a night, too. Socorro, or Magdalena, where there were girls to spin and kiss, and hold onto in the back room, in the dark.

The door came open under his knock and he stepped back unwillingly. Of course, it was Burn English, black hair too long and wearing a collarless shirt much too big for him, highlighting the pallor of his indoor skin. The man was unsteady, but the thin mouth grinned.

"If it ain't Hildahl. Come back to see what you done? I been waiting on you."

"Well, I been waiting to see you, too, English. Standing, that is. Don't look to me like you're going to die the next minute or two." He could have been more choosy about his words, but the angle to English's mouth, the gleam in those damned fire eyes, they told Davey this wasn't a friendly meet.

"You set me up, Hildahl. I ain't going to forgive that."

Davey rubbed his face, stalling for time. He was tired and angry, and now this. It took some remembering to know that English's mind was back two months or more, when all that hooraw about the wild horses and the wire happened. A lot of time had passed, but English had had no part in it.

"Friend, I had no doing with the stampede. You heard us coming and ran. We wanted to talk, is all. Meiklejon's a reasonable man . . . he come up to talk." Being sensible was rough. Davey tried again. "I tried to warn you about the wire. Tried to turn that gray before . . . before you got killed."

Hate remained in the green eyes.

Davey sighed, wiped his face, and found his fingers damp with sweat, his mouth turning salty. Then he heard a small sound, raised his head, and saw Miss Katherine staring at him. He had nothing to say to her, either, so he left.

Two days later, Davey came in early, leading his bronco. A pulled shoe, a bad stone bruise, and he had had to walk. He pared away the bruise and swabbed tar on the infection, reset the shoe. Then he put the bronco in a pen, vowing to poultice the hoof later when the tar had worked into the bruised sole.

He was tuckered out, hungry, and still mad. A cup of coffee, maybe a warmed-over biscuit or a slice of fresh bread, and some of that blackberry jam would ease him. So he pounded on the kitchen door, and, when no one answered, he limped inside, headed for the cook stove. There the enameled pot was shoved to the back of the stove.

No one showed. Meiklejon was out, at least the pacing grullo he favored was gone, and Souter had the men chasing a bunch of cows off of Blind Mesa. But Miss Katherine should have been here. Then it struck him. She was here, alone with Burn English. What he imagined then was against his upbringing and inclinations, so he made himself pour a cup of the thick coffee, laced it with canned milk.

What he was thinking was wrong. But he went through the house to the back room, sipping his coffee, not calling out Miss Katherine's name or asking for Burn English. Not saying anything out loud at all.

Burn's stomach injury bled occasionally so it was necessary to change the bandaging twice a day. He never exhibited any physical discomfort or, indeed, showed any reaction at all as Katherine pulled back the soiled cloths, removed the herbs that *Señora* Ortega insisted still be used. Katherine did not mind doing the simple chore.

Barren of children, she had not known the flesh of any human the way she knew that of Burn English. Now her fingertips, so lightly, delicately out of concern for any pain, traced the skin and muscle and bone of a most singular human being.

Burn English was not handsome, nor was he a gentleman, but he carried a quality that struck Katherine. He opened a need. She could not equate the terrible urgency when around him with any common rationale. He beckoned her, and she responded. He lay supine on the bed, eyes closed, hands flat, palms turned up, waiting. She knelt beside him, close to his dry skin, and she knew the fluttering lids of his eyes watched her through their transparency. She needed to remove the old bandage from his midsection. The scent stopped her—a smell of herbs mingled with one she believed was purely male.

Her mouth was moist and she wiped her lips. In raising her hand, she brushed over his ribs where his heart would be. His hand grabbed her, held her wrist. Katherine counted in Latin to keep calm. His eyes opened, and he must have known, for he smiled as she bent down and kissed his forehead.

"Burn." The name fluttered through her lips.

Davey watched them from the doorway. Fury took hold, for the woman and the mustanger, for himself and his indecency. He forced weight onto his foot, dug the boot heel into the wood floor, turned, and went back down the hall. The hot kitchen, empty of all kindness, mocked him as he searched for the bottle of brandy. Its fire choked him. He slammed down the bottle, stalked outside to inhale the thick summer air.

Burn sucked in a breath; he could not do this. Even as his body drew him to her, he could not. He willed himself flat and dull. She must finish her task, change his bandage like changing a baby's diaper, and then leave him for her other chores. Burn bit his mouth. His body quivered where he could not stop his heart.

Her hands were cool, quick-moving, no longer lingering over his exposed flesh. She was letting him decide, she was stepping away even as she sat beside him on the sagging bed and ministered to his physical need.

Burn let his eyelids draw back enough to filter what he needed to see. Her skin was pearl white, her body tight against her dress, so close to him he could taste her pulse. He had no business dreaming, wishing for the weight of her hand on his wounded skin. He enjoyed his pain for it brought her close to him. Indecent, using suffering as a reason for love. There could be no illusions. She would give herself from pity, and hate herself for the act, hate him for accepting it. He closed his eyes and held still.

Davey couldn't settle down. He ached and his gut was empty. He could see those hands rest on the mustanger's hide. Her kissing him. He went to the stable and made up a poultice, wrapped it on the grullo's hoof with an old gunny sack, anything to keep him from thinking about Miss Katherine in there with the *mesteñero*. But he couldn't stand it; he couldn't let him touch her.

He stormed back to the kitchen, making lots of noise at the door, sending a chair against the wall. The gesture didn't matter. English was at the small corner table, wearing another one of those flapping shirts. Miss Katherine stood near him, her hands on his back, up near his neck. Hands that rested gently, too kindly, hurting Davey even more.

He forced himself to go to the cook stove to pour out cold coffee, refusing to look when Miss Katherine did not step away from English's chair. He heard a deep groan that echoed inside him. Davey drained the cup clean of the stale coffee and stared at his opponent over the rim, unable to look at Katherine. He attacked, with words for once, never having done that before. "No man worth his salt'll take a good woman's reputation so light, *mesteñero!*"

White with effort, English rose from the table. Katherine's hands went to her face. English placed both hands on the wood table. The raised, damaged knuckles shimmered against the mesquite grain.

"You got a bad mind, Hildahl. To think this woman'd do anything wrong." Then he pushed away from the table's support. Miss Katherine stepped back in anticipation. English's voice was harsh. "I can't fight you, Hildahl. Not now. But I can hold you to a settlement, come a month or so. You're mean wrong."

Katherine Donald started forward, hands raised as if to soothe over the conflict, but English shrugged to stop her and Davey witnessed what the simple gesture took from him, saw a long spasm cross the bony face and settle deeply in the mouth's drawn corners. It took a strong will, but English managed to reach the hall doorway

English's voice was soft, pleading. "Ma'am, it's not what you been doing out of pure kindness. It's his thinking." English steadied himself against the door frame a moment before he disappeared into the dark house.

Davey was left to face Miss Katherine's anger.

In the morning, when the crew came for breakfast, Red announced that the boss's favorite traveling horse was gone from the pens and asked whether Meiklejon had gone out this early. Miss Katherine put down the wooden spoon she was holding and said very quietly that Burn English was also gone.

Souter took a drink of coffee. Davey's face was red.

Katherine looked clearly at him while talking to Souter. "He left a note. Said he took the grullo as it was easy riding, and that he would leave the animal at Quitano's as soon as he could. Said he'd been here long enough."

★ ★ ★ ★ ★

JACK HOLDEN

★ ★ ★ ★ ★

Chapter Sixteen

He slowed the quick-stepping dark bay and held himself quietly, listening, cocking his head to question a sound, drawing in quick gasps of air to check what else he could learn. He'd ridden the cañon often before. Its walls were high and narrow so that even in the hot summer heat the sun barely greened the few trees and scrub bushes. It was not a safe place for any man to be caught, even more dangerous for a man with a warrant on his head.

Jack Holden released his hold on the dark bay. The horse bolted, spooked by the walls that hung in on either side. Laughing, head thrown back, body rocking with the frantic horse's stride, Jack let the handsome bronco run.

The cañon widened abruptly, spread out to a small valley covered with sparse grasses and low juniper. Finally in agreement, horse and rider stood, motionless, both sweating, winded, skin and hide black with soaked dust. It had felt good to run, good to risk everything on a turned rock, an unseen coyote den.

Jack guided the bay to a pool of water glistening in the afternoon sun, its surface rippled by invisible life. He let the bay drink sparingly, then got down and hobbled the animal, slipped its bit, and turned it loose for some graze. He shucked off his clothes, hung them on a bush, and shivered as he put one foot into the water. Holden was tall, lean, battered, yet well-formed and handsome. His dark curly hair touched the back of his neck; he felt its weight and knew he was in need of a shearing.

Ranchers didn't treat a man with long hair well—could be hiding the sign of a notched ear, the badge of a known horse thief.

Jack laughed as he stepped deeper into the pool and felt his groin and belly shrink back from the cold. Caught out now by an irate rancher, he would be mocked and ridiculed, and hung naked for a horse thief, cattle rustler, lover. All titles belonging to his sins, any of which would lead to his inevitable early death.

He wanted only to breathe the clean hot air and feel the pool's cold water cleanse him. It didn't matter that the bay gelding, now grazing peacefully, wore the familiar brand of Son Liddell. The old bastard hated everyone. Jack knew he'd never hang for stealing that particular man's horses. Most likely it would be an irate husband quick to fire as Jack climbed out of a bedroom window.

He'd changed his habits lately, out of laziness. It was easier to take cattle locally than to make an effort of riding west, or north, to find contributions to his way of life. He didn't take many; these locals couldn't complain of his excessive thieving. He needed only enough cattle to buy necessities. Women didn't cost much in actual coin. They wanted *him,* not money.

He rolled over in the water, let his long body float in the shallow pool. He looked down his chest and belly, hollowed out by being too long on the fugitive trail, and saw his genitals floating on the water's surface. Beyond them were the two white columns of his thighs, the bony protrusions of his knees, and his feet sticking up in the air, white and pale, toes shaped by the narrow boots he wore.

Men weren't much to look at naked, Jack decided again. Now a woman had her curves and softness, a pleasurable sweep to her buttocks, a loving roundness to unburdened breasts. But a man was angles and planes, thickened muscle too easily led by the passions of weak flesh.

He laughed while forgetting he lay on a fragile surface, and immediately half sank, took in water, and, choking, rolled over, struck out with his hands, kicked with his feet and legs, and scraped his hip on a submerged rock. Once he extricated himself from the churned water, he lay gratefully on the rocky ground, still laughing and choking from the immersion, spitting out sand and mud. After he stood and gathered his clothing, he saw the bay was far down the valley, hopping valiantly on tied legs, desperate to get away from the monster that had emerged from the once safe watering hole.

Jack dressed quickly, caught the bay that seemed grateful to come to Jack once it recognized its master. Jack unhobbled the animal, led it back to the pool. Then he kneeled down, leaned out, and studied his reflection in the moving shadows. The face was long, with flat cheek bones and a straight nose. The eyes were a bright blue, blue enough to shine in the water's mirror. The curly dark hair fanned out in back of the flat ears. The mouth was too wide, the lips full, the teeth white and strong. A handsome face, Jack was often told.

He grinned at his wavering reflection and stood up. The bay side-stepped quickly, shook its head, then its whole body, dust spinning in a fleeting cloud. Saddle strings popped, stirrups banged, and the bay jumped from the noise, broke wind, and jumped again. Jack laughed, and mounted. He sure wasn't much of a horse thief if this bay was the best he could steal.

He was to meet a man to discuss the sale of someone's twenty head of longhorn cattle. Jack's hand rode close to his pistol, but he didn't touch the weapon, nor did he pay much attention to any side noises—leaves rustling, birds suddenly flying up from nesting trees. His mind catalogued these sounds and knew their meaning. The bay walked quickly, carrying Jack's weight easily.

Motion in a stand of piñon spooked the bay. Jack patted the horse's neck and let the animal whinny. If it was his man, he'd soon know. If another, they would fight or pass pleasantries. He pushed back his hat, wiped his damp forehead, and remembered with great clarity the taste and feel of the cool water, the force of its current over his flesh, and he smiled to himself.

Jack spoke toward the piñon. "It is funny for you, *señor?* To startle a man seeking shelter from the miserable sun?" Jack settled the hat, shifted in the saddle. No telling what the bay gelding would do next, and Jack had an aversion to being thrown on rocky ground studded with cactus. "Come here, *señor* . . . to where we may speak and see each other's faces." Jack's Spanish was passable, but he still heard a chuckle from the brush as he spoke.

"That, *señor,* is a most reasonable idea." The voice spoke English in a deep, unruffled voice.

A horse split the bush, a light roan with a long Roman head, and a quick, pacing gait. Jack shook his head as the man rode in, and his gesture was understood, accepted.

His new partner had a brand of humor. "Ah, *señor,* I have heard of your fondness for these fine animals. That one, he is a beauty, but look, he is trembling and afraid. Is that the mount for a professional thief?"

Jack responded in kind. "Well, *señor,* I see you choose your mounts by their ugliness. Does this make you a better thief? The one you ride . . . it must be of the very finest, for I have rarely seen an uglier bronc'."

The dark-skinned man frowned, then leaned back and patted the roan on its rump. The horse twitched its tail, as if spanking a nuisance fly, then returned to its interrupted nap. "Yes, señor, it is an ugly animal, but it does not waste time and effort on jumping from that which will not hurt it."

The man's English was definitely superior to Jack's Spanish, so they agreed, with a shrug, to continue in that unmusical tongue.

The two rode a half mile off the trail, into one of the many narrow cañons that crossed through the mountains. As they rode, Jack was conscious of towering over the man and his pacing roan, and often had to check his bay's nervous trot. But when they found the most suitable place and dismounted to discuss their future together, Jack saw that it was the horse's size that was deceptive, for the man was almost as tall as Jack, and much wider in the belly and shoulders, much stronger through the span of his hands.

The Mex spoke: "You are Jack Holden. I am Refugio."

Jack could hear the doubt in those few words, and nodded casually as he extended his hand and the Mex responded. Refugio looked to be in his thirties, with the usual dark hair and eyes of his breed. A scar across his face—from his right eye to the corner of his mouth—marked the journey he had taken to manhood. Jack watched Refugio's eyes, saw their black reflection as they traveled up and down Jack's own frame, taking a similar inventory. When the man's face opened in a dazzling grin, Jack found he could not keep himself from the same gesture. Never mind their opposing colors, they were matched where it counted.

Refugio began: "It was whispered to me in Springerville that you know to speak with those who would buy cattle branded, but with no bill of sale. I have a small herd, gathered slowly through this long winter. Many cows, several steers, even two bulls that I know will bring much money. But I cannot trail them, or sell them to the *gringo*s who have the money. This is why I come to you."

It was hard reading Refugio's face. The dark eyes smiled, but no pleasure framed the mouth, the head was half turned. He did not know his man, so Jack squatted, leaned his back against a convenient rock, and stared out at nothing, leaving room for Refugio to do his own thinking. The man watched the sky a bit, then looked down at his own hands, spread them wide and low, squatted next to Jack. In no hurry, confident, the Mex waited a few moments, then brought his hands together, rubbed them dry.

"I know, *señor,* that I am but a man not always right, wanting only to do his work and get by. More than that, to be a judge of who lives or dies . . . I do not wish such things for myself."

Jack spoke. "Have you changed any of the brands?"

"No, *señor,* I was waiting."

Jack shrugged. "Well, let's get it done."

They rose together. Refugio nodded. He laughed a few moments later when Jack got on the bay and the horse jumped sideways, scraped the side of Jack's boot before he could settle in the saddle.

"You ride a better horse for work, yes?"

Jack nodded. "Whenever I can."

It was a lie, but Refugio laughed. "Then I have taken the right partner, *señor.*"

They parted company at a narrow fork. There was no dust, no sign of the man's visit. Jack sighed and slapped the bay, felt the explosion of air from the horse's gut. "*Amigo,* we are both great fools." Then it came to him. He'd angle over to Gutierrezville and pick up whatever mail might have accumulated for him over the past month or so.

There was one letter for him at the Gutierrezville post office, written in a hand he did not immediately recognize. It was obviously that of a lady, which he knew through long familiarity with such letters. The envelope was frayed and stained, and held no scent, although it could have started its long journey sprinkled with lilac or rose water.

Dear Jack, the letter began, and he smiled as he read the most ordinary greeting, still not knowing the scribe's identity. *We have not seen each other in many years, but I am asking this favor of you as the only member of our family in which I may place my trust*. These words stopped him cold, froze the smile on his face, and seethed in his heart. He had no family. He had ridden away from them more than thirteen years ago, when he was only fourteen.

My son, John, named after you and our father, is proving himself to be a young man in need of guidance. Through inquiries I have determined that you often reside in the southwest New Mexico Territory, which is well known even here for its wildness and the severity and hardship of its life.

Jack reinspected the letter wrapping, which bore any number of faint markings across its front. It had been a long trip from Kansas, detouring in Chihuahua and San Antonio before finding Silver City and then Gutierrezville. He pondered briefly on the whys of such misdirection, as the printed address boldly stated Jack Holden, New Mexico Territory.

John is much like you, dear Brother, in wanting to see the world and in caring little about the feelings of those who love him. Jack paused here to re-taste the hurt and anger that had driven him from the home he had once shared with a sister, a tired mother, and a hated father. His "feelings" had been bruised by his final departure; he had left carrying the distinct and bleeding marks of his father's rage and anger across his young back. There had been no one to ask about young Jack Holden's "feelings". The pity inside him, quick to find a raw opening, swelled up and out, and Jack felt the rising pain, fought to crush and stamp it down, where it must lie dormant and banked, let out only upon rare occasion.

I would ask you to take the boy, start him with the knowledge you have won through these separated years. He is not a bad child, not in the way his grandfather speaks of him. But he is wild and ready, and will not stand for such treatment as is often meted out. Jack fought a heavy breath that choked in his throat and wanted to strangle him. *I know you too fought this same battle. Therefore, I am sending*

John Thackery to you, with a few dollars to be used to purchase the clothing and gear necessary for his new life. He has signed on with a herd of cattle being driven to Springerville in Arizona, which I hope is close enough to where this letter finds you. I do not wish him to be a burden for you, dear Brother, but I am no longer capable of standing between my son and my father.

I wish you all my love, and hope that your life is what you had sought it to be so many years ago. Thank you before you even know what is to be asked of you. Thank you for taking in your kin to shape his young life.

It was signed *yours truly,* and with her name. The same last name that Jack no longer used.

CHAPTER SEVENTEEN

The unexpected request forced a shiver through Jack. She did not expect her child's return. The boy was on his way, and Jack must take what arrived and not disavow the obligation that a barely remembered woman placed on him. Nephew—the word he needed to accept. Blood relation—a boy from a sister's passion. No mention of a father, no married name. By his calculations she would have been carrying the child when he left. That galled him, to have left her to face their parents' violence.

Springerville wasn't much of a town. The hurry-up of its founding showed in the shacks nailed together with gaping holes below the roof, signs posted advertising lumber, general mercantile, bank, even lawyers. But there was no doubt on Springerville's heart. It wanted money and it offered goods and services in alarming variety to insure that little cash made its way through town without changing hands at least once. It was Jack's kind of town. He had made money here as well as spent it. Cattle a man didn't have to raise and fret over sold real quickly at a bargain price, and that same money bought what passed for pretty women and all the good friends found in a whiskey bottle. There wasn't much more Jack Holden wanted.

The child who came flying out of the office near the shipping pens was not part of Jack's expectations. The boy had Jack's sister's bright red hair that came from some long-departed ancestor. The boy stopped at the office door, a knife appearing in the boy's hand that he used to clean his nails. *A pretty child,* Jack thought. When the boy finally moved, perhaps because of noises from the office interior, Jack saw it in the boy's direct stare and knew he was trouble. Pale gold eyes flecked with darker color and set deeply in the skull, and shaded by thin lashes so pale they held no color. Jack's father all over again.

Jack always had thanked his ma for her looks that had become his own oft-mentioned handsomeness. This boy was Jack's pa— pure trouble. Jack removed his off-side boot from the stirrup, introduced himself, and offered the boy a mount up. The youngster climbed on, and Jack let the nervous bay prance through the tangle of shipping pens so familiar to him. At his back he could hear voices and the inevitable sound of a rifle cocked and readied.

"What kind of hell'd you raise back there?"

There was a simple answer, and it came in a familiar twang that brought the full realization of who rode behind him. The voice was his father's, and no mistaking its irritated tone.

"I asked to be paid, and the man said he owed me nothing. So I hit him."

"You got a horse, or do we have to find you one, and the outfit to go with it?"

The boy had few graces. He shrugged. Jack could feel the gesture.

"Got a bronc', and gear. Bought 'em near Salinas. They belong to me."

The voice rose at the end of the declaration, and Jack knew the kid had been challenged to keep his outfit. Older hands on a drive would chouse a kid, give him the bad jobs, the rough unwanted broncos, the tail end of the drag, meaning to find out the kid's worth before they had to depend on him.

Jack guided the bay as the thin hand pointed out a small pen holding a sorry yellow mare. The boy slid off the bay without talking, and Jack pulled leather when the horse leaped forward and began bucking hard. When he brought down the bay, there was the boy, holding the saddled mare, watching with bleak eyes at the bay's antics.

"That bronc' ain't much," the boy said.

They talked some. The boy, who answered to John, said he'd come in three days past. He had slept in the shed, fed the sorry mare from leavings out of the pens, but didn't think he'd taken enough to equal the $5 he had paid for the mare's keep. John also had had to fight for his $20 for the drive, which the boss had not wanted to pay. By the boy's account, he'd won the battle, had the mare and a $20 coin in his pocket.

"How'd you eat, boy?" Jack was curious.

The kid looked at him with contempt. "Ladies to towns . . . they feel sorry for an orphan kid like me. They feed better'n any company office could. Take me to their bed, iffen I wanted them to." The last was said in defiance, and Jack looked away, careful not to see too much of himself in that anger.

"You got a last name, boy?" Maybe this would give him a handle he could use.

"Ain't the same as yours . . . the one you use. Ma told me I was to keep the family's name, not change it like you done."

"You do what your ma says, boy." The image of his sister birthing out this throwback felt strange. Jack shook and put the bay off stride. The jolt put some sanity back in his thinking. He was stuck with the boy, and there was a job to be done.

The thought that he must change entered his mind briefly—find honest work, not meet up with Refugio. It wasn't much of a thought and didn't last long, not past looking sideways at the boy and seeing those odd eyes and the angry mouth. He was nothing more than Jack Holden. The eyes flickered, and Jack knew he was caught.

"I know you're a thief . . . Uncle. Heard it in Springerville."

The harsh wording stung Jack. *Uncle.* There was a pause in which both parties counted time and held back on temper.

"Don't expect your ma thought any different when she sent you. Word travels far, and she knew how to find me." He paused, letting the boy sort through that thought. "Tells me you already got a head start in trouble back home." A ghost of something hidden in those flecked eyes, and Jack half bowed, mocking the recognition from his wayward kin.

"Ma said you was quick," John said. Admiration was clear this time but only for a moment. "Got the same thing done to me that the old man done you. I paid him back, the son-of-a-bitch. Sold off his best bull, spent the money on whiskey and women."

Jack took another good look at the scowling boy. "Well, kid, you ain't but fourteen yet."

The boy laughed, his wide mouth stretched thin, but the smile and sound never got to his eyes. Looked something like his ma for a moment, as close as Jack could recall, but she had a sweetness that this kid would never handle.

"Yeah, it took the old man bad that a boy got him. Laid on the belt hard enough, but that bull didn't come runnin' back . . . that money already got spent out of a whore's purse." The laughter again; Jack winced. "Guess it took me 'bout as long as you to get tired of the whippings. Guess I wanted revenge and you just wanted out." The child had no mercy.

Jack's voice echoed inside his head. "I got business ahead. Man I got to see. You ride with me, you work. No questions . . . no talking 'bout what you see. You take orders, you'll get a decent horse, get enough to eat. Won't offer more'n that."

"No matter to me . . . Uncle. Guess I'm your boy now."

The words were straight, but Jack heard an disturbing undertone. Nothing this boy did would be for less than his own gain. But right now it was necessary for him to work for his Uncle Jack. Jack shivered. "You keep your mouth shut, boy. Do as you're told and we'll get along."

They went looking for Refugio in one of the many unnamed cañons of the backcountry. Jack's eyes moved quickly as they entered the narrow file. The rock walls, up too close, suggested the confines of a prison cell. The boy rode behind Jack, forced into silence by the pressing rock. Jack didn't trust the boy at his back. Refugio was far more honorable.

He reined the bay left around a fallen boulder, and the cañon opened up to a surprising valley, with lush graze ringed by a flowing stream. Cattle bawled and stamped and grazed like everyone's cattle. The dumb beasts knew nothing about ownership or stealing. They only knew the indignant pain of altered brands and the eventual knife across their blood-drenched throats.

Refugio separated himself from a low fire and walked to greet his new partner. Two other men, indistinct except for the vague shadows of their moustaches, looked up, shrugged, and went back to their chores. Irons stuck out from the fire like an angry porcupine. "Ah, *mi amigo!* You have brought a friend?" Refugio stared at the boy, then studied Jack's face. "He is of your family, *señor.* I did not know the outlaw Jack Holden had kin in these parts."

The kid's words were bitter, but not much of a surprise. "I ain't workin' for no Mex, Uncle Jack. Ain't never workin' for no greaser."

The air chilled. Jack felt the itching wind across his back.

Refugio maintained his steady smile and waved a thick, work-stained hand. "We are all of the same color here, *niño*. Outlaw. You will do to mind your manners for we have more weapons than the one rifle and pistol of your sainted uncle." The words came laced heavily with scorn but did nothing to quiet the boy.

"You say what you want, Mex. I ain't listenin'."

Jack pulled his horse around and backhanded the boy across the mouth. The blow knocked him clean off the horse, hands flailing, grabbing for anything. The yellow mare moved sideways, dropped her head to graze. The boy lay out on the ground, and his pale, flecked eyes found the face of his uncle.

"You learned a lot from the old man, didn't you, Uncle?"

The boy had a way of saying "Uncle" with equal parts derision and bitterness. The thin face bore a red handprint across the cheek, but the eyes never blinked or cried.

"Boy, you work or ride on. Don't matter to me," Jack said, calming his bay, watching the kid try to figure things out.

The boy's eyes went to the grazing yellow mare, saw the ribs and bony quarters, the white hairs around the muzzle and above the eyes. They took in the patched saddle, the lack of rifle or scabbard, the thin bedroll tied on with mended strings. Then those eyes came to rest on Refugio, the still grinning man, before moving on to Jack.

"I'll work, Uncle."

Jack nodded. "Keep your miserable thoughts to yourself."

The boy nodded, hate right there in his eyes.

Jack shrugged, uncaring. He'd seen that very hatred before in his own father's face.

Preparing the cattle took two days because Refugio was in no hurry. And the boy kept getting in the way, dropping things at the wrong moment. Testing, Jack thought, deliberately acting dumb, setting the steers running, chousing a mama cow from a *vaquero's* long rope. Around the largest of the two stolen bulls, the boy was quiet and competent, yet, whenever Refugio or one of the other men had a steer caught by its heels and on its way to the fire, the boy lost the iron in the dust, or the knife jumped from his hand.

Refugio knew what had to be done. Jack nodded his agreement, then stepped back. The rope from Refugio's hand went over the boy's thin chest. The boy spun in anger, helpless, and caught sight of the grinning Mex who had roped him, and began to rant and curse with words even Jack did not often use. Refugio laughed, and touched his spurs to the sturdy pacing roan. The animal jerked back, the boy came plunging forward, landing hard on his face and chest.

Refugio coiled the rope as he guided his roan in toward the yelling, struggling boy. Refugio leaned down, keeping the rope taut, never letting the boy have a chance, and said: "*Niño,* you are no more than a fool, and a very young one at that. You make more work for yourself and your esteemed uncle. I will show you the way, *niño.* I will take you out into the world and you will find what awaits you there. For your words and your hatred are nothing against my rope."

With that he swung the roan in a tight spin and kicked the little horse, which quickly hauled the boy across the rough ground. Jack was still, relaxed even; Johnny had asked for this and deserved it. Jack trusted Refugio would not deliberately kill the boy. The boy bounced and jumped until he got lost in the dust, but Jack took note that the roan bucked against Refugio's hand on the rein, and that most of the cactus and rock were missed. In a few minutes the lesson was over. The roan halted, the rope shook loose and coiled up against Refugio's saddle. The boy lay still. Jack did not go to help him. Refugio turned his back, after nodding to Jack, who saluted in return. It was easy with the Mex. Words were not necessary, only quick glances and shrugs. Their lives ran parallel, the boy an unwelcome ir-ritant.

Johnny crawled to his knees, shook like a sweaty bronco, stood carefully, and rubbed at his face, wiping dust from his shirt and pants. And still Jack did nothing but sit on his bay and wait. It was inevitable. The boy caught Jack's gaze with his hot eyes. There was an exchange—a rapid fire of hate and fury. Jack smiled. The boy would not be with Jack too long.

The remaining steers were cut out and the brands reworked quickly, easily, with the aid of a bruised and torn young boy, whose face was tracked with muddy tears, but whose mouth was blessedly silenced. Only the eyes showed a fury, but eyes did not kill a man.

In ten minutes or so the herd was gathered and readied. The boy did his job, saying nothing. Jack gave him the same courtesy. They rode out, Johnny Thackery to the left drag, punishment for his sin of hatred, for the wind blew from the east, lifting a cloud of dust and dried manure over anything in its path.

Four days later the cattle were sold, south of Gallup, to an Army gent who'd forgotten he knew how to read a fresh brand. It didn't matter, the government's hard cash was good, and Refugio with his two *amigos* rode off, counting their shares. No parting words were said; none was expected. Jack would see the man when they needed each other. Till then it was *"Adiós"*. Jack liked and trusted the man. But he had a shadow riding too closely—one Refugio would not risk his life in saving. Jack could hate his nephew, he thought, if he studied on it long enough.

CHAPTER EIGHTEEN

Out on open grass, thunder told them they were in trouble. Jack kicked the bay as he picked out a shallow depression in the ground ahead and went to it at a run. The kid followed, mostly because he didn't care where he rode, and the yellow mare was too herd-bound to leave the bay.

They'd come from Red Hill, headed south, near the soft contour of the hill that gave the little settlement its name. Jack always suspected this land—it rolled and turned green fast, but hidden underneath was red dirt and rock, and the green wasn't the green of grass but a thin useless weed. Bush and scrub, but still, if a man didn't expect much of beauty, the area was pleasing. Except when a storm came hurrying across the hills, blasting thunder and rain, digging into the ground with shots of lightning. There were no caves or gullies where a man and horse could wait out the fury. It was too wide open which was why Jack pushed the bay into a gallop. He could see the outline of a depression too far away, the lightning hitting too close. Hail made the bay reluctant to face the wind, and Jack needed to spur and beat the gelding to keep it running.

Jack did a skidding dismount and dragged the horse with him, caught the bay's head at the bit, and drew it around to touch the saddle. The bay staggered. Jack threw his weight into the horse's shoulder and the terrified animal went down hard. Jack lay across the horse's neck, and prayed.

A shape rose up in the rain; a voice called out with its bitter taunt. "You scared, Uncle Jack?"

Damn fool boy. "Only idiots don't fear these storms. Get down, kid!" His last words were drowned out by thunder. Close on its heels came a flare of light. Jack saw the blue-white streak cut through the dark sky over Red Hill, and the accompanying sulphur smell overwhelmed him. The ground under him shuddered with the blow. The bay screamed, tried to throw Jack, but suddenly quit struggling as Jack twisted a tender ear. Then fire hit Jack on his left wrist where it touched the buckle of the bay's headstall. The fire traveled through him, crackling and searing his insides. He smelled burned hide, felt pain travel his left arm, then his heart stopped beating, and his eyes no longer closed against the driving rain.

It was his heart that let him know he was living. That area of his chest rose and fell painfully where the heart tried beating. Jack counted each labored pump, could hear the driven blood pulse in his ear, could almost feel it run through the ends of his fingers, down his legs, and back across his thighs, deep into his groin, his belly, and back into his overworked heart.

No rain, no clouds, no more lightning. Not even a whimper of distant thunder. He lifted one arm above his head and saw the fist open and close, felt the deep pain travel to his shoulder and back. The shirt sleeve was torn. The flesh beneath it streaked red and charred. He gently rested the arm on the ground and he rolled back, saw the corpse of the bay gelding about ten feet from him. His last memory was of the bay's rolling eye close to his own face. Hell of a storm.

He came to his knees, then slowly fought to get up from the ground. He saw the legs of a pale yellow horse first, then a boot swinging endlessly in the stirrup. He finally lifted himself high enough to see the rest of the apparition. Johnny Thackery. The boy grinned. Jack winced at the realization.

"Hell, Uncle Jack. Guess we got to ride double now."

The mare was poorly built for a passenger. Her quarters sloped badly, giving Jack nothing to sit on but a raised spine and a tail held to one side in a delicate, almost feminine gesture. The mare plodded—the only gait she could manage with the double burden. Jack clung to the saddle, cursing under his breath.

The boy knew enough to keep his mouth shut, which was a rare blessing. They managed to quarter back to Son Liddell's horse pasture. He cursed, thinking about his omission. His saddle was tied to the dead horse. It would get eaten by critters drawn to the fried meat. He had removed the bridle. The bit had been melted, but the crown and cheeks were intact, and one rein only lightly scorched. He could twist a hard nosepiece into a crude bosal. Liddell had good, broken stock; one of them was likely to be a bosal horse. Hell, he thought, he'd come out alive. What more could a man ask of such a storm.

The odd trio drifted over the edge of one more red hill. The mare slipped to her knees twice in the greasy mud, and then quit and no spur or whip would move her. Jack reached for his pistol on instinct and found it gone.

Now it was a matter of getting into Liddell's pasture, and catching up a horse, a good one this time. Not flash and color, but some heart and ability. Liddell had to own at least one horse matching that description.

Jack roped out a blocky paint. The animal's back was well-rounded. It was a long ride to his saddle and gear, so the smoothed back was important. He fashioned a bosal on the paint's nose. The patient animal showed it wasn't keen on being ridden bareback, but would accept the humiliation if Jack insisted. After a brief discussion, the paint stood quietly and let Jack make a fool of himself climbing aboard.

Once up, it still was an uncomfortable trip back to the red hills and the dead bay. Jack and the boy rode mostly at a slow jog, a gait the paint kept to easily. They cut through the smooth wire fence again, taking too short a time to repair the strands. Jack didn't want the horses out, didn't want to lose his free stock to the land's endless miles of grass.

The boy obviously struggled to keep from asking the question, but finally broke down and spoke bitterly to his kin. "Why you botherin' with all this work?" The boy's thin, colorless hand waved over the twisted strands of wire. "They ain't your bronc's."

"Liddell and I, we play our game. If I step too far, then the old man'll have the law on me. But we kind of agree . . . I steal and return, he complains and don't do nothin'. It's a matter of pride, boy. Simple matter of pride."

He could tell by the eyes, restless and unfocused, that the boy didn't get the point, maybe couldn't understand. Jack found a cut tree and used the stump to get back on the paint. Hell, maybe he hadn't explained right. He wiggled on the paint's back to find that one comfortable spot. He'd vowed not to climb down again, but he also hadn't trusted the boy to fix that fence properly.

Single file they proceeded through the dusk, keeping to the slow jog, never stopping. And he would have missed it if the paint hadn't shied, stumbled, swerved hard to the left, and lifted its head, snorting and blowing like a racehorse. Something hung from a dead pine near the trail's edge. It turned out to be Jack's saddle and blanket. It was enough to spook anyone, Jack thought. He sat on the paint, eyed the gift of his own gear, and tried to figure out the why. He snorted when the answer came. He rubbed the soreness of his burned arm lightly and swung down from the quieted paint, pulled the ends of the rope, and slowly let the gear down, until it sat waiting for him on the nest of needles and cones under the high, dead tree.

Sure enough there was a message pinned to the blanket, only a few words: Señor, *this is to hurry you. To the arroyo of the cavalry.* The man had a way with words. Jack grinned. The same cañon where he had gone swimming.

"This place ain't bad, Uncle Jack. Kinda pretty."

Jack nodded, surprised the boy even noticed the cañon they rode through.

"It's a nice place to bury a man." The boy couldn't keep shut and leave a good feeling, he had to go and say the wrong thing.

It was a pretty place, and too well traveled now for Jack's comfort.

They rode the left side of a forked cañon, where wildflowers were scattered through the high grass. That was its name—Wildflower Cañon—but he didn't tell the boy.

Wildflower opened up with lots of pine spread under with grass, a few clusters of high fir, even a waterfall came through broken rock. It sounded nice and calming. Both horses pricked up their ears and turned toward the noise, eager as their riders for water and time to rest. Jack eased up in his saddle and thanked Refugio again.

He dismounted from the paint and let the horse drink its fill. He found himself rubbing his sore arm, and knew it was infected. He cursed as he knelt down to drink, then rested the arm in the cold water. The chill hurt for a moment, and then soothed. After a few minutes the arm was numb, and Jack could relax.

"I'm ready to go whenever you are, Uncle."

The boy still had a way of rolling "Uncle" off his tongue that goaded Jack. He caught up the paint, retightened the saddle, and mounted, silently blessing the simple use of a stirrup, the easy way a man's backside settled in the saddle's seat.

They rode quietly for several hours, Johnny making no more attempts at talk. They had to ride in the day's heat, with their hats pulled low to mask the sun, shirts quickly darkening with sweat rings. They rode with their horses' gaits—the paint jogging easily, the yellow mare stumbling sometimes, the boy cursing ugly words and threats that did not make the mare any easier to set.

A flash of distant lightning, a crackle of thunder. Jack's arm hurt more, the walls of his throat tightened, and he felt edgy. The paint threw its head, slipped into a short-strided lope. Jack could not stop himself from searching for the darkening clouds, nor could he keep from turning his head to listen for the thunder, to find its direction. He rubbed his arm unconsciously, and the boy laughed at his Uncle Jack.

Refugio was sitting on a rotted pine, smoking a foul cigar. "So, *señor*, what is it we do this time?" He asked even though he had left the note.

Jack pushed himself from the paint's back, stood on the uneven ground, rubbing his arm again. The sore was becoming more than a nuisance.

Refugio took out a second cigar, lit it, and offered it to Jack, grinning through the smoke. "It is a man's cigar, *amigo*. Not like those imitations that the bankers and the Englishman smoke. Try one, *amigo,* you will find out soon what a man smokes in Mexico."

Jack puffed on the smoke and felt rather than saw Refugio leave his perch. A moment later he returned, in his hand bits of dried grass. "*Señor,* this will help your arm where it is burned." Jack allowed the man to sprinkle the wound with the grass. The ugly wound leaked fluid and the weed clung to the moisture, prickling the skin but adding little to the discomfort.

Refugio resettled himself. "There is a village not many days' ride from here. A small place called Jewett. There a man has started his roundup early, hoping to confuse men such as us. The man is cheap and thinks only of himself. Those cattle he brings together, those handsome and fat calves, they will become ours, to sell so we may eat through the long winter. It is a fine idea, no?"

"It's a stupid idea if you ask me." Johnny Thackery throwing in his unwanted opinion. The boy was ragged and sullen, had grown dirty in the days he'd ridden with his uncle.

"You are not asked, *niño.*" Refugio's voice was soft, but the words hard edged.

Jack shrugged; nothing would change between these two. The boy had forgotten about his dragging lesson, forgotten the power behind Refugio's polite requests. Jack wanted to save the uneasy peace. "Johnny, you ride with me and do what I say. Refugio and me, we're talkin'. You tend to the horses, boy. See they don't drink too much water. And watch out for the paint, he'll kick you, boy, you mess with him."

"Sure, Uncle Jack."

There it was again, but the boy went for the stock and left the two men to themselves.

Refugio stared at Jack, as Jack watched the boy. "It is the posturing of a child, *señor*. There is nothing more to him than to any growing boy. You are not, perhaps, used to the rôle, *señor*? I have three daughters, and their mama and I know something of a child's mind."

Jack thought about that, thought about Refugio as a father, watching the boy slap the yellow mare when she pushed to get into the stream. He shook his head. "No, Refugio, he is not just a growin' boy. Some of them come up to be killers, remember that."

Refugio's thick hand clapped Jack's shoulder. "Let us ride to those fine cattle that wait impatiently for us. There the boy will find enough action and excitement to keep him busy." Refugio looked away from Jack as he continued. "I know hatred, *señor*. I have felt it many times. It does not come from you. Your sister was right to send him to your care. You are good for him, *señor*. Although I suspect that having the boy in your camp sometimes spoils a good night's sleep. You do not think in color, *señor*. You think only of stealing cattle, and horses, and women." The man glanced slyly at Jack. "It is not much for a man's days, is it, *mi amigo?* But it is better than hate."

He wasn't living a high moral life, Jack thought, and Refugio was right, and knowing it was a scalding tonic. Jack swallowed hard. "*Señor* Refugio, I thank you." He extended his hand.

Refugio laughed. "Let us ride to our cattle, *señor*." And then he shook Jack's hand.

It was well after dark when they made camp on the mesa.

Refugio told the boy to set up a picket, cut grass, and portion out handfuls of the precious grain for the horses. They would need the extra strength in the coming day, and it could not be risked to hobble the broncos and turn them loose.

Jack laid his left hand on a bleached pine log and stared at his long fingers, raising each one and feeling the strain of each particular tendon. Since the lightning strike, his hand hadn't worked right. It puzzled him to see his fingers fail to respond to simple commands.

When the boy was done eating and had fallen asleep, Jack and Refugio sat together companionably. Refugio gave Jack more of the crumbled herbs to spread over the burn. It looked better than it had this morning, and Jack nodded his thanks.

Refugio talked, more to hear something than for any reason. "This rancher we are to visit, he had ranged his herds up on the mesa on grass that was claimed by another man. His cattle have been driven off, so he will be an easy target for us. The others will not come to his side and fight. This will make our life easier, eh, *señor?*"

It was simple with Refugio, no need to play any rôle, no need to be more than a lazy thief.

Well before dawn they saddled up. Refugio led them to the mesa that ended abruptly, the rim scarred with flat shale, slab rock, small prickly pear, and stunted juniper. The roan casually headed over the edge, flipping its tail high as its rump disappeared over the ridge. All Jack could see at one point was the top of Refugio's faded hat.

The boy followed Jack, fretting with the yellow mare. Jack headed the paint downhill. Halfway down, there was a small bench, and he caught up to Refugio.

"See, *señor*, there is Slaughter Mesa. We have saved more than a day's ride."

Jack followed the motion of Refugio's hand and saw in the

newly breaking sun a glittering shaft of light on a boulder set precariously into a straight run of shale and trees. It inspired awe, how the boulder clung to that hillside.

"Believe me, *señor*. You can ride from the top of that mesa straight into that rock and there is a trail that follows its base, which brings a rider down to the bottom. It is not a trail to be used lightly, but a man with nerve and a good horse can make the trip." Then Refugio laughed. "Of course the steady horse is important."

Refugio lifted his reins when the yellow mare came puffing and blowing in beside them. Time was wasted letting her recover. Refugio covered the time by talking. "It is beautiful, is it not, *señor*?"

The boy's face was drawn white; his hands barely kept their hold on the reins. The two men ignored these signs of nervousness; there was no other way off the small mesa.

Jack agreed with Refugio. It was truly beautiful to look out and see into the distance. The sun was against the top of Slaughter Mesa now, turning the flat expanse blood red. Small dots could be seen—cattle moving, bawling for their sleeping calves. The sound carried lightly on a quick breeze. Refugio sighed contentedly.

Below them the trail turned back on itself. Refugio's roan gathered its hind legs underneath to jump a fallen pine, and Jack watched as Refugio leaned back slightly to help balance the horse. The roan easily evaded a series of tangled branches and walked out to a smoother section of the trail. Jack let his paint have a go at the treacherous descent.

Something floated past Refugio's head, slowly at first, then picking up speed with the wind. Floating out over nothing, it caught a current and dropped quickly, sliding down the roan's shoulder, flapping between the horse's front legs. The spooked horse threw up its head, tried to swing about on the narrow trail. Refugio' face turned up to Jack—the dark skin was pale, the eyes wide. Then the roan buck-jumped over the object— John Thackery's hat—stumbled, and one hoof slipped from the trail. The animal snaked its heavy neck, staggered, fought to stop sliding. Refugio threw his weight with the roan, but the slick-shod hoofs could catch on nothing but mud, wet pine, and moss. The roan tumbled off the trail's edge.

Jack hauled back on his trembling paint. He thought he could see the side of Refugio's face; he thought he could feel the terror and fear as horse and rider tumbled into aspen and pine.

The faded hat lay in the trail. Jack urged his paint forward, spurring the horse over fallen logs and tangled branches, but the horse would not pass by that hat. Jack rammed in his spurs, and the paint backed up from the signal, responding more to panic as Jack called out but heard nothing in response.

He scrambled from the saddle, falling to his knees on the slippery hillside, catching hold of a shaky pine. Listening for Refugio's voice, for any sound. Nothing. So he stuck out his feet and skidded them downslope, following the deep gouges of the roan's fall. He looked up once and saw the yellow mare's underbelly as she too leaped from the trail.

Jack could barely protect himself from the branches that slashed him, the rocks that pounded his legs and backside. He dug in his boot heels, planted his spurs, and rode the slick hill. His fall was broken by the half-buried rump of the roan. Jack fell forward, grabbed a tree, yanked himself upright.

A call drew him to a clump of tangled aspen, young trees that had given way to a stronger force. A boot was caught between two slender trunks. Gently Jack knelt and freed the boot, laying Refugio's leg carefully on the mossy ground. He heard the accompanying groan. He made himself crawl closer. He had smelled the smell before in a gutted horse, a wounded bear, a deer taken with a bad shot.

"*¿Señor?*" The voice was weak.

Jack braced one trembling hand on an aspen and lightly touched the undamaged side of the man's face. "*Mi amigo.*" He choked out the words. "I didn't know you wanted to fly."

"It seems, *amigo*, that in truth I cannot fly at all."

Jack did not flinch or betray his horror, for it was Refugio and not a broken animal. He had never seen an eye torn from its socket before. The ruined face made an effort at a one-sided grin.

"It is good I was not handsome before, *señor*. Not like you. For now, indeed, I would be very angry." Refugio tried to lift one arm, but it was broken at the wrist and again above the elbow. Even so, the weak effort caused a spasm through the body.

Jack sank back on his heels and closed his eyes. When Refugio coughed, he opened them. A dark stain widened around Refugio's shoulders, more blood soaked into the ground by his hips.

"*Mi amigo*, you have a task ahead that is not often asked of one friend by another. But it is necessary. I will die. Nothing and no one can help. But you . . . you can let me know I have had one good friend in this life which we all must leave." He looked with that awful, single, bloody eye at Jack's hand, which by instinct rested on the butt of the pistol.

This was asking too much, but it would be done.

"*Gracias, señor. Muy hombre . . . ah, la Santisima.*"

The one eye stayed focused on Jack as he pulled the trigger. Standing slowly, pistol gripped in his hand, Jack looked down at the corpse, trying not to see the remains of what had been a good man.

It was the plaintive whinny of a horse that broke the spell that had formed around him. The sound carried all the pain and fear, all the destruction that lay at his feet. Wherever he looked, there was blood. He could smell nothing but fouled manure and gasses, voided bowels, and emptied bladders. Not even the trail of broken aspen and shattered pine, their hearts exposed to the hot air, could hide the incredible stink.

The whinny reached him again. He twisted his neck, tried to stare uphill into the bright sun. He could not bury Refugio for he had no tools for grave digging, no hope of finding enough rocks in this grassy place to cover him. And his shot might have caught the attention of curious men—ranchers and cowhands—who were now riding to investigate.

Jack knelt again in the ruined earth and, with his knife, shaved two sticks from a dying aspen, twined them in a cross, using rawhide strings cut from Refugio's own saddle. There he jammed the cross into the bed of moss and leaves at Refugio's head. A poor marker for one life. Then he pulled his way out, returning on the trail left by their falling bodies.

When he climbed over the lip of the trail, he was surprised to find the paint gelding waiting. Jack used the near stirrup to haul himself to his feet and found, as he looked over the paint's back, that the yellow mare was huddled behind the bigger horse. There was no sign of the boy.

Jack called out but only birds sang to him. A small animal scurried through the underbrush behind him. He backtracked the mare and found the boy near the base of a sturdy pine. Jack knew nothing would ever wake the child. The head was tilted, the bones in the neck snapped clean. Jack wiped his suddenly wet mouth, glimpsed his hands soiled with Refugio's blood. There was no blood around the boy.

He shuddered once and grabbed the boy's boots, dragged him slowly downhill, talking all the time to the horses. The animals were eager to hear his voice. The mare took several steps toward him, reached out her muzzle, and brushed against his back as he labored with his burden. He lifted the body and

185

let it slide onto the mare's back. The boy was barely fourteen, never had grown much height and never had weighed more than a three-week old calf.

Then he went to the paint. He'd bury that old saddle with the boy, he'd bury all the kid's meager gear with him, but he'd have to do the burying without Johnny Thackery's hat. He knew right where he'd take the kid. Wildflower Cañon, where the boy'd talked about it being a pretty enough place for a dead man to lie.

I regret Johnny's death for it was an accident of a kind seen too often here. Man is at nature's mercy in this land. I can say that he did not suffer at the moment of death.

Here he considered the harshness of the word "death" but could find none kinder. The more civilized folks used words to deny death's importance. "Passing" was one, a word Jack hated. It destroyed the death itself. Dying was no passing to anything, it was the end, right here and now, at the time that the last breath fled through clenched teeth.

It was even more difficult to be polite when he recalled Refugio's single eye watching him at the very second of his own death. There would never be a word to describe the act and its consequence. Making such a death civilized by talking around it was something Jack could not accept.

He finished the letter and took up a bottle of tequila. It was another full day and night before he could stand straight and take the letter to the Gutierrezville post office.

The same smiling man took the folded paper and told Jack the fee for its mailing. They exchanged coin and Jack was finished with his contract.

"*Señor*, we are sorry to hear of Refugio and wish to thank you for his final care."

Jack's boot stuttered on the puncheon floor. A small, squat, dark-haired man with heavy whiskers shadowed Jack's elbow. "His wife . . . she is my cousin. We are in your debt, *señor.*"

Jack could not speak.

The killing was known. The thought made him sick. He pushed past the sad-eyed man and hit sunshine, walked to the pens where the paint was stabled. Jack Holden was a thief, not a murderer.

★ ★ ★ ★ ★

KATHERINE DONALD

★ ★ ★ ★ ★

CHAPTER NINETEEN

Her fingers trailed over the floral material, a gift from Mr. Meiklejon, sent from England by his fiancée. Her employer would be marrying soon and the question of her continued residence in a bachelor's house would be resolved.

Katherine let her thoughts run away while she worked on the final seams of her dress with its fine, smooth finish and tender pattern, and she laughed at herself for her mental indulgences.

Men had so many freedoms while women could only taste small ones on the sly. It was a poor exchange, marriage for loneliness, independence for security and obedience. My but she was bitter this morning. Katherine knew the source of her anger. Burn English. There had been no improprieties in a physical sense, yet if her moments with him were known, she would be called terrible names for her tenderness.

Tied to a reprobate father, cooking and caring for him more than fifteen years, refusing the suitors he deemed proper, seeking out men who showed more life, more daring than would make a good husband, she was perceived as less than a middling success, barren and still virginal. And angry at the world pushing her into the mold it preferred.

The needle slipped, her finger bled two drops to stain the lovely pale green lawn with two small, perfect circles of red. She knew all about blood; she would have to wash the stains before they set. She did not move, composed, erect in the straight-backed chair in its corner of the small back room. Where she

191

had held guard over Burn English. The material spread over her lap, she put the pricked finger to her mouth and slowly laved it with her tongue, sucking gently, tenderly, remembering other tastes and different times.

So much had revolved around this room through the spring months, so much pain and doubt, so much anger and distrust. She had known, when she looked into those eyes, that it was the core of Burn English, the heart that beat on despite the wounding, it was the strength of soul that had kept life in the wasted body.

It might be horrible to admit, but she missed her patient, longed for the need he'd had for her. His life and daily comfort had been placed in her hands. It was what she wanted, that terrible need from another human being. Not this soft, endless repetition of cleaning and cooking and smiling and deferring to whatever a man wished.

She shook her head. There was Davey who had changed so in the past weeks. She had continued to conduct herself in a calm and distant manner around him, very much the lady, and Davey was responding as a reflection of her attitude. This was the explanation of his change, his new remoteness, the absence of his obvious affection.

She kept a constant internal dialogue to remind herself about Davey, that he had the ability to read her thoughts and guess her feelings. Since the morning it was discovered that English had taken the pacing grullo and was gone, Hildahl had looked at Katherine as if he were witness to the raw side of a woman he had held in high esteem. Whatever it was that bothered him, Davey Hildahl had a forward, bitter touch to his words now, and Katherine knew she responded in kind, with a quick, sharp word and a hard stare whenever he confronted her.

She did not know what was happening to her ordered world, but it was frightening, and exciting, at the same time. Maybe she was being granted the merest taste of an unorthodox freedom.

Her father, however. She had not been surprised when he had put out the word that he was claiming the mustangs branded with his Bench D. Edward Donald saw a chance to take something to which he had no earned right. Since he had officially put in his claim and had signed a warrant, she had not spoken to her parent.

Her hands began to play with an escaped lock of hair. Sweeping and cleaning, baking cakes and pies, all were more difficult when her thick hair came unbound and into her eyes. She would cut it but for the weight of it on her neck, the pleasure of throwing back her head and feeling its bounce. Unseemly, her father might say, a sign of wantonness in an otherwise good and righteous woman. But there was so little she could be vain about, so little to please just her.

She had a quiet, secret memory of one morning finding Burn English with a book out of Meiklejon's library. A leather-bound copy with faded gold script and an odd dark stain on the cover—Rudyard Kipling. English had sat with his back propped against the wall, his hands wrapped around the book, working over the words. When Katherine had entered the room, he had dropped the book under his covers.

Since his departure, there had been no word from English, or about him except that he continued to escape the law's highly ineffective attempts to take the mustangs from his stewardship. No word from Jack Holden, either, but lots of stories about rustling cattle, scrapes and fights in too many small villages at the same time to be possible. Gossip about him and the Blaisdel girl, which had a nasty turn. And Davey Hildahl, bitter and harsh, barely smiling. Too many men and none of them belonged only to her.

★ ★ ★ ★ ★

Jack rode in to town to see her. Just her. After two months of being deliberately ignored, Rose had resolved not to respond to him. But he rode to the back of the hotel, where he had first found her mid-winter. And she was there again, getting vegetables from the root cellar for one of Mama's heavy stews. Nothing had changed about their meeting except the time of year. The humid sweetness of late summer replaced the bitter wind, but that was all.

Jack leaned on the low cellar door, and, when Rose turned around, a basket full of carrots and onions on her arm, he was there watching her. She hugged the basket to her belly like a child and felt her heart pound. He was as handsome as she remembered—the smile slightly vague, the eyes still blue. He had come in just to see her, he said. Here was her power, her strength. An outlaw wanted by the law, hated by everyone, and he risked his life to come to her.

There was little tenderness in his hands. She was casual, breaking away from the urgent caress to put the basket on the damp cellar floor, and then pat her hair, work at the buttons of her skirt. She did not want his lovemaking here; she hated the smell of the place, the crawling insects and other varmints.

He came back with his hands to raise her skirt, and, when she tried to cry out, he covered her mouth with his hand. She stared into his eyes, which mocked her as he finished his labored, dispassionate act.

They separated and did not look at each other. Rose attempted to clean herself while Jack did nothing but stare out past the cellar's heavy posts to the bright air beyond them.

She revolved slowly, brushed against Jack, and brought his attention back to her. Then unexpectedly he leaned down and kissed the top of her head and Rose knew the man she loved had returned.

"Rose Victoria, you are a pretty thing."

She didn't want this, as if she were nothing more than a child. Then her mother's shriek called for her, and she sighed deeply, again aware of the gesture and what it accomplished. Jack leaned over her as she sorted out the vegetables and wiped the last of the dirt from her hair and face. He picked a twig from her curls, put his face to her bosom, and kissed her skin in a loving, long, delicious kiss. Rose quickly rebuttoned her shirtwaist and went out into the misery of the noon sun. When she risked a look back, Jack Holden was gone.

Chapter Twenty

Gayle Souter and Davey Hildahl rode up to Quemado where Melicio Quitano wanted to know if he would ever get his fee for having returned Meiklejon's pacer. Souter paid him, then got a tidbit of old gossip for his troubles. Burn English was riding the dark colt branded with Donald's brand, and Jack Holden had another Liddel mount, a stocky paint this time.

They were also told that Stan Brewitt had come in one night and offsaddled his badly lamed red dun. Said the horse had stepped in wire and panicked. He'd been up checking on the Red Durham bull, and said there were wild mares in the fenced-off pasture.

Souter looked sideways at Davey, but neither man spoke of the mares after that.

The wire cut had turned sour, and, despite three weeks of care, the only answer was a bullet between the ears for the red dun, and a meal for the coyotes out in a distant wash. Brewitt moped around. The dun had been his best mount, but he perked up when Souter brought in a rugged buckskin and let Brewitt have the horse.

One day Eager Briggs rode in on a scrawny palomino gelding. His broken leg was still wrapped in a hard cover and stuck out to one side of the horse. Briggs, as usual, had some gossip. Said that Edward Donald was pushing a warrant on Burn English for horse theft. The old man stared at Davey while giving out the information, as if Davey would naturally have something to say. Briggs would make his rounds and soon enough the whole territory would know about Donald's greed.

Briggs had more news: two corpses had been found near Jewitt. A man and a horse. The man was a Mex, buried in a shallow grave with a rude cross near his head. Powder burns said the killing was done close and after the injuries. Only one eye remained in the skull. That last bit of information upset most folks, Briggs told his audience.

Other riders came through after Briggs's first visit, passing on more information, looking for late strays. Briggs came by often toward the summer's end. It seemed like the whole southwest corner of New Mexico was fired up about Jack Holden and his thieving and Burn English and his damned horses.

Summer turned quickly to fall in the mountains. The San Agustin plains became muddy and dangerous with late rains. Three cows got bogged down, two were saved, one was shot before it choked to death. Red Pierson got thrown from a rank mustang and broke his wrist, but was out hunting L Slash strays two days later.

Stan Brewitt learned his buckskin gift was a better mount than the old dun, and bragged on the horse, mostly about its speed, until a course was set up and bets made, all on Sunday. Stan was more than $50 ahead, a real high roller, until a passing Mex beat the buckskin racer on a flea-bitten gray.

New trouble started, so the ranchers held a meeting at the Morely place. The rains had come late, but soon enough for the grass to green up before winter. Patches of the best graze were being eaten; hoof prints of a small band of horses could be read in the damp earth. Attempts to follow the horses led up narrow cañons and impossible trails where no sane man would ride. The ranchers were angry. This was their grass, their feed, and they depended on it for the wintering. Horses were stealing their grass. But there was no solution, and the meeting ended in anger.

English's name wasn't spoken around the L Slash Ranch. Miss Katherine got thinner and quieter, and Meiklejon was caught in his barbed-wire hell. Then he got called back to England. His parting orders to Gayle Souter were to pursue any leads that might finish the reign of theft perpetuated by Jack Holden.

Katherine was able to lose herself in ironing, a task she rarely enjoyed. Today it used her energies and calmed her thoughts. Until a noise outside the window distracted her. She blinked, looked out, and saw Davey Hildahl riding in.

She watched Davey dismount, groaning softly with him as he took those first steps in the awkward walk achieved from being in the saddle too long. Katherine knew Davey was searching for Burn English as well as Jack Holden. She blamed her father's unconscionable act for Davey's exhaustion. Davey still harbored a burden of guilt, believing himself responsible for any trouble chasing the *mesteñero.*

Katherine stopped reflecting as another horse raced into the yard. She opened the kitchen door and went outside. No man who rode for Gayle Souter treated a horse in such a manner unless something terrible had happened.

Red Pierson's face was flushed, his voice high. "They've cornered Jack Holden on Slaughter Mesa, near Indio Cañon. He ain't been in Arizona . . . he's holed up with a lot of cattle got changed brands." He spat, took a drink from an offered canteen. "They sent for Lawman Stradley. Word come down English is with Holden. He's thrown in with the rustlers and been stealing cattle all summer."

Katherine's hands shook and she held them together.

Then Stan Brewitt appeared on a spent horse. Behind him came the new man, Spot, on an equally tired mount.

In less than ten minutes the men had roped and saddled fresh mounts while Katherine prepared food. Now she sat at the kitchen table, cradling her hands around a cup of warmed coffee, taking an occasional small sip to keep herself occupied. These men, who had talked shyly to her of their dreams and their distant families, their small hopes, would ride out and kill two men she loved.

She buried her face in her hands, tipping the coffee. She was close to crying, something Katherine Donald did not ever do. The sack of supplies waited on the table, a plain, matter-of-fact token of what was about to happen.

It took her several moments to realize Davey Hildahl stood next to her, dusty hat clenched to his belly, fingers turning the brim endlessly.

"Miss Katherine, I don't believe it's English neither. I know the man . . . not like you maybe . . . but he ain't that kind. Holden and him, they couldn't get along. Ain't nothing in English that'd let him steal another man's cows. You take heart, ma'am, I'll make sure they don't hang English . . . if they even find him to the mesa, and I don't think they will. Don't you worry, it won't come to hanging the man."

She smiled to thank him. He'd promised nothing about Jack Holden. No one could stop that massacre once he was caught. Jack lived the life, now he would die the death.

Davey half opened the door, held it, and found the courage to say the rest that had been on his mind. "You know, Miss Katherine . . . you heard 'bout some horses loose-herded on good grass . . . kind of stealing graze from all the ranchers. Me, I think that's the only kind of stealing Burn'd ever do. Getting his mares fat on other folks' graze now that we got good rains . . . stealing something that'll grow back."

The men left in a tight bunch at a long trot, and Katherine felt the edge of despair again. She would like to ride with these men to Slaughter Mesa and the craggy, rugged depths of Indio Cañon. She would like to hold off the rustlers and chase the bandits, herd the bawling cattle. Any work a man could do, she wished to try. But she had been hired as a housekeeper, a civilizing woman on a ranch full of men, and she must do what was expected.

Katherine returned to the table and stared at the coffee stains, studied the shape they took as they soaked into the scoured wood. She rested her head in her cupped hands and watched the sun's reflection on the glass window disappear, saw the light day air turn to dark.

The rebellion was growing, and she reveled in its bitter freedom.

CHAPTER TWENTY-ONE

The new man called Spot rode in two days later. Katherine warmed him a plate of stew and poured out fresh coffee. Spot ate fast, then packed a lot of ammunition in two saddlebags and caught out a fresh horse for the return ride to the mesa. He offered no new words on what was happening.

Spot's quick departure left Katherine alone and more aware of the ranch's isolation. Few visitors came by on their way to another place. She tried to concentrate on cutting up the old hens and setting them to stew, then she attacked the few vegetables she'd grown in the poor summer garden.

Next she set bread to rising, covered with a heavy cloth, and placed it near the stove, as out of drafts as she could manage. The hens were well seasoned and started in their broth, simmering more slowly now, cooking into a semblance of tenderness. The knowledge weighed on Katherine. The men on

Slaughter Mesa would shoot or hang a man, and return to her
kitchen hungry and tired, expecting her to feed them even
though they had become killers. She would fulfill her duties,
knowing these ranch hands turned killers were children under
the guidance of older but not wiser men. She would not think
about the consequences, she would make her pies and cakes to
please them, she could not envision murder. It was a hard land,
a hard way of life. Survival here was insured by measures that
were strict, sudden, and of necessity without mercy.

What she did after the hens were boiling and steaming on the
stove, the bread was covered and rising, was something she had
only dreamed of doing. She went to the corral and the only
animal that came up to her was Davey's bay. She petted the
bay's face, and slipped on a neck rope, then twisted the end
around the long nose, spending far too much time fashioning a
way to lead the horse. Men had always caught and saddled an
animal for her. She put her hands on the bay's neck and spoke
firmly until the horse was quiet. Her courage returned, and she
laid the blanket on the horse, lifted the saddle to her thigh, then
heaved it up and over. The bay accepted the familiar burden
with a deep sigh.

She had witnessed the rigging of saddles, so, when she pulled
on the latigo and the bay distended its belly, Katherine brought
up her knee into the animal's gut and the bay blew air that
smelled of fresh grass and sweet grain. Katherine laughed, and
patted the bay neck. Success.

The bridle was another matter, but in the end she was satisfied that, if the bay tried to run away, she would have some
control. The metal hung low in the bay's mouth but the animal
could not spit out the bit. She decided it was time to climb
aboard, after retightening the cinch as she had seen the men do.

Katherine pulled, and heaved, and cursed, and eventually
found herself in the middle of the saddle before the horse

walked away from the fence. Having been witness to the many contests between horse and rider, she was delighted that the bay was so quiet. This happened, she supposed, from its having been ridden hard over the past days. She would not ask much from the horse; this ride was meant solely for pleasure.

A side-saddle held a woman captive, left her awkwardly hanging to what was called a leaping horn, legs dangling, supported while strangled by the saddle's confinement designed to insure her female safety. Riding astride was forbidden, unmentionable, a daring act no respectable woman would consider. For visits and chores, a woman more often chose the utility of a sensible horse and a fine wagon, harnessed and brought to her, of course, by one of the ranch hands.

Eventually, finding her balance easier with legs placed on both sides of the horse, Katherine began to study her surroundings. She was already well away from the ranch, seeing only grass and tall trees, the shadowed mountains, the overwhelming sky. This was a freedom she had longed for. She let the reins slide loose and kicked the bay, and it was as if a force propelled her backward. She needed to open her mouth wide to inhale gulps of air. Her eyes watered and the tears blinded her, but she was fearful of loosening her grip on the saddle horn to wipe them away.

There was no time or distance, only the horse and the air— the motion that she had not ever felt. The bay was beginning to tire; she knew from the slowing strides, the deep, harsh sound of the bay's breathing. It was how she felt, also, and it was strange to be in silent agreement with an animal that could neither talk her language nor understand her need.

The horse walked and Katherine leaned down, laid her face on the black mane and spoke all the words she could not say to another human being. The bay tossed its head and moved on.

Then bay stopped abruptly, throwing Katherine forward, and

she sat up, outraged. A horseman came from a narrow draw to her left, and the bay swung its head to watch the stranger approach. It was Jack Holden.

He reined in his sweaty paint and nodded to her, tipped his hat. "Good day to you, Katherine Donald. This is not where I would expect to find you. Out hunting?"

Katherine stared at Jack's face. He had changed—black shadows marred his handsome features. But he still sat his horse with the usual air of grace, one hand on the reins, the other ready to hold a pistol or reach for Katherine.

He was hurried, that was evident by the rise and fall of the paint's ribs, the white lather showing under the saddle skirt, along the horse's neck, between its front legs. The paint was thinned down from too many of these hard runs. Jack definitely looked shabby, but he had not yet been caught and hanged.

"I thought you were on the mesa, Jack. Surrounded by every man within a hundred miles or more, and you fighting for your life." She did not screen her words and did wince after she had spoken them. "You have been fairly identified as a thief, Jack. Why the change . . . why would you now begin to steal from the ranchers here? They are even linking Burn English with you, and, because of what you have done, they will try to hang him, also."

She thought she had spoken the words in a neutral tone, but there must have been a note in her voice, for Holden smiled for the first time in their chance encounter.

"Ma'am it's good to see you, too. But I swear English is not counted among my friends or associates, and he is most definitely not on Slaughter Mesa. I've never met him, unless you count the time I tried to swap horses with him." Jack laughed, and there was a dreamy look to his eyes, a memory of something better. He took a long breath. "He stood that mustang broadside and dared me. Offered me a short ride, knowing I wanted his bronc'. There weren't nothing I could do 'gainst that kind of courage. He couldn't have weighed more'n a hundred something pounds, like a scrawny cat tackling a bulldog."

Then: "Ma'am, I got a favor to ask." Jack looked directly at Katherine and did not flinch at what he must have read. "Ma'am . . . I lost a good friend, and word's come back they finally buried him. Would you get a name put on a cross? Name's Refugio, that's all. Refugio."

She nodded yes, of course, remembering the sorry tale brought to the ranch by Eager Briggs. This Refugio had been a Mexican bandit and a friend of Jack's.

"There's another favor, a tougher one," he said, looking away. "I know there's always a girl. But this one . . . I wronged her, Kate. It makes me ashamed of what I done. Please." Here he quit, at a loss for the right words.

Katherine watched his drained face, and thought of the summer gossip.

"It's Rose Victoria, isn't it, Jack?"

He nodded, relieved of having to speak the name.

"Well, I can't guess what you have done to her. She's not pregnant, is she? She's not carrying your child?" This should be a feared subject, too basic to be mentioned between unmarried men and women.

Jack's face was white, but he told the truth. "I've taken her, Kate. Several times, and she's come willingly to me. But this last time, I was wrong."

Whatever lay on his conscience, Katherine decided she would not make it easier by mouthing those useless, magical words of it not being his fault, of his being blameless in having a girl, a mere child.

"I took her, Kate. Can you understand what that means?"

Yes, Katherine thought, *I can understand.* But she would not condone his doing so. Still the man had been accused of worse, and the girl had been with him of her own accord. It wasn't fair, she wanted to cry, it wasn't right for him to take a lovely young thing who had a chance at marriage. He had his pick of the wives and spinsters; it was unfair that he took the pretty girls, too.

"I won't be able ever to explain to her. Would you please . . . ?"

Katherine had been too deep in her own thoughts and not listening to him, for she had no idea what he'd requested. But she nodded, looked straight at him.

"I need her to know it was wrong. She needs to know men can be better than I ever was."

Katherine would try to explain to Rose Victoria, but she was not convinced the girl even knew she had been wronged.

They watched each other, two lonely people, and each saw the hurtful truth.

"Kate, enough of all this. It's only years and time . . . it is of no importance to anyone but me. Come here . . . please?" It was the first time he had ever asked.

His kiss was sweet and gentle, not demanding, simply offering tenderness, and pain. They drew apart, their horses shuffling to accommodate the shift.

Jack tipped his hat to her, said the last few words left to speak. "Ma'am, I stole that kiss from you . . . my last act as a thief. Now you ride home. It ain't safe for a lady to be ridin' alone, not with all the riff-raff coming through."

She would have spoken, but he touched his hand to her mouth, and against her lips she felt the weakness spill from him.

"Ma'am, you are always a lady. I'm a gentleman no longer. Please, Katherine, go home. You'll be needed soon enough."

★ ★ ★ ★ ★

The bay was content to walk and that gave Katherine too much time to think. She cried, shedding tears, the nodding bay gelding as her witness. Davey's bay gelding took her to the corral of the L Slash headquarters and stopped. Once the horse was turned out, Katherine was alone. There was no one at the house, and for the first time ever Katherine was afraid.

She forced herself to approach the house. She entered the kitchen quietly, suspecting all manner of invasions. But the room smelled of stewing hens and rising bread and nothing else. She had been gone on her rampage less than two hours.

After changing back to a prim dress and washing up, she returned to work. But she was altered inside, where it did not show. She moved easily, yet her legs ached from the unaccustomed riding, and each bruise and reddened patch of skin was a welcome reminder.

As she peeled the carrots, a different scent warned her and she spun around, knife in hand. It was Burn English, more ragged than ever, a softly curling beard shading his thin face. He was bloody, of course; one hand held the other arm at the wrist. She would have tended to him immediately but for the eyes, which stared directly at her, with no sign of deference or longing. Even Jack had only glanced at her, unwilling to insult her with a stare. English was different; he was always different.

"Ma'am, you call off your pa," Burn English said. "If he don't remember we're partners, then he's dead. I ain't got much left to lose."

Katherine responded the only way she knew. "You are the thief . . . using the ranchers' good winter grass. What do you call that but thieving?"

He grinned unexpectedly, and it made him almost handsome. "Ma'am, I'd call it investment. None of these boys'll give me peace enough to find my own graze so I use theirs. They'll get a chance to buy good stock, so they're sort of paying now for what they'll want to buy later."

Katherine hadn't expected him capable of such devious thinking. It was hard not to smile at him and the calculated charm of his words. He took away her need to say something, anything in response, by letting his arm hang at his side. Immediately it leaked blood droplets onto the kitchen floor.

"You clean up that cut, Mister English . . . so it doesn't stain my floor."

He couldn't grin any more; the effort put a bleak grimace on his face. "Ma'am, I run out of clean a while back. Ain't had much chance to do a wash lately or find time to take my Saturday bath. I need your help for this one."

She offered him a large rag soaked in cool water.

He wrapped the arm, licked his dried lips. "Thanks again, ma'am, for the rescue. Can I get a drink of water . . . maybe a few biscuits? I've been riding hungry too long. Seems folks think I'm a cattle thief."

She poured him coffee and put out old, cold stew, biscuits, molasses, and half of a leftover pie. He ate everything she put in front of him and looked like he could eat more. She took her chance to lecture him while he ate, figuring he would remain only as long as there was food. "The outlaw life doesn't suit you, does it? You've damaged what took so long to heal. You might well have killed yourself this time."

He dropped a biscuit onto his plate. "Ma'am, I ain't no outlaw. Even your boss admitted his wrong and pulled off the law. It's your pa, wanting what ain't his, doing this to me. I ain't no outlaw."

A verbal contest was a waste of time. She rested her hand on his shoulder, and he winced. Her voice was sharp. "Mister English, if you are running only from my father, stop and clear it up. Or are you running more from habit than circumstance?"

He shook his head and the shaggy hair covered his eyes, rolled over his filthy shirt collar. "Ma'am, your pa and I had a deal, witness and all. As for me reasoning with the law, I got a killing to my name. Two men down in Texas." He waited, seemed to know how she would react.

Katherine went to the stove and stirred the boiling hens, appalled that he would speak so easily of killing.

"There, ma'am, you're doing it again. Not knowing why or how, you only know I was wrong, whatever I done. Like those ranchers up there wanting to hang me with Jack Holden. I killed when I was sixteen. Two men who tried to rob me. My family were dead by then, so it was up to me." His eyes were hot now, his voice harsh and strong.

She rested her hand on the knife handle, finding comfort there.

"Being called a thief by your pa seems small next to what you think of me." He stood, and it was an awkward series of movements. "Ma'am?" This time the word was gentle and she shuddered. "We knew each other those months while I healed. You know me well, yet you judge me wrong." He was a gentleman; she saw in his face how carefully he chose his words. "Ma'am . . . I'm beholding to you for the meal. Add that debt to the ones I already can't pay." His breath came out in short gasps, smelling of stew and coffee, and sickness. "I won't go after your pa, ma'am. Not like I would any other man. That's the best I can give you to pay off my debt."

She put a hand on his ribs and felt the raw structure of muscle and bone. He shifted, and she leaned against him as his good hand stroked the back of her neck. She gasped in pleasure. At her sound, his heartbeat quickened and she could feel the race inside him.

Suddenly Burn pushed away from her, and Katherine could not stop a small cry.

"Ma'am, I can't come to you like this. You be more careful

you don't let men like me around you. It ain't safe."

Before she could reach for him, he put out a hand to stop her. It was the arm wrapped in the now bloody rag and again droplets of blood stained her floor. "I'm a damned horsebreaker, ma'am." He grinned that wonderful, unexpected grin. "I keep swearing at you, ma'am, to get you to listen."

"Sit down, and don't pretend you're all right," Katherine ordered. "Let me doctor that arm . . . and pack you some food." She used the words and the act of running water into a pan to recover. When she looked back, he was sleeping lightly, his head cradled on his good arm. Left alone, he began to snore.

A horse came into the yard. She peered out the window. It was Davey Hildahl. He dismounted and began tending his mount. Katherine waited. No other riders came in with him. Returning to Burn, she gently unrolled the reddened cloth, and still Burn did not wake. The cut was long and ugly, stinking of infection—most likely a wire cut. As she began her work, she found herself strangely pleased. She glanced at the back door, where she knew Davey would appear. And she touched the back of Burn's neck, threading the soft hairs around her fingers. Harsh words had been spoken, warnings given, but for now, with the man needing her and another about to return, she was content.

Chapter Twenty-Two

Davey knocked on the door. Beneath her fingers Katherine felt Burn's body tighten. She kept washing the deep cut, focusing on the marvel of human muscle and bone, and did not look up when Davey entered.

He nodded at Burn as if expecting to find him there. *Of course,* she thought, *he saw the tracks of Burn's horse.*

"You been riding that colt rough, English. Be too damned . . . darned bad to ruin another good 'un."

Burn's reply was filled with anger. "So you got a bronc' to lend me, huh? A nice big steady bay gelding . . . or maybe a fine-legged grullo that'll do the work of that gray." Davey's head jerked as Burn kept talking. "Two bronc's killed under me. Remember?"

"Ah, hell . . . heck. You can't lay the death of that roan on me."

Burn flinched as if the words had drawn more than blood. "Hildahl, I ain't blaming you for neither bronc'. You're the one placing blame. I'm doing what has to be done. That colt's a tough one and he's all I got."

Davey Hildahl sneezed, a loud and blustering intrusion that startled Katherine. Burn's body twitched, then resettled, but Davey grinned like a little boy. "English, it ain't bad seeing you setting quiet. I've been hearing summer tales about you. About some ranny put his mares on other folk's pasture. That's close to stealing."

Burn turned his head, focused his gaze steady on Davey's form. "How can a bite be stealing grass left to grow?"

It sounded like a Chinese riddle to Katherine, but Davey's round face puffed out in a laugh.

Katherine began to ask questions. "Mister Hildahl, how far behind you are the rest of the men? Have they found the outlaws they sought? Are any wounded . . . what do I need to know?" By calling him "mister" she had withdrawn their tentative friendship, and it was obvious from the tightening in his face that he understood.

Burn stood, and by that act drew both onlookers into his world of suffering and deprivation. It took time and a tightening of his body to rise from the chair. His torso swayed as if a wind blew through the kitchen walls.

"Davey, I've got to ride," the *mesteñero* announced. "Ma'am, thanks for the cleaning up."

209

Both waited for his next move, fearing a harsh breath or a quick turn and he would collapse.

"I never rode with Holden. You know that. Ah, hell . . . Davey." Burn turned slightly. "Ma'am, you tell your pa my debt to you is the reason that I don't go after him."

Burn held up his arm, nodded again to Katherine, and made his way to the door. He hesitated, then looked back at the two silent people who watched him.

"If I ain't careful," he said, "I'll get used to having friends."

Davey's head jerked back as if yanked. Katherine felt her pulse quicken within her breast and throat.

Burn opened the door, paused again. "You take care, Hildahl. We'll cross trails again. Ma'am, it's been mostly a pleasure. Thanks." Then he was gone.

The silence held as they watched Burn disappear. Then Davey coughed and Katherine wiped her forehead.

"Mister Hildahl, you must be hungry. May I fix you some dinner?"

"Ma'am, I came off Slaughter Mesa when I found Holden's tracks heading this way. I followed them till they mixed with other prints, tracks I know well." He stared at her knowingly, and she dropped her eyes.

"It is a fine animal, and, yes, I met up with Mister Holden, who suggested I return to the L Slash where I would be protected. There were outlaws and killers on the loose, he said, and I would be much safer here."

"Ma'am, that's what worried Burn and me . . . the change in Holden. Still we know he ain't a killer."

Katherine would not look at him. "Mister Hildahl, how about some reheated stew and fresh biscuits?"

While they ate a good meal in the Meiklejon kitchen, Jack Holden stole the flashiest bronco out of Son Liddell's pasture—a sixteen hand black gelding with high stockings and a star, a small eye hidden under a thick forelock. He left the worn-out paint in trade.

CHAPTER TWENTY-THREE

They were one day off the mesa, and, when Gayle Souter got up from breakfast and walked out to the corrals, the men followed. He parceled out the chores quickly. Despite the useless siege, the fall work had still to be done. In ten minutes each man knew what the day held. The young stuff needed to be choused out of the upper range. Souter ticked off the landmarks, reminding Bit Haven it was a tall, burned cottonwood, not the puny aspen hit last summer, he was to sight on and turn before. And if any man didn't know the difference between a cottonwood and aspen, he ought to quit his riding job and work for a shopkeeper.

Souter sent Davey Hildahl riding north to the fenced sections where the red he-devil patrolled his wire kingdom. Davey's orders were to ease into the herd, cut out those meant for market, and leave the breeding stuff alone. Souter might send help later, but, for now, Davey and his snip-nosed bay would do.

Souter and Red Pierson would trail Jack Holden. Souter hated setting out to ride a man down, but the hole-up on Slaughter Mesa hadn't caught the outlaw, and Holden knew the unwritten laws. He'd stolen from neighbors; now he would be hunted and killed, like any animal that turned on its own.

Davey had said that Holden rode a paint that toed out in front, so in the beginning the tracks were easily spotted. Soon enough Holden would need a new horse, for the paint's stride was labored and uneven. The trick was to get close enough to the man, so any change in mounts wouldn't lose them the trail.

Souter reined in his red dun, let the boy catch up.

"Red, we're cutting this trail, knowing Holden's going for

Liddell's bronc's. You see anything to make you think different?"

Red shook his head, and the pair lined out their traveling horses toward Liddell's pasture. Red found fresh prints through the broken fence. The bronco tracked up short on the near hind, a flaw Holden wouldn't have seen when he roped out the gelding.

Eager Briggs liked the ancient palomino he'd picked up in Magdalena. The Mex who sold him the bronco wasn't clear on ownership, but Eager himself didn't bother with such niceties. Not many ranchers would care about one useless gelding tired enough so that a broken-legged old man could ride it. He called the horse Gold—he'd done some prospecting in his time and the deep yellow horse was the closest he'd come to a rich vein of color.

Now that his leg was healed, Eager'd taken to riding north and east every two, three weeks, staying out maybe two days. He told himself there was no reason to his wanderings. Most times he'd not go back home but, instead, would make camp and wrap up in Gold's saddle blanket and watch the fire he'd set, thinking about all the things that would fit in his curious mind. On these trips he made sure to take extra bacon, beans, coffee, and the makings for a smoke or two. Not his particular habit, but there were some who got struck by the need for that putrid stuff in their lungs. Now Eager, he liked a good cigar, one of those soaked ones that come out of Mexico. Hell, then a man knew he was smoking something with courage. Mornings he rolled up and got out of the blanket, folded it and put it on the palomino's back. It was too much effort for an old man to pack up the extra food, so he would leave it hanging by a rope from a nearby tree. Keep it safe from varmints until the next time he rode up the same way. Of course it was never there when he would come back, so he always packed more, not wanting to go hungry.

Eager might be old to some folk, but he still did love his victuals. Not like that young one he caught sight of now and then. Riding that big dark colt. The boy had got some manners to the colt now, not like the first time Eager had seen them in Quemado.

And Eager remembered the boy as clear as day—tough, moody just like his pa, old John English. English used to laugh when he told it, the family joke. The family was Welsh, named English, living in Wales, Texas. The boy was the spitting image of his pa, excepting for size.

What food Eager left for English in the trees wasn't enough to feed a man full up, but the mountains had their own food on the hoof—elk and deer, bear if you were hungry enough. The bits Eager put out were more for variety, the makings of civilization. Although Eager much doubted the English boy had a strong hankering for anything civilized.

This time when Eager got to his camp, he hobbled the palomino and dug a pit for the fire. He found himself talking out loud to himself; there was a lot an old man didn't know, even coming to the end of his life. A lot he'd forgotten, about being young and going after the whole world.

He sat and chewed on a Mexican cigar and talked about the outlaw, Jack Holden. The word was Holden had taken another Liddell bronco, and that Gayle Souter and the kid, Red Pierson, were tracking him.

If those three met, there would be killing, for Souter wasn't a forgiving man. Eager stated his feelings about killing, his old voice getting louder, and the palomino looked up from its graze, wiggled its long lip after a choice bit of grass. Holden against the two L Slash men wouldn't be pretty.

It was a shame to think of Gayle Souter shot down by the

likes of Jack Holden. Or Red Pierson dead; the boy was growing up right. "A lot of might-be in the world," Eager told his horse. His next topic was Davey Hildahl, riding fence on those wire sections. "Looks can deceive," he said to Gold. "Can't judge a man by the form he takes, got to see inside a man to know his soul."

As he guessed on it, a shadow drifted into his fire light. A thinned bay colt led by a man lamed on the offside and leaner than the horse. But the voice came out always the same.

"Thanks, old man. I've been out of coffee and beans a while . . . they'll taste good with elk."

The English boy handed over a rump portion of the elk, and Eager got to slicing thin steaks. Hadn't had elk in a long time, didn't know if he could gum his way through any more, but, by God, he would try.

The colt was unsaddled and rubbed down, hobbled, and left next to Gold. The ancient bronco was pleased with company, and the horses nuzzled and nickered some, then went back to eating. Only then did English come in to the fire's warmth, where Eager could get a look at him.

"It's good to see you still alive, boy. A sight this old man don't get to enjoy often. I know where you been, 'cause I been there before you."

The boy had come a far piece since his tangle with the bob wire. Eager pushed the wrinkles up on his forehead, wished he had his store-bought teeth. That elk was beginning to smell better than good.

English watched him, then spoke. "I know you now, old man. Eager Briggs is what they call you here. That's a summer name. You come up from Texas."

He'd known the boy was studying him the last two times or more, but the cut about his name still hurt. It wasn't the name he was born under, but he'd owned it a long time. He waited.

This wasn't done yet. Then the English boy caught Eager by surprise.

"You think Hildahl's in trouble, old man?"

It took a moment, then Eager nodded. "Yep, boy. He's right plumb in the middle." Then the old man did his own jumping. "The name was Leutwyler when I rode with your pa. Bert, it was. My name. That's why I called that ugly, no-count mule Bert, so not to forget my mama's naming me. Your folks was good to me."

It was downright foolish, two men sitting across from each other, a fire burning between them, charring up good elk rump. The boy's eyes widened; Eager grinned and wiped his wet mouth.

English spoke quickly. "You rode a big dun. I wanted to ride that bronc', and I asked you one day. You said the dun was a man's horse and to come back when I was growed big enough." That hung quietly. "What'd you think now, old man? I growed big enough for you?"

The gall of those misspoken words rose in Eager's belly. "A man can say things he don't mean. I 'pologize now . . . for what I said then. Old Bert Leutwyler, he died in that Texas country, and a new man rode on up here. A better man, I'm hoping."

English nodded and parceled out the charred elk steak, took some beans. Eager sliced himself a cut of meat, shoved it between his gums, and worked hard swallowing, all the time grinning and watching John English's boy.

Burn wiped his fingers around the tin plate, and wished the old man had made biscuits. God, he was hungry, could never get quite full. Where he rode was determined by the mares and foals, and often that meant running off game, forcing him to live on cold water and chewed hide. But he wasn't going to quit the mares, not after all this time.

"Boy, what you planning to do with winter's coming? And

how come that stallion's letting you run his band?"

Burn didn't want to think on it. He'd found the mares, and the stallion, and they remained on his conscience. He shivered, rubbed the healing cut on his arm. He'd found the stallion ribby and infected, cut to pieces amid wire, but still standing, unable to escape the coil circling his front leg. He'd cut the stallion's throat and had taken on more horses than he could handle. With a lot of hard work he'd caught five of the bachelor colts—broke to ride, he'd sold them only last week over in Springerville. The sale had given him enough cash to buy a bit of land. The dream still could be taken from him. So he sat while the old man looked at him.

Burn ran his tongue over the inside of his mouth, tasting sweet elk, spiced beans, the fouled coffee. "Briggs, you say you think Jack Holden's going to end up where Davey is?"

The old man answered quickly, as if he, too, was glad to get away from the more personal talk. "Yeah, I read Holden's tracks pointing this way, 'stead of to Springerville. He's got two men coming fast behind him . . . Gayle Souter and that kid, Red. Only Davey's in his way. It'd be a shame to lose a man like Davey Hildahl to such as Jack Holden."

"Hildahl saved my life," Burn said, "much as any man ever done. Guess I owe him the same."

It could have been surprise on Brigg's face that got his jowls to quivering. Burn was set to ride after he slept some. It would be a luxury, knowing nothing would sneak up in his sleep. He trusted the old man that much. Old Briggs seemed to understand as English rolled himself up in a blanket. Looking like his pa a lot then, he was John English's boy and that man had never quit, had never given in till the illness had taken him. It was a hell of a legacy for a boy to grow into, and it had nothing to do with size.

Briggs stayed alert most of the night, a rare feat for him. He did fall asleep along toward morning, and, when he woke, he was covered with a damp blanket, with the old palomino standing over him, head drooping, lower lip hanging close. When Briggs snorted and coughed, trying to sit up, the horse flapped that lip, yawned wide enough that the old man could count its back teeth, and went right back to dozing.

The fire was banked. A pot of coffee hot to the touch waited. English hadn't been gone long, and the first rays of sun came hitting over the rocks, making a pink and red wash on the boulders. Briggs stretched hard, pushed Gold out of the way, and drank the coffee right from the pot. The boy had taken the only cup.

Mama yelled from the kitchen that she needed a meat order from Hargreave's. Now, Mama said, and come get the money. Old man Hargreave always had to be paid in cash.

Rose let the coins roll in her fingers as she walked. They felt good, as if she held a sudden power. She passed a number of horses tied to the railings in front of the different stores. A child ran in front of her, clutching a wrapped package. This was the sum of her life, errands, demands, everyone else's needs but her own.

She went to Billy's livery and told the old man she needed to rent a quiet horse. Billy nodded and grinned, showing his few remaining teeth. "You in a hurry, huh, little lady?"

Rose accepted the quaint leer and comment with no hint of disquiet, for she was bent on following her desire.

Out of sight of town, Rose let the horse amble at an easy pace. She had little idea of where, exactly, she was going, but she knew Jack was out there somewhere, running for his life. All those men were chasing her Jack, but she would be the one to find him. She knew that in her very being; she would find her love and stay with him, protect him.

Three hours later unbidden tears drenched her face. She was exhausted, and alone, night was coming, and she was nowhere that she recognized. The horse climbed up a steep hill, following a narrow track that went on indefinitely. Rose wiped at her tears and yanked on the pinto's mouth as the animal turned to go down a particular trail. They would go where Rose wanted, not where the stupid horse chose.

Black night through early morning and then mid-morning with its searing, shimmering heat. Rose was crying when the Mexican found her.

"Buenos días, señorita."

A polite greeting, but Rose knew better than to trust the man—her mama had taught her well. She quickly wiped her face clean; it would not do for this Mexican to know she was lost and crying.

"Here, *señorita,* let me offer you some water."

He was still being very polite and was not that ugly, she rationalized. She let her tired horse drift in closer. "Well, I guess a small sip would be all right. Thank you." She took the canteen and hurriedly opened it, dropping the cork but not caring as she poured the delicious water into her mouth. It spilled down her chin, soaked into her dress, but she didn't stop drinking.

"*Señorita,* it is not good you drink so much. You will become ill, please, *señorita.*"

Finally she was done, and the pinto horse she rode shivered and swung its ugly head around and licked its lips. Rose politely handed back the empty canteen, ignoring that she had lost its stopper. Her head was swimming now, and her stomach felt odd, heavy and bloated. She dropped the reins carelessly, and pressed both hands to her belly, noting that the Mexican had gotten off his horse and was running his fingers over the ground, looking for something. *Good,* she thought, *he won't bother me.* Then bile filled her mouth and she leaned over the pinto's side and vomited. The watery liquid spewed from her and she could neither speak nor sit up as the fouled water spilled on the animal's legs and stained her once pretty dress.

The Mexican said nothing, but took the pinto's reins and began to walk. Rose Victoria had no voice to complain.

The humiliation was complete when, in a clearing in front of a sturdy adobe and stone hut, she tried to dismount and fell instead, landing heavily on the stone-carpeted ground, legs wide, skirt pulled above her knees. The Mexican had done this to her. Rose fussed and cursed and wiped her wet, stinking mouth. She needed Jack Holden now. Where was he, why couldn't she find him?

CHAPTER TWENTY-FOUR

Davey Hildahl's bay showed no interest in hurrying, so Davey let him wander while trying to count up what cattle he saw, guessing where the others might be hidden. When the bay spooked, he was ready. Bones were scattered around or still caught in old wire. He patted the bay's wet neck and let the horse stand and blow, felt it quiver under him. He was spooked, too, but finally the bay settled.

His camp would be simple. He stripped down the bay, and fed out a cup of oats. Then he rolled himself up in an extra blanket, pulled his hat down over his face, and slept. Come morning it was jerky and coffee, a small fire almost enough to warm him. By mid-morning he'd found a cow. He had first heard her bawl, and then the bay had gone to the sound. Damned fool cow was rolled in wire, cut right up to the hock. Her calf grazed on nearby grass. Ten sections of graze and the cow had had to have that blade of grass over the fence.

Davey slipped from the bay, uncoiled his rope, and got ready. Once he had one leg roped and tied to a tree, one snagged up to the good bay, he was able to doctor the cow's cuts. The calf got curious and ambled over to watch, decided the bay was its new mama and tried to nurse, and got a hard bite on the rump for the insult.

It was tricky sliding the cow loose while keeping away from her swinging horns, but with Davey back in the saddle and the bay alert and ready, it wasn't so hard, after all. After the cow trotted off, the bawling calf following, Davey got back to work.

It was a tangled mass of wire, so he dismounted and hobbled the bay, slipped the bit to let the horse eat while he worked. The fence needed to be spliced before the bull found the exit and left for higher country. His fist was wrapped in a coil when he sensed the approach of a rider. He didn't recognize the fancy black, which was traveling short on the left hind. It had to be Jack Holden, though—and that meant trouble.

Gayle Souter caught himself rubbing his upper lip again, and frowned. He and Red Pierson had stopped at a settlement near Datil Wells. A man there had told them a town girl'd been found on the plains. The man described the girl, and Souter knew immediately it was the oldest Blaisdel child, Rose Victoria. The man's wife spoke of Jack Holden, saying the girl had been crying for him. Souter and Red had watered the horses, filled their canteens, and asked a few more questions about Holden before they left.

Now they were headed north as Red caught the scent of new tracks and climbed off his bronco. The boy was trembling as he picked at the dirt.

"Look here, Mister Souter. It's that barefoot colt the mustanger rides. You figure he's riding to meet Holden . . . or chasing him?"

A short hour later they hit more tracks. A team and wagon far off any decent trail. Souter thought: *Edward Donald. No other fool would drive a wagon this far up in the mountains.* Souter shook his head. A country was too settled when a man couldn't ride five miles or more without crossing fresh tracks.

It was a long run, so Red and Souter held their broncos to a slow gallop, gathering them for the downslopes, urging them up onto the next rise. These two broncos were no good on the end of a rope, no good chasing cows, but, by God, they could run.

Katherine burned two loaves of bread. The other three were thin in the middle and scorched on one side. Meiklejon had returned from his overseas jaunt full of energy about the impending arrival of his bride. He asked Miss Katherine for news and she gave him an edited version.

This morning she had climbed out of bed quickly, tingling from a dream and knowing the day could bring nothing but bad news. She forced herself to work, but her hands rebelled, and the last of the dried apples flew onto the floor. Tonight it would be half-baked bread, steaks, and canned peaches again.

Two men approached the wagon from the rear and Edward Donald reached for his whiskey bottle, but it had rolled under the wagon seat, glistening in the sun. He slapped the lines against the rumps of his team and, in reaction, got one twitching tail but no actual response. When he got hold of good horseflesh, like the mares that English had branded for him, he'd have a fine team that would move out in a steady trot.

Donald spared a glance over his shoulder, thinking he recognized Souter and some boy. *The old fool will meddle and lecture with that superior look and calm, level way he talks*, thought Donald. So he slapped the team again and pretended he didn't see them riding up closer.

"Mister Donald, you haul in those horses!"

The voice was an unwanted intrusion into Donald's world consisting only of sky and trees, sandy red hills and tufts of high, swaying grass.

Gayle Souter wanted his say. "Where you figuring to go, Donald? There's no way that team can drag you much into those trees."

Donald looked at the team's broad backs littered with old harness. He could see two ridged backbones and count the ribs on the near horse. His thoughts must have wandered, for a look passed between Souter and the boy, and it was not a particularly kind look. Donald rubbed the back of his neck that had been burned by the sun.

"Mister Souter, why are you so concerned about me? I'm not up to any mischief," Donald said as he tried to turn the wagon, but a wheel stuck on a rock, and no matter how hard he whipped the tired horses, they could not get free.

Souter stepped down from his saddle horse, moved to the wagon seat, and took the lines. He sat a moment, the lines resting in his enormous hands, and then began to cajole and croon to the team as his fingers sent their message. Two equine heads came up in unison, long ears swiveling to listen, and, with a few light tugs and twists, the animals bent to their collars, surged forward, and began a series of half steps that brought them around and pointed downhill.

"Donald, why don't you tell it around," Souter stated, "that you've given up title to those horses belonging to English. Save all us of a lot of trouble . . . but mostly you." He gave the lines over to Donald and stepped from the wagon seat onto his waiting bronco.

Donald thanked the old man, and included the silent Red Pierson with a polite nod. Then he alternated clucking and slapping the lines to guide the team back along their own tracks. He would end the long day with a drink. Then he would begin his campaign to decline ownership of the English horses.

Red watched the wagon's bumpy, jolting departure. Donald

had a big mouth and a wealth of words, but nothing to say. He didn't need to empty the bottle to get to the truth.

When it came to a choice between horses and men, the lines got blurred. One man's life could be worthless compared to a good horse. Burn English kept pushing the dark bay colt, thinking about Davey Hildahl and the woman. She was part of this—the tension and debt owed between him and Hildahl.

He found signs of a cold camp outside the wire fence. Reading the tracks, it was obvious Hildahl had slept there. Burn loped the colt some, came up to the old fence he'd built, and saw where the wire beyond it had been cut and repaired. He led the colt through, made his own hurried repairs, and remounted. The tracks of Davey's bay were fresh.

Fresher tracks cut the bay's prints. Burn put the colt to running, past the bones, past more of the damned wire. The colt shied but kept on. Burn leaned forward to stroke the colt's neck. He didn't slow down, or draw out his old Walker, or even put a hand to the Spencer under his leg. The colt wasn't broke to gunfire.

The colt skidded to a halt, blew loudly, snorted, and pranced under Burn's hand, too excited to obey, too keyed up by the running to stand still.

It was Jack Holden who brought his horse around, staring at Burn with widened eyes. Hildahl was kneeling, crude pliers in hand. The earth around him was ground up and bloody, plowed in wide, useless furrows. A cow had been caught in the wire, Burn guessed. Now it was Davey Hildahl who had gotten caught.

"Holden." Burn nodded to the man, paying no attention to the pistol in his right hand. Then: "Hildahl, you look like a nester down there in the dirt. Best stand up, if your guardian will allow it."

Hildahl stood up, unrolled was more like it, and Burn was again conscious of the man's lean height and awkward bones. He had that baby look to him still. Maybe they could play Holden between them and get Davey free.

The colt took a dislike to Holden's fancy black. The bay snorted, flattened his ears, and snapped at the bronco. The black arched its neck and swung its muzzle in defiance at the colt, and Holden absently smacked the bronco hard on its crested neck. The pistol never left its target. The *crack* of the blow was startling.

Burn took a gamble. "Holden, you best not keep a cocked pistol, riding that bronc'. He's ringy as hell. It could be you'll shoot yourself . . . never mind Davey or me. I ain't much of a gun hand, but I can pull the Walker loose real fast, and Davey's got a Colt to his side. You can't get to both of us, not from the back of that god-awful lamed son-of-a-bronc'."

Then a different tactic leaped to mind. Burn shook his head in apology even as he spoke, but the words were what he had been thinking. "It ain't like you to kill, Holden. Not like you to shoot that Mex on the mesa like you did, or that boy you buried. Killing ain't what you do." He read the startled look in Holden's eyes and kept banging away. "You must 'a' put a bullet in that man's brain 'cause he asked you. You two were good friends. What happened to the boy you put under in the cañon? How'd he come to die?"

Holden turned red, then dead white, and Burn saw the fingers tighten on the pistol trigger. He slammed his spurs into the edgy bay colt. As Holden's pistol fired, the colt jumped and hit the black at the shoulder, knocking the horse down, and then leaped over it. Burn stopped the colt, reined in hard, and spun the horse around to find Holden climbing on the black as it staggered to its feet.

Hildahl stood, his pistol pointed at Holden. Davey was pale, but he spoke calmly. "Now, cattle thief, see how it feels having a man ready to kill you over nothing." The tremor in Hildahl's voice gave him away. He could kill right now, but Burn knew that murder wasn't Davey's specialty.

The *mesteñero* put his own six bits in. "Holden, there's two of us to check fence, gather them cows. It's bad odds for the likes of you. So I guess you better turn that fancy horse downwind and ride. If Davey'll let you go that is, and from the look to him, he's ready to pull that trigger."

Holden rubbed his mouth, spoke as if he hadn't heard Burn's warning. "That boy I buried, he was kin. My sister's kid." He hesitated, looked away. "Horse bolted, kid broke his neck. Ugly, damned ugly." Then the old Holden resurfaced briefly—a grin and shining eyes and no care in the world. "It was bad luck, boys. I didn't come up here to steal . . . just bad luck runnin' into Davey. I didn't even know who it was, and then this thunderbolt rides into the middle of us, and we all shoved out pistols and started bluffin'."

Burn ended the stand-off. "Holden, fancy words don't change what needs doin'. You shuck the bullets out of that pistol, then ride out. We don't want you nearby." Burn could feel Davey bristle at his words, so he addressed the tall rider. "Hildahl, he may be wanted, but I ain't going to be the one to take him in. Whole territory's after his hide, he's got enough running him."

When Holden raised the pistol and spun the empty cylinder to show Burn and Davey, the black raised its head and its eyes rolled white. Lather showed thickly on the shiny neck. Burn patted the now quiet bay colt and watched as Davey let Holden pass. He kept the spooky black to a slow prance until they disappeared into the tight pines.

Burn let out a hard breath, coughed, and wiped his face. He was shamed by his fear until he saw Davey doing the same thing, adding a tug to his pants in the actions. It wasn't funny, but there was no stopping them. Burn slid off the colt, leaned against the shoulder, unable to stand on his own two legs, and started laughing along with Davey.

When Burn cleared his eyes of the tears of laughter, he saw Hildahl was tensed up, pistol in hand. Then Burn listened. Two horses approaching on the same trail that Burn had followed. He slid the Spencer out of its boot, kept the bay's reins close to him, using the colt as a shield. Sweat dripped inside his shirt. He smelled the fear, felt its tight pull at his belly.

It was Gayle Souter and the kid, Red Pierson.

Davey would have laughed but his sides already hurt. He suspected from the look on English's face that the man was going through the same feeling. Davey did the talking this time; it was his boss's range.

Souter never took his gaze off of Burn, except to give the bay colt a good study.

Davey tried to make his point. "Holden aimed to shoot me, Souter, and Burn stopped him. Last we saw, Holden was headed north on a black Sunday bronc'."

Souter surprised them with his answer. "Miss Katherine sent us this way, said Holden'd been to the ranch. We turned her pa back some time ago. Davey, you finish your chore . . . gather up what you can. English here'll help you drive the stuff in . . . as payment for some of the grass his mares been grazin'. Me and Red, we're trackin' Holden, and we'll get him this time or run him off our range."

When they got on Holden's tracks, Souter let the boy do the work. He gave him encouraging words when it got rough, but most of the time he sat his red dun and thought about the two men they had left behind. Hildahl would be Meiklejon's best choice to take over when he himself had to quit. He hated to think that way, but the past few days had told him he was no longer young. Davey Hildahl would do as boss in a few years.

Red hauled up, pointed to where Holden's tracks climbed a shale slide.

Souter patted his bronco's neck. He couldn't second guess Holden, even with the information about Holden's direction. The tracks went straight up. Souter and the boy followed.

It took a long half day to ride the rest of the section. Pride kept Davey and English from admitting the truth, even when it plain hurt to keep working. Finally they spoke up about the horses, saying the broncos were done in and needed a rest. In the colt's case it was true; even a greenhorn could see the youngster was worn to a nub.

They camped outside the bull's territory, roasted a tough hare and boiled old coffee, even cut open an airtight of peaches and took turns spearing the fruit. No need to talk. The horses grazed. The colt even got down and rolled in the hobbles and got back up with no trouble. In the morning they'd push the market stuff over to the burned cottonwood, leave them for Bit Haven and Stan Brewitt to bring in.

The last quarter mile, right before they could see the ranch, was hell for both men. Davey cursed under his breath; he was delivering Burn English to Miss Katherine again. A woman as fine and tender-hearted as Miss Katherine, she found more in a man than was really there. He was the fool, after all—big, dumb Davey Hildahl putting a rival in the arms of the woman they both loved.

They rode that last quarter mile in silence, full of memories and forlorn hope.

Katherine was at the kitchen door when they rode in. Their terrible exhaustion was evident, yet they spent time caring for the horses before they took care of themselves. At the door, Katherine watched.

Bothered by her private thoughts, she fed both men as much as they could eat, marveling at their capacity. Davey was the first to finish, sipping at cooled coffee while Burn ate a second piece of pie. They had not spoken except to ask for more biscuits or another platter of meat. Unless she asked a direct question, they were too busy to talk. She knew the range etiquette—a meal was for eating, talk came later.

Burn stood up and thanked her while Davey offered to wash the dishes. She stared at them in wonder. There was pride and grace in Burn English, with fiery eyes and temper, the heavy black hair and thin body. Then Katherine moved her gaze to Davey who fiddled with the dishes, holding one up in his long hands. Sweet, child-like, steady, and strong.

She knew without either of them needing to tell it—they both were in love with her.

Burn was the first to hear the two horses. He tensed, glanced out the door. Gayle Souter and the boy, Red. The old man climbed down from his red dun, stiff as Burn ever saw a man. Souter headed for the kitchen. Burn saw the look on the seamed face and knew it was bad.

Katherine walked to the door. Souter entered and refused coffee. Katherine backed up until she could almost touch both Davey and Burn.

"Ma'am." Souter removed his hat. He looked down at the swept floor marred with boot scuffs. He couldn't get the words out so he began again. "Ma'am. We found your father, Miss Katherine. Shot through the heart. He died quick."

It was as bad as Burn knew it would be.

Souter droned on, doing his job the only way he knew. "We found Jack Holden nearby." Souter coughed. "From what we could read off those tracks, Holden met with your pa and . . . don't know why, won't ever know . . . but Holden shot your pa." Here Souter faltered before continuing. "It looked like

228

Holden's horse bolted. The spill broke Holden's back." There was a long pause this time. "He was dead . . . time we got to him." Souter had finished.

Katherine took a half step closer to Davey. As Davey put his hand on her arm, a look passed between him and Burn English until Burn had to turn away.

EPILOGUE

When he wrote the final words, Gordon Meiklejon realized the sun was glittering through fast-moving clouds. It had taken him five days of steady writing to come to the end. Now Gordon ventured outside to look up and see the distant blue of the sky. When he raised his face, he could feel the sun's warmth on his winter skin. He sighed, and a voice called out: "What'd you think, boss?"

Gordon turned, watching as the man walked toward him, long legs pumping through the drifts. Davey Hildahl stopped next to Gordon, and the two men exchanged pleasantries.

"This will do for the spring grasses, won't it?"

Davey nodded at the boss' statement. "It's what Souter would have called 'poor man's fertilizer.' A spring snow'll melt quick and that pretty green we been waiting for'll grow up fast."

They'd come a long way since that terrible fall. Davey and his wife lived in the old house, the one Littlefield built in '84. Gordon had offered to build them a new home, but Katherine said her husband liked the place and that she'd grown fond of it, also. Several rooms had been added to accommodate the Hildahl children as they were born. First was Henry, born in '94, and then little Gordon. And Edward, who had lived only a month. Fanny and her sister Elizabeth shared a large room.

It was a full house, one Gordon and his wife envied. Roberta was unable to bear children, but she shared some of the child-rearing work with Katherine. Only on very rare occasions did

Meiklejon catch her gazing at the Hildahl children with sorrow in her fine eyes.

Once Hildahl left him, Gordon sat down at the cluttered desk and re-read the final words of his story, thinking of all the events that had followed. He would not record these, for it had been his purpose to write his impressions of that first year, since it had served as his introduction to New Mexico.

Rose Victoria Blaisdel had never recovered from her ride. She had laid, semi-conscious, for days until word filtered back to Socorro of Jack Holden's death. The child had then gone through the hotel shrieking, and it had taken Dr. Lockhart several hours and a bottle of laudanum to quiet her. She had been sent East "to visit an aunt," as the family told the story. By the following spring, no one spoke of her at all.

Both her sisters married. One lived on the L Slash with her husband, Red Pierson. The boy had thickened as he matured into his promise, and was a good hand on the ranch. The other sister was in Socorro with her second husband, running the Southern Hotel.

Gayle Souter was buried on the ranch. He died simply—a horse shied, stumbled, and Gayle came off, lay stunned for a moment, then got up, remounted, and never said a word. But he'd been busted inside, and it was Burn English who brought him in. He had packed the old man's corpse on a horse like a side of meat, but there was no other way. English said he'd found Souter up by the burned cottonwood, head propped on a rotting log, bowed legs sprawled out with the boots still on.

Burn English. Here Gordon looked out through the window. He was still puzzled by the man. Neither Katherine nor her husband would talk about English. The last time Gordon had tried, about three years ago, there had been a look shared between them that promised much but gave up nothing.

English had stayed in the area for a number of years. He had bought land, put in piped water, and built sturdy corrals. He raised excellent stock from the wild mares, using the dark colt as the sire. No man ever complained that an English-bred mount lacked stamina, speed, or good sense.

Eager Briggs still leered toothlessly at the world when he would tell his tales. He lived in Gutierrezville, where he'd found a widow to take him in. Briggs didn't ride any more, but he could and would tell his stories, except if asked about Burn English.

It had been Red Pierson who rode in four years ago, saying Burn English was gone, his cabin destroyed, his horses set free. No one saw the mustanger again. Not around Magdalena or Socorro, over to Quemado or Springerville, or even near Horse Springs. He had disappeared, leaving behind only the legacy of good horses and a lot of embroidered speculation.

ABOUT THE AUTHOR

William A. Luckey was born in Providence, Rhode Island, but later went West to work with horses. "I've spent the past forty years dealing with rogue horses using my own methods to retrain and make them useful—I've evented, shown dressage, fox-hunted for twenty seasons, worked cattle, gone on five-day trail rides. I've owned over 150 horses personally, going back to when I was seven. I've actually been riding now for almost sixty years, and have taught riding for over forty years." *High Line Rider* appeared in 1985, the first of eleven Western novels published to date. William A. Luckey's next Five Star Western will be *Burn English*.